THE GREEN MAN

Henry Treece's new novel is set in the heroic age of migration after the fall of Rome. He has placed his stark young hero Amleth—the Green Man of the title—against the various backgrounds of grey sea-scoured Jutland, crumbling Roman Caerleon and restless Caledonia; and has brought him face to face with many of the monolithic giants of the time in the fulfilment of his compulsive destiny.

The story shows a Europe sinister as a twilit forest where every gleam of torchlight reveals one predator or another busy above his prey. Brother seeking a throne kills brother, wife plans husband's death, servant spies on master. In the full flood of passion, son avenges father; and in the name of tribal ritual, sister seduces brother. It is a world ignorant of chivalry; where Christian teaching either has not penetrated or has been forgotten, to let the pagan tide roll back on land that once had been reclaimed.

It is a story of barbaric men and women, confused by the numerous voices of the ancient past whispering in their ears, urging them this way or that until they lose all knowledge of direction and, almost in desperation, act as much by instinct as the animals about them. At the same time they are capable of deeply-felt friendship and of loyalty, of laconic bravery, of gentleness and mercy shown in most ironic circumstances.

The Green Man

HENRY TREECE

THE BODLEY HEAD

LONDON

© Henry Treece, 1966
Printed and bound in Great Britain for
The Bodley Head Ltd
10 Earlham Street, London, WC2
by C. Tinling & Company Ltd, Liverpool
Set in Monotype Bembo
First published 1966

CONTENTS

Foreword, 9

I Jutland, 11

II Britain, 109

III Pictland Dream, 191

IV Vendilsgarth, 227

Afterword, 253

AUTHOR'S NOTE

This story is prompted by the assurance of authority that the meek shall inherit the earth. It is based on a text entitled *Amleth's Revenge*, published in 1961 by the Press Department of the Royal Danish Ministry of Foreign Affairs in Christiansborg.

The first writer of this story was Saxo Grammaticus, a shadowy assistant priest, secretary to the Archbishop of Lund and founder of Copenhagen, who died about 1220. Saxo's great chronicle was the *Gesta Danorum*, or *The Exploits of the Danes*, in the course of which he told a story which is as old as mankind, although he pinned it to a northern prince who may have lived roughly about the time of King Arthur.

It is probable that all stories which have somehow filtered through from prehistory are erotic-heroic, as Polonius could not have brought himself to say, which may be because there is only one story that men feel the need to hear told again; this is the story of sowing the field, reaping the crop, and burning the stubble. Or, of man's coming, his delight in his full strength, and his going back into the ground as manure, the Sown Man as they say.

With these primary colours there is possible a great variety of mixtures. Set above the essential birth-copulation-death triad, there are all the emotions of glory, fear, hope, greed, despair, patience, disgust, laughter, contempt, tenderness, stark horror and sheer loving.

All myth, most legend, and much of history follow the archetypal pattern of the seeding, burgeoning, dying year. Sometimes this pattern seems to be a coarse one; but it is one which we know to be real. Just as we know all the words that must be spoken to reveal that pattern. We may not like them, but we know them to be the words of the language, the thoughts of the men.

H. T.

FOREWORD

To the Duke and Honourable Pastoral of Puteoli, Golden Mouth, Lord Manuel Chrysostom in the Hand of God and at the Foot of Mary: from the humblest of his servants, Gilliberht of Fiesole, monk in the House at Arles, in the year of Our Lord 526.

My Lord and Patron in the name of the Father, the Son and the Holy Spirit, greetings from the bowed knee. May your roof still stand, may the Terror have passed you by, and may this come to you safely though the heel of Theodoric bears down hard.

Here we have suffered. The Barbarians have put the sword to fourteen of the Brothers, have burned down the vines and have filled the fish-ponds with heathen rubbish. By God's Grace, we hid the candlesticks and altar-cloth which Your Serenity gave us, before they came upon us in their iron.

Yet now, since there are but three of us left and no House to live in, we must shift as best we can until the times are gentler. Lucian has gone on foot towards Valencia in Spain; Eusebius has taken ship for Athens as an oarsman. May they reach their appointed peace. I am hidden in the fish-cellar of Arbogastes at Marseilles. May God keep me undiscovered here until your honoured answer comes.

This is my request, Lord and Patron, Golden Mouth: that I be granted the means to travel north to Scania, or Gotland as some call it. A horse and a mule, or two mules, would see me overland. A little bag of silver no bigger than your dear daughter's clenched fist would feed us, since I should buy only what I could not beg; and do neither where corn still stood and fish swam in the rivers.

Should Your Serenity fear that my purpose in travelling to be the ignoble end of saving my own worthless body, I here take the liberty of outlining my intent:

The land northward of Frankish Colonia lies in darkness, and there I would journey (by my Patron's good will) so as to cast Christ's light through that obscurity.

My Only Lord, to tell of these Northmen in full would be to disgust Your Honour and terrify His children. In short, they remain as our honoured fellow-Roman, Tacitus, once wrote of them: immoderate guzzlers of barley beer, who howl into their shields like beasts; drunken, they dance naked among sharp spears, ignoring the blood they shed. Hercules is their god, though they call him Orwendill or Vendil, and praise him for bringing back the sun. Their goddess is Isis of the dark groves, whom they call Nerthus of Earth and whose secret cart is drawn by sacred kine when she goes to see men impaled so that the grain should sprout. The women in general are as hard: they wear their breasts uncovered in the sternest wind, and bring weapons to their chosen men as dowry. No woman among these stern people is thought worth the name unless she can examine the battle wounds of her menfolk; husband, sons or brothers; without weeping.

When I reveal to you, Mightiest, that these pagans paint themselves black before combat, wear the tusked heads of boars as helmets, sing drunkenly upon the burial-mounds of their dead, and, when their passions are suddenly aroused, strike dead the nearest slave at their bench, then you will see in what degree such beastly brutes have need of Christ.

A horse and a mule, Most Generous, or two mules, together with a little bag of silver, delivered after dark at the fish-cellar of Arbogastes. So I will go forth, Lord, as Our Master's pupils did, counting no cost too great in this saving of souls.

And when the dark North is lightened, Your Grace, and Romans can tread there in justice and holy judgement, what honour will come to Your Memory, O Generous Giver; what gratitude of the pious.

Your meanest but most devoted servant,
Gilliberht of Fiesole.

I
Jutland

KING VENDIL was getting into the wall-bed when he heard a scratching at the courtyard door. It was the seventh day of Yuletide feasting and the kept-men lay on their backs in the straw with their mouths open and their axes forgotten. Queen Gerutha was sleeping with her arm about her woman in the upper bower until the drinking was over and the men safe again by night.

So King Vendil must answer the door himself if it was to be answered. He was heavy with ale and had not long come from one of the kitchen-girls. He was not pleased to make the journey along the dark stone passageway in his bare feet. When the scratching went on, King Vendil turned from the bed, hardly able to keep his balance, and kicked at the nearest of the kept-men in anger. But the man only rolled over and spat in the straw.

King Vendil put the curse of the hanging Odin on the man and then went towards the dark old door himself, tumbling against the stone walls many times before he reached it. When he had drawn the forged iron bolts at top and bottom, the white light blinded him for a spell and he could see no one there.

Then he saw two men wrapped in cloaks of dark stuff, standing one on either side of the door just in the yard. He could only make out their eyes and teeth in the moonlight, but he knew who they were and tried to shut the door again. The ale in his belly made him slow and one of the men put his knee into the opening while the other man took Vendil by the iron beard and dragged him a little way outside.

When the king saw what they meant he tried to shout out. But the first blow rendered his mouth wordless and the second took all the strength out of his heart.

He crawled for a while under the moon, sliding in his own blood and trying to point his finger at the taller of the men. But the other man laughed and kicked his hand from under him.

13

Then they trod him down on the midden in turn and put the sword into him three times. And when they had done this they sprinkled him with last autumn's black straw and went away. They left the castle door swinging in the sea wind. Anyone could have got into Vendilsgarth during the night, but no one inside knew that. They were all sound sleepers, and the soundest was King Vendil, and the coldest.

The winter sea off Crabland was so icy that a man falling into it gave up the ghost after drawing three breaths. Yet with the pale sun glinting on its salt and the humped green island rising and falling beyond its swell, it looked almost gay, as though it danced for the glory of Frigg the Merry Mother. A small ship made its way towards Crabland with four oarsmen rowing and a square hide sail painted in red ochre. Its sign was a sun with the rays coming off it. This was Vendil's own sign, and Vendil's son held the steerboard of that ship, reining it in when it ran too headstrong at a breaker, like a stern rider holding back a wilful horse from a fence.

He was a tall youth, somewhat stooped in the back but of sturdy growth. His arms were thick and covered already with a mat of yellow hair through which a broad gold bracelet glimmered red in the sunshine. His head was long and horselike, its light hair cropped close to the bone so that his kettle helmet should sit the firmer. His skin was strangely pale and his eyes blank and staring, until something caught his notice; then they sharpened like those of an owl that sights a mouse and were not pleasant to look into. His lower jaw was no prettier; it seemed that Odin had given him a stallion's teeth, for they pushed outwards at the thick lips so that he seemed always about to bite whomsoever he grinned at. In Vendilsgarth one of the bolder Jarls once said that this youth could suck a plum dry without opening his mouth. But in the eyes of the women there he was a proper enough man and most of the young ones dreamed at some time or other of lying with him at Barley-feast or Straw-burning, though there was no woman in the castle, or in the village that lay under its north wall, who could honestly say that he had as much as

14

put his hand under her skirt. His mind was set on other things; it was in his heart to become a hero, although as yet he bore only a long knife and not a true sword.

At his feet as he steered the small ship sat a dark-haired man with long black hair and a grizzled beard. In his first coast-raid against the Weders, a crofter-chief had struck him a back-hander with the axe so that now he was hunched from neck to waist. His name was Torfi and he had never loved a woman half so much as he loved the youth at the steerboard.

There was another man of note in that small ship who stood at the prow shielding his light blue eyes from the glancing winter sun. He stood so tall that men used to say he could piss over a longship with its sail up. But this was not true. Men called him Gautrek the Mild because he had eight men's lives to account for and had been an outlaw so many times that now he had lost tally whether he was still under sentence or free. And no man dared come to him and tell him which.

He turned from the prow and called back over the rowers' shaggy heads, 'Hold in towards the pines on the headland, Amleth. That is where we are to meet the Geat-king.'

The man at the steerboard spoke down to Torfi and said: 'This Geat-king, this Beowulf, should I kneel to him when we meet?'

Torfi said, 'You, from the loins of the Sun King and the Barley Queen, who is grand-daughter to Rorek Ring-giver? Who is this Beowulf? The blood that runs in me is as good as his.'

Amleth said, 'It is my wish to join his warband and gain fame. To bend the knee costs nothing. Besides, last winter I killed a stag he had been following for three years. He might hold that against me.'

Torfi spat over the side into the water. 'That is not what he will hold against you, Amleth,' he said, 'unless they have lied about him.'

Then Gautrek came down among the men and stood by them. He said, 'If you kneel before the Geat I shall knock you flat myself onto the sand. I have not had the managing of you all these years to see you behave like a bitch on heat. Remember, when we cut our

15

wrists and became blood-brothers, you swore never to go against me?'

Torfi said, 'If you kneel, our King Vendil will get to know of it. You will dishonour him. He will shut the sun from us and bring thunder and lightning round our heads. And the queen your mother will not let the barley spring, then what shall we do for bread and beer?'

Amleth was silent a while. Then he said, 'You talk as though they are gods. You do not live close to them as I do or you would know.'

Gautrek smacked him across the face, not hard but hard enough to leave red finger-marks. He said, 'They are gods. The people will tell you that. If Vendil should ever die it would be a bad day for us in Jutland. We should know bad times. Then it would be the moment to kneel and beg your bread and your life from a Geat-king. But not till then.'

Amleth said, 'Vendil will never die. The man who could kill my father has not yet formed in the womb.'

For seven days the king's body lay under a calfskin at the end of the feast hall where any free man who wished could satisfy himself that Vendil was truly dead. His brother Feng was the man who lifted the hide most often and even raised the waxen eyelids each morning to see if life might have come back into the glazed pupils. And after each raising Feng would throw the hide back over his brother and shake his grey head and say, 'Ocho, but if I were a weeping man then you could look to wade ankle deep in brine.'

Then always he went off to the curtained war house where the henchmen played chess and drank with them until the place shook with laughter and snoring. And all this while the Queen Gerutha, who had not yet come to her thirty-fifth year and whose body still burned with the last flames of youth by night, rocked in her horn-beam chair alone and cried that the sun had gone away from the earth, that the barley corn would not spring again, and that no salmon would make their way up the streams towards the nets any more. But when she was in another mood she would rage into the

16

women's bower and pull hair and pinch breasts and tear at robes saying, 'All you whores can find a man when you want one. Why must I be left alone? Why must I dry up by day and never have a king on me any more? Is it reasonable for the field to stay unsown because the first farmer dies?'

A thin-faced girl called Sibbi said to her once, 'If I were a witch born of seven witches I would see that I got another king, if I had to make him out of clay and breathe life into him myself.'

Gerutha gave this girl a very stark look but did not have her thrashed as she would have done to the others. Then she went back to her own chamber and sat in the hornbeam chair and gripped its arms with a fierce grasp. She shut her eyes fast and said in a whisper, 'King, king, come back to me. Come as a bear, come as a tree. But come before night-time and lie by my knee.'

She got a little relief from this but did not entirely believe that her powers were still in her. To test this she opened her eyes and placed two seashore pebbles on the tiles of the chamber, one blue, one russet, a hand's length apart. Then staring at them, she said through hard-bitten jaws, 'Roll, little stones, and touch one another. Move when your queen bids you, stones, and kiss.'

She waited a long while and nothing happened. Then all at once her body went most cold and she began to shudder in every limb. Just before her senses left her she saw the two stones move and hit together on the floor. Then just as suddenly they rolled apart again and lay quite still as they had been before.

Then she went into a sort of cold sleep, and did not wake till a kitchen-thrall ran in, dressed only in his leather apron, and shouted out, 'Lady, a bear has come into the kitchen and is tearing at our meat.' He had to slap her face a while before she understood. Then she felt sure that the king had come again as a bear and she cried out, 'Let him feed his fill. See that none of the men hurts him. I shall put on my red feast-robe with the silver lace at the collar. A king must be greeted as suits his station. Go, man, and tell them all to stand back.'

The thrall went away shaking his head but when he got into the long stone kitchen again he found that three kept-men were holding the bear in a corner with long bullock-poles while the youngest of the kitchen-women were stabbing at him with fire-irons and forks. The new king, Feng, was there, laughing and encouraging the girls. He was promising a gold ring to the one who brought the bear's thing to him and so they went at it like hunting bitches, screaming at one another to stand clear. While they did this the kept-men roared and took liberties with them to spur them on.

He was only a small bear and too old to fight back as he once would have done. His teeth were yellow and broken, his claws were ground down and blunt from grubbing among hard stones, his pelt was grizzled and worthless, with bare places showing along his arms and back. He was too far gone to roar and rage at his tormentors and could only squeal with shrill fright from time to time. One of the women got a bacon-hook into him and pulled his legs apart and from under him. Then the men got tired of this poor sport and knocked the tumbled beast about the head till he stopped screeching and shuddered and lay quiet.

The woman was just showing her trophy to Feng when the queen came sweeping in at the door, wearing her scarlet robe and a throat-ring of bronze. When she saw what they had done her face went as white as a bone, then she ran at the woman and tried to ram the red part into her mouth. The kitchen woman howled with fear but did not dare strike back at the queen. King Feng took a hand at last and held down Gerutha's arms by her side while all the men and women scuttled from the kitchen.

The queen kept crying out, 'He came at my bidding and you let them kill him. How many kings must you kill before you are satisfied, Bastard?'

His anger was so great at this, he forgot that she was a queen above him and flung her onto a bench and held his red hand over her mouth so that the others should not hear her words. She bit at him savagely and tasted his red salt. He was so hard a man that he wiped his wounded hand about her face until she was almost as ruddy as the bear.

She kept shouting out, 'If my son was here! If Amleth was here! He would quieten you, murderer.'

Feng laughed and said, 'What, that oaklog, that fool.'

Because of the little dead bear they both shouted words that had only been in their heads before, lying silent. Gerutha yelled, 'I know who murdered Vendil and took his place on the throne chair.'

And Feng cried back, 'And I know who gave birth to the girl, Sibbi, and then put it about that she was a fosterling from among the Geats. You know what they do to women who lie with thralls, Gerutha. You have seen them over the log and howling. You have seen their hair go white before it was finished. What if I tell the lords who Sibbi is?'

Then with all this struggling and shouting, they both wore out their fury and lay on the bench gasping. Then Gerutha felt the king in him rising beneath his torn calfskin kilt and took him but tried to punish him at the same time. And at last he grinned down at her and said, 'There, woman. Would you barter me for that little bear? What had he to offer? Only a snail. A small snail.'

In the windswept fields each year when the skimming black clouds first let through the pale glow of the new sun, Gerutha always strode as the Barley Queen, and stretched her long white hands over the little green cowering shoots and said, 'Barley, Barley, rise and come to me! Barley, come up with your little green pricks. Pierce the cold earth and show yourselves.'

Sometimes this needed more than words and waving hands. Sometimes the little barley points would not break the dark earth until it was made darker with blood. If there was no captive-warrior for the earth-wetting, then it would be a wandering stranger who had slept in Vendilsgarth. That is, if he had not eaten the salt there.

Then sometimes it would be an old man who was weary of the slow winters and the windy summers, weary of dry bread and watered ale. One who wished to see his dead family again. Then he would go under the old stone axe and help the little barley pricks to rise again and feed the castle-folk.

19

Gerutha was the best Barley Queen for a day's sailing. For her the little green points rose up as proudly as hot men. She was fifteen when she married Vendil the king and had spent all her life on horses, racing the other Jarls' daughters, or in boats dragging in the herring. But when Vendil paid her father the bride-price of forty oxen this life ended, and her new husband carried her under his arm like a basket and flung her onto the wall-bed. He said out of his bushy beard, 'Now you are something. You were nothing before. But now you are something.'

He shouted for the women to wash the salt and fish-scales off her and when they had done this and had scrubbed her in brine till she was glowing and kin for a king, he said, 'Now you are to be the Barley Queen in Vendilsgarth. Look, I will show you things.'

He was very harsh on her like a ploughman turning over the earth. He showed her many things that she had not known about. And when she had learned these things, she felt a power coming to her and then she was brave enough to handle the king roughly as well.

When he lay across the wall-bed with his eyes wide and his beard upward, she laughed and bit him and dreamed she was a bitch-wolf. But when he tired of this he swept her onto the rush-floor with his hand and said, 'Nay, nay! You are still only a lass from a fish-Jarl's cottage.'

She scratched him with her rough nails and bit him again, kneeling in the rushes, and said, 'I am the Barley Queen! I can make it spring up when I wish. See what I have done already and with a king.'

But in the morning she knew why Vendil had laughed at her. The field-Jarls took her out and tied thongs to her wrists and ankles, laying her with her body to the earth. And they they hitched the thongs to two young stallions and whipped them over the furrows.

The sandy earth and the stones in the earth spoke sharp words to her pride. And when they took her weeping off the thongs after the acre was furrowed, she wished only to die. She had forgotten her name or which meat she liked best to eat.

The women tended her smiling; the king rode away to talk with some Frisian cousins without saying farewell to her. If he had looked through the curtain with his red eyes and bushed beard she would have screamed with fear.

She lived on ewe's milk for a fortnight and could not shift to help herself.

But that springing-time the barley rushed out of the red soil as though Loki were at its heels with his hot spear-point. There had never been such a crop at Vendilsgarth. A man could not get his thumb between the green shoots, they were so thick. In the castle-town there was stout bread and strong ale for a full year after this furrowing. The folk made songs to Gerutha and would not have let her leave them for the Hoard of Jerusalem.

Vendil praised her and said she was the most fruitful queen he had taken. But now when she saw him her body closed like an oyster-shell. She went ice-cold and had to bite her lips hard to keep from yelling when he laid his hairy pelt upon her.

He said to her: 'It will pass, wife. You will come again in time. Get the women to see to you. They know how to make it come again.'

He left her and used the castle-women instead until she could be his queen again. But she never was. Then one day an ashen-haired spinster called Katrina whispered that she should avoid men with hair on them and see whether she could grow warm with a smooth man.

Gerutha said she would do anything not to bring dishonour on her father the fish-Jarl. Katrina brought a stable-thrall into the little holly-wood beyond Vendilsgarth Dunes, and he let them put a sack-bag over his head. Then Gerutha tested herself and found that she was not dead from the barley-field after all.

Vendil was away fighting the Finns for a year. Gerutha had her daughter in a cow-byre near Aarhuus. Katrina called her Sibbi and took her as a fosterling.

When Vendil came back hacked from the Finns, he was only half a man and was well pleased that the queen gave him Amleth. Though that last child of his getting was hunched like a bear and was very slow to walk or talk.

21

Vendil, consoling himself in his chair with the hot ale, was pleased enough that Amleth had teeth like a war-horse, yellow and jutting. He said, 'Since there will not be another in Jutland it is up to us to call him the model of what men shall be in the coming years.'

Feng, the king's brother, smiled behind his hand and said, 'A proper prince. Aye, a proper prince. This one will kill monsters unless I am very greatly in error.'

No one listened to Feng then. He was an envious second son with poor hands for a horse and had never killed a man over the age of fourteen.

These things came back to Gerutha the day the little bear was slaughtered in the kitchens. She looked up through her tumbled hair and said to Feng as cold as ice, 'Only a snail! A small snail! That could be enough. That could be better than a chopped lump of bog-oak, brother, gnarled and black.'

Feng at the bed's far side bit his beard and snarled at his title, brother. He drummed with his heels like a man with a lance in him.

'Joch! Joch! I have seen things that would make you howl if the castle-Jarls knew.'

'A chopped lump of bog-oak, brother, gnarled and black. Better a snail, a small snail.'

He spat out a piece of his russet beard.

'If they knew how like you this Sibbi is, below the chin.'

'Gnarled and black, brother.'

His great lips were raw. 'If your son were caught in the beech-woods, coming back from Crabland, we could make bog-oak there too.'

The queen did not laugh then. She took him by the hand. 'What lies between us, one thing. He has harmed no one. Let him be.'

'He is too much the fool to harm anything. He is good for nothing but field-fodder. His hulk would rot down well for the barley. Pigs would relish his orts.'

The queen beat her hands against her head.

'You would not hurt him, the king's seed! Your water would run red from you, to spill his blood. Your hand-bones would dissolve, reaching for the sword. To bleed king's flesh—to make veal of a prince! How would you dare, Bog-oak?'

Feng kicked the clay water-pan across the room in his fury and broke it against the far wall. He looked a while as the straw drank the water, then said: 'Why do you adore the king's seed, thrall-lover? Do you take him back into you, gobbling him, Barley-Mother? Is that your love? And this Sibbi: do you suckle her still? Or does she suckle you?'

Gerutha put her hand out to clench him but he drew back laughing: 'Or do you set them together, blood to blood, left hand to right hand, to make issue? Is that your secret barley-sowing? Is that your sin?'

The queen stood tall at him and said, 'You, king-killer. You tell me my sin. Savages you are, the men. Redder savages, the kings. Is there no cleanness in the world? Is there no clear water, no bright sun?'

Feng coughed and spat and latched on his silver belt-buckle. He said, 'I will tell you something, little queen. You were afraid of my brother Vendil. He was like the north-wind to you; like a tall pine; like an ice-rock. He was too big for you. Too hairy and big.'

Gerutha Jute-queen put on her worsted mantle and said, 'Yes, I feared him, Feng; but I do not fear you. Come barley-sowing and I could have you sweating against an oak-stake, watching your seed sprinkled in the furrows. I could have you tied powerless, Feng. The castle-Jarls would welcome such a saviour giving what they feared to lose themselves.'

Feng stood well back from her, fingering his raw beard. He said, 'We are wedded, Gerutha, and must make the best of a bad job. But I shall set spies to watch the mad prince. I shall watch your thrall-bastard, Sibbi, myself.'

The queen bared her pointed teeth at him and said, 'The girl Sibbi will wrench you to your knees, old bog-oak. She has earth in her, and that can smother a fire and a man.'

23

Sibbi lay on a pile of sheepskins in the dark spruce-hall of Yule-tide, while a young thrall named Runolf made rough play with her. She flinched but said smiling, 'Steady, farmboy, or you'll lose your fingers.' He laughed down on her and smacked her. 'You,' he said, 'a queenly-thing, and so thin! They are fatter along the west shore, the broth-wenches, with their big hips. They could take a war-horse and not shout.'

Sibbi nipped him and said, 'With the pot-grease on you, why do I bother? I could have princes in the green bracken, so why you?'

Runolf drew away for a while not knowing what to do or to say. Then he whispered into her mouth, 'You, Sibbi, a thin beanpole, you! With those other women there is warmth and rolling in the damp hay. With you, only this squealing, this pulling off and talk of kings. That saddens a man. It is like ice on him.'

Sibbi screwed up her blue eyes under their tight ash-fringed lids and said, 'If the prince came back and found you on me, he would do something you would never forget. You would never be the same again.'

Runolf glanced aside and said, 'He is a fool, he is a gelded calf. He and his two companions live in a dry dream. He and Gautrek and Torfi—three dreamers who have never had a woman or got a man. They like it cold on the hill, not hot in the hall. When this world ends, as end it must before long, they will say that the god ordained it—and will never think that they brought it about with their hesitation of putting new men onto the earth to keep things going.'

Sibbi slid from his hard hand and wiped her face with her mantle that lay across a stool. She said, 'I cannot trust that the world will end as you and the other thralls say. It has been going so long. I have heard travellers tell that it was here even before the Romans. It was here when there were Greeks and Egyptians. There was a little wizened man here a month ago in the castle hall bartering silver bowls who said that we should be stupid to think the world would end this year or even for another twenty years. This man had seen great red stone palaces that stretched up to the sky, where kings and queens lay in rows, shut in their golden boxes, and never a stink coming from them because of the herbs. And he had put his fingers into the sand in another place in Greekland and had pulled up face-masks of gold that had been on kings' flesh in their time. Oh, the things he had seen and touched . . .'

Runolf said laughing, 'I am touching something now, but it is not a Greek's, Sibbi!'

She lay a while to consider it, then moved when the time had come and gone and said at last, 'Yes, peasant, but I am trying to tell you of the things that stretch beyond this minute. This traveller who called himself Count Daedalus, but whose slave said his name was Delos, told us all in the feast-place that the world is merely a great estate. There are many kings in it and each one has his own company. Each one has his own house and statues. In Rome there is such a king, with fifty virgins in white to wait on him. In Greekland there is another who builds columns of black stone into a labyrinth, and round every black column a white snake carved in alabaster.'

Runolf drew her to him again and said, 'I do not care whether the snakes are black or white. Let us think of our northern snakes that are neither—but, oh, how they can wriggle and sting!'

Then in a while Sibbi said, 'You must see that the cooks give you the thickest beef-broth, Runolf-snake. You will die else. Then what shall I do until the prince comes back from Crabland? With you cold and stiff, ah, no!'

Runolf could find the strength to roll over a little and say, 'Cold, yes; but stiff, oh no! Not stiff—not then!'

They were both laughing about this and pulling each other about over the hay-bed, when a kitchen-woman came in and said, 'Runolf, look what the old man gave me for getting the hook into a little bear.'

He took what she held out and said, 'Odin, Odin, a gold ring! A gold ring! Shall we marry on this, you and me?'

Sibbi covered herself with the mantle so that the kitchen-woman should see less to carry back to her mates. And when the woman had gone she said to Runolf, 'Why do you open your mouth so?'

He was already pulling on his breeches and said, 'And why do you? Yours may have no teeth in it but it bites a man down to the very root. From now on, Sibbi, call someone else when you are afire, I shall go with the ring-woman. She carries more meat on her bones. Besides down in the shippen the men say that you are like one of those rotting apples that spread the taint to the next fruit that touches you. I shall go to the woman with the golden ring. She is clean.'

Sibbi did not show that she heard him. She raked her ashy hair with a silver comb then put on her mantle and belted it round her with a twisted thong girdle.

And when she had scented herself with cat-musk and rose-water, she went down to the kitchen to see if the women had kept the bear's thing. She had never seen one, much less handled one, and yet the men were always talking about them as though they were dumbfounding, like thunder.

Yet when she held the thing she wondered why such a mystery was made of it. A small boy was stouter she thought.

And while she was rolling it one way and another in her fingers, the horns blew and Feng rode out on a black horse past the open window. He was red-faced and furious. She shook the thing at him in mockery, but he only glared and frothed at the mouth. He had the little black bear's carcass over the horn of his saddle. It hung down on either side as thin as a wolf-skin.

Always that was how life turned out: great songs and stories were made of it but when one saw the thing it was nothing. Runolf had seemed great in her slithering dream—but now he was nothing. Even flint-eyed Gerutha was nothing. Even the dead king who had seemed like a rough pine-tree once when he held her against the wall was nothing. She began to wonder if even the prince was nothing; Amleth the wide-eyed shambler. Was he nothing too?

In a narrow fiord on the west side of Crabland, off Sealand, stood a low booth of grey stone roofed with brown sea-kelp. Two men sat before its door holding axes across their knees. Twelve paces

26

away, in the tall coarse grass sat forty men bearing lances and swords. Their gear was brightly polished and bore the emblem of the raging bear. But the men at the door wore poor clothes, of iron kettle-hat and horsehide. Their legs were wrapped round with harsh brown linen.

But that was the only poor thing about them. One was a fierce-faced man with a grizzled beard up to his eyelids; and stood almost seven feet tall. The other was hunched and black, with hair to his breast and a nose like an eagle. His backbone was bent but his face was like a king's. About his bare thick-thatched arms he wore four circles of red gold set with red garnets. Every movement he made when speaking, though in whispers, was one of a harpist. His right eye was dark brown, his left the white of milk. All his motions of the head were to the right, towards his axe-hand.

Inside the booth, bent over a slow fire of driftwood and piled sheep-dung, sat two other men. The one in the heavy grey bearskin was middle-aged, about thirty, and wore a short-cropped beard about his fine chin and cheeks. The other would be eighteen and had little beard yet. But his crop of yellow hair made up for it. He had no eyebrows and his eyes were as colourless as flint. His hands were large, and the red of them reached halfway up his thick arms that were dense with corn-coloured fur. His mouth jutted forth, because his top and bottom teeth were as big as a horse's and as yellow.

But both were proper men, who would have stood a head above all others in a market-place full of folk.

The one with the big teeth spoke gently to the other, almost like a thrall. The one in the bearskin smiled a deal and answered slowly, like a priest giving counsel. His name was Beowulf and he was a king among the Geats. The other's name was Amleth, and he would one day be king in Jutland, unless he was killed before his uncle Feng died.

And Amleth said to Beowulf: 'What is there for a young hero to do, my lord, up here among peasants?'

After much thought, the king of the Geats said: 'All the mere-

27

monsters are dead: I put an end to them. And there are no men, except in Spain among our folk the Vandals.'

Amleth kicked the smouldering fire with his cowhide boot and said: 'Then what can a prince do, to show himself to the people?'

Beowulf picked up a glowing stick and blew on it. Looking under his eyes he said: 'In Greekland there is a great captain called Belisar, or Belisarius as the Romans there call him. He is a great doer and always calling forth for other horse-captains to join him. A man could gain gold coin and fame, riding with him.'

Amleth said: 'I would go, and happily.'

Beowulf answered: 'It is two long seasons off by longship down the bad rivers. And this Belisar would have you kill men who speak your own tongue.'

Amleth said: 'That is no bar. Men are always killing other men who speak their own tongue up here for no coin or fame. So why not in Greekland among the Romans?'

Beowulf said: 'You speak shrewdly. But what we do up here is our own business: and what we do out in the bright world is something else. I for one would hardly care to put the axe to another Geat, once we were south of Kiev. Indeed, I would hardly speak harshly to a mere-monster or a woodland troll, unless I knew he came from the north.'

So they talked on a while, and the men outside picked their teeth with thorns and wondered how to pass the slow time.

Amleth said, 'This Belisar, his city is a great one full of gold. A Jute-prince with twenty axe-friends might come away rich, might he not?'

Beowulf scratched at his beard and spat into the fire. He said, 'When I was a young man in Hrothgar's time I thought the same. That king's city was Heorot and you would have thought a wandering warman would get rich there. The streets were paved with coloured stones, the Hart-Hall was overlaid with gold, its roof lofty and wide-gabled. Inside against the dais-wall he had stag's horns plated with gold and his tables were as long as a ship. You would

28

have thought he was free-handed enough to see the gold on his woman's neck and the good swords his carles carried.'

Amleth said, 'He did well by you, didn't he, king?'

Beowulf said, 'I brought a boatload of Geats with me, so there was something to pay for what we did for him. But what I got mainly for my trouble was a lecture against pride and a kiss on the cheek. The gifts he gave out I had to distribute to my own lord when we made landfall. My king, Hygelac, was never slow in holding out his hand when the warmen came home again.'

Amleth said, 'At Hrothgar's Hall you had trouble with old Unferth. He called you a fool. They still speak of that at Vendilsgarth.'

Beowulf said, 'If I could meet him again, and he a young man, I would shorten him by a head's length.'

Amleth said, 'His son holds a steading outside Vendilsgarth even today. He is my uncle Feng's close friend. He calls me a fool, too.'

Beowulf said slowly, 'Perhaps one of them could be right. Why do you not take the axe to him and see what he says?'

Amleth smiled. 'I would rather sail south and serve the Roman Belisar. There might be more profit in it than you got from Hrothgar. Times have changed, men ask a higher price now.'

Beowulf said, 'Times may have changed, but kings have not. Belisar would first set you all praying to his god, Kristni the White-Warlock. When your knees were raw and you could hardly climb into the saddle he would put you on killing your own folk down there. You would be better at work for the Roman duke in Britain. He is softer in the head than Belisar.'

Amleth thought of this for a while then said, 'This Kristni down at Micklegarth, what sort of god is he, then?'

Beowulf said, 'He is the same god as all gods. Up in the hills they call him Theos with a hammer in his hand. Others call him Tonur Thunderer. Down there by the blue sea they say Kristni. But it's all the same; they hang him on the tree and put a spear into him just like Odin up here.'

He began to laugh and then to chant:

> *I know that I hung on the windy tree*
> *For nine whole nights,*
> *Wounded with spear, wounded for Odin,*
> *Self dies for self.*

Amleth said, 'I would not put the point into myself. Now that would be a madness!'

Beowulf said, 'Some men have a wit as thick as a horn-lantern. Only small light shows through.'

He got up and groaned as he stretched his legs. It was damp in the booth on the sea shore. Green moss grew on the inner stones and white mould came under the footings close to the earth.

The Geat-king said at last, 'Amleth, a king on a tree is a king on a tree. There are no two ways about it. They are the same king. Romans put the lance into Kristni's side; Odin put it in for himself, to finish the agony. It does not matter who finishes a god as long as he goes at the year's end. There have been old Greeks who jumped off high rocks when their time came. That is good. When my time comes I may jump back again into the sea; or I may feel cold in the winter and leap onto a funeral pyre. It matters nothing. The king dies for himself to be eased of all the things he has to do for the people. It is a sweet parting of the ways; he does not regret it. Consider, he is a tired old man worn to the bone by serving his folk. He wants rest.'

Amleth said, 'When I go it shall be with trumpets blowing and red flags in the fierce breeze—no putting the point into myself.'

Beowulf said, 'That remains to be seen, boy. Even this famous White-Warlock, Kristni of the Romans, cried out to himself when he was on the black beam. He said, "Father Elias, let us have done with this now. I have had enough".'

Amleth scratched his thick hair at the root then said, 'But that is not crying out to himself, to cry to his father.'

Beowulf said, 'This Elias he shouted to had another name among the Micklegarth-folk. He was Helius who drove the sun across the sky. And this Kristni who called himself the Fish-god, or at other

30

times Poseidon, was that same Helius, whose other name was Zeus, whose other name was Helius. Look, youth, I have spent a lifetime trying to work out which god made me do this and that; so do not come up here from Vendilsgarth and try to right me now.'

He was pulling at his beard and his lower lip was showing so much of his fangs that Amleth thought it well to pause a while. This Geatish king was too powerful for a Jute to anger at the moment.

At last Beowulf calmed and said with a stark smile, 'Do not try to think of everything, boy. Listen to the old men who have already thought of it all and they will guide you. See, this Kristni Warlock is Odin hanging on the tree, as all other gods have hung in their day. So why take the pains of sailing down to Micklegarth to serve him? Why not go where there is fresh-minted coin, and no god to speak of to serve? Why not sail to Britain and shovel good Roman meat and wine into your mouth? The duke there is a fool, he does not know which side his arse hangs on. Go to Arthur the Bear and join his warband. Then when the sea-chests are full, come back and sit upon the throne chair in Jutland.'

Suddenly he put forth his hand and took Amleth in the inner part of his thigh near the root and gripped tight. He said, leaning towards him and smiling, 'We of the north are not the fools men make us out to be, eh Amleth?'

The prince drew himself away. 'Get a queen,' he said. 'I am a man.' For a moment, he came near to dragging out his knife. Though he thought that this would be a poor weapon to stand against the great blade the Geat had at his hip.

Then all at once Beowulf was grinning down on him and was saying, 'There, little one! There! It is only between one king and another-to-be. We kings do not rain the common earth with our favours, you know.'

He drew away and then Amleth wondered if he had done right in being so angry at a king touching him.

King Beowulf saw him to the door of the booth. He said, 'It should be a fine day tomorrow as you go into the haven at Vendils-garth. You should sail in with a following wind and that will let your pennant stream out to the waiting folk boldly. Also it will let you go in without the tents up on deck. It always looks better for a prince to sail in without cover. These tents look cowardly, boy.'

Amleth nodded his great head. 'I shall do as you say, lord.'

Then Beowulf leaned over to him and whispered in his ear. 'Be not so afraid of a kingly touch,' he said. 'One man strengthens another, remember. It is only the women who geld a man.'

Amleth turned away and whistled to his comrades, Torfi and Gautrek. His face was so flushed he did not dare look back at King Beowulf who still stood outside the Thing-booth on the rocky shore.

It was only when they were ten arrow-lengths offshore that Amleth said to tall Gautrek, 'That Beowulf is a proper man for dragon-killing.'

Gautrek spat over the side into the water and said, 'Aye, lad, proper enough for getting old fish-wives under waterfalls and calling them mere-monsters—but what he would look like if a real man ever took a sword to him, Odin knows!'

Black Torfi hobbled up and said laughing, 'Come away, Amleth lad, or this Gautrek will spoil you. Come and watch the seals floating.'

Gautrek, who held the steerboard, called after them, 'I would never spoil him but that Geat would! Amleth needs real men to tend him not that old woman!'

They pulled into Vendils-Haven the next day just about sundown. It was a cold damp afternoon with the drizzle slashing across the shore, turning the sand to mud. No one was there to see their ship make landfall so they did not hoist the pennant, nor did they take down the deck-tents. There was no wisdom in making a princely show if no eyes were there to see it.

The way up to the castle went first between tall dykes that held the green-scummed water away from the low fields and then it passed across a stretch of waste on which only the wiry heath grew and no sheep grazed. Beyond this place the land plunged down again

32

and knee-high grass grew green and rank. Here there were woods as thick and untended as they had been since Odin had his shrine there. Great brambles straggled between the firs and pines as thick as ship's ropes. In its season the staring phallus of the cuckoo-pint showed itself without shame, garlanded by its lady-sheath in the shadow of the woodland. The old women of Vendilsgarth flung their aprons over their grey heads and went mumbling past this place; hardy boys from the fish-Jarls' steadings dragged fatherless girls there to show them the pretty flower and did not let them go until they had made some try at following its example. Then all ran back, some laughing, some weeping, to the single street of driftwood hutments that led up to the stone walls of the garth.

When the three voyagers came to this woodland, Torfi crossed his first two fingers and held them up above his monstrous head. Gautrek the Mild slapped him on the hunched back and said, 'There are no ghosts here now, you fool. That is all past. Men rule the earth now.'

But Torfi said, 'You cannot hear what I can hear, flap-mouth.'

And then they walked into a thick grey salt-mist which stayed with them until they came to the wood's far edge. Here Amleth held up his hand to halt them. 'Hark,' he said, 'there is someone there. Get down behind this gorse.'

They crouched and stared through the greyness and saw a dark shape moving back and forth, back and forth. It was Feng hunched on his shaggy black horse, bent like a troll, wet through with sea-fret, the tussocky grass up to his stirrups. He was cracking a long whip-thong and crying out, 'Joch! Joch! Forgive me, Vendil, I meant no harm. See, I have hung up an offering to Odin here. Joch! Joch!'

Torfi whispered, 'He is a man in agony.' But Amleth put his hand over the dwarf's mouth and squeezed it tight shut. 'Listen,' he said.

Feng was riding again and again at a leaning oak tree, slashing with his whip at a draggled carcass that hung there and crying out with each stroke as though he felt the lash himself.

Then the sudden rain came down and still crying out Feng swung

C   33

his horse round and cantered heavily through the muddy grass towards Vendilsgarth. The three came from behind the gorse bush and went to see what hung in the oak-tree. It was a small black bear so torn and beaten that it looked hardly more than a worn black bag of mangy hair.

Gautrek said, 'This man must be in sore trouble when he offers such a beast to Odin. See they have cut off its parts—what manner of offering is that to the god?'

Amleth said, 'He called out my father's name. That I did not understand.' Torfi said, 'Nor will you ever understand if you stay here in the rain fumbling with a stinking hide on a tree.'

They ran through the rain, wrapping their short cloaks over their daggers to keep the rust from them, and reached the castle just as dusk came down and the gate-guards were dragging the stockade timbers into place for the night. Amleth called out to them to hold back a while. One of the men said starkly, 'What, leave the gate open for it to come up out of the wood and fetch another king?' Amleth shook the man by the hair a while for his insolence but in the garth-yard he turned to his friends and said, 'Fetch which other king? Are they all mad here?'

Torfi and Gautrek left him at the hall door, for they were not allowed in among the kept-men. Amleth strode onward towards his mother's bower.

Queen Gerutha was sitting in her chair, biting her white lips. All day she had tried to make the two pebbles roll towards each other but no power came out of her to shift them. Now she felt weak and very empty and when her son ran in through the spruce-boughs, she did not dare look him in the eyes. He kneeled before her and said, 'Queen, I have come back.' She nodded; 'So I see,' she said. 'Did you learn anything of use from the King of Geats?'

Amleth said, 'What is my father doing, queen? Where is he?'

Gerutha bit at her lips again and began to weep. Amleth reached up with his great hand and wiped the tears from her cheeks. 'Has he been harsh with you, queen?' he asked. 'Has the king hurt you?

When the time comes for me to roll him off the throne-chair he shall know what he has done before he dies.'

Gerutha shook her head, she said, 'You must not speak like that, my son. You must not even think of doing harm to the king. Only ill-luck can come of such thoughts.' She leaned forward and held him to her, his great staring head against her soft breast. He closed his eyes and nuzzled her as though he was a babe again. He thought how right she was; the king was so great and powerful, with such a black troll-head and starting eyes. Vendil must surely be made in the image of Odin, so giant-like that no man could overcome him. Even the scent that came off him was enough to frighten the war-stallions into kicking their stalls to pieces; and when he as little as coughed the fierce boar-hounds ran under the trestle-tables with their tails between their legs. Once when he was a little lad Amleth had heard his father making water against the stable wall after a feast and it was like a great river gushing out. Once when the thralls were driving the steers up to the castle-butchery to pole-axe them before winter came on, a four-year bullock broke loose and ran at the king in its madness, scenting the blood of its fellows in the troughs. And King Vendil clenched his fist and struck the beast on the neck and everyone in the shed heard the neckbone crack like ice breaking. Then the bullock fell dead against the king and he stood his ground until the butchers dragged it away; and then the women found that Vendil's leg had been broken in that fall, but he had given no sign of it. They bound his leg within green willows and he was off hunting the day after, riding first among the men and shouting the loudest. Amleth, mouthing gently at his mother's breast, was a child again, and knew that his father was a god. He shuddered to think that he had dared threaten him. Then Gerutha began to shudder too and pushed him away roughly.

She said, 'Go and see Sibbi. She may have news for you.'

Sibbi was sitting with the other unmarried women, teasing sheep's wool into yarn which would go onto the queen's wheel to be spun in time. They sat in the straw at the far end of the Maidens'

35

Bower where the men did not come and so there was little modesty among them. Some sat cross-legged with their shifts drawn up about their waists for comfort; others who had dressed felt freer without their bodice-thongs tied. Sibbi herself wore only a blanket about her shoulders for she sat the closest to the hearth-fire in the middle of the chamber and did not feel the cold.

They were talking of women's things, of men and of dreaming, when Amleth pushed aside the hurdle-door and strode among them. The girls winked at each other, seeing that he made for Sibbi, and gathering their wool went through the back-curtain into the sleeping-booth.

Sibbi smiled up at the prince but did not stop her yarn-teasing. 'There is a space beside me by the fire, Amleth,' she said. 'Sit and tell me of your journey. Did the Geat-king welcome you well? Did he give you a place in the warband?'

Amleth kneeled before her and took the wool from her hands roughly and flung it down. 'I have come from my mother the queen,' he said. 'What news have you for me?'

Sibbi leaned back a little then put out her hands to support herself with the blanket falling away from her and the fire glowing on her body. She said, 'What news should I have that the queen does not know, Amleth? They killed a little bear in the kitchens and Feng has hung him on the tree as an offering. It is a poor offering but perhaps better than nothing.'

He was nodding, blank-eyed, and running his hands over her absently as a man does along the shaft of a spear. She moved to make it easier for him since he was more clumsy than most. He said to her suddenly, 'Why should Feng make the offering? What right has he, with a true king in Vendilsgarth? Is that the news you are to tell me?'

She smiled sadly and moved his hard hands a little way so that he should not hurt her. Then she leaned towards him and put her arms about him gently in the warmth of the log-fire. 'You ask so many questions,' she said. 'What would you do if there was not Sibbi to ask?'

36

Now he lay against her, almost smothering her with his great bulk. For a moment her hand came behind his head and pressed it to her breast. He nuzzled it with his mouth, his great teeth about the nipple like a child. It gave him a strange comfort and for a while he forgot his questioning and was still. Sibbi looked past him, her eyes wide and painful. She whispered, 'Let us move away from the fire-light into the straw in the corner.' But he did not hear her. Then she tried to untie the thongs of his belt but he lay so heavily against her she could not find the knot.

Now his face was so damp on her body that she drew off a little and said, 'Amleth, have pity, I am not your mother, have pity.'

He rolled away and sat up, wiping his horse-face with the back of his great hand. 'When I am with you, it seems that you are my mother, Sibbi,' he said. 'There is something the same about you both. I do not know what it is.' Then he bent forward and laid the blanket across the girl's legs and wrapped it about her shoulders. She stared at him with wide dark eyes almost weeping. But he sat a pace from her and cracked the knuckles of his fingers and ran his tongue round the edge of his great teeth.

He said at last, 'What is the news then, Sibbi?'

She clenched her jaws bitterly and got to her feet. With her back towards him she said, 'Vendil is dead. The thralls found him trodden into the midden three nights after you set out for Crabland. That is the news, since it is news and nothing else you seem to want.'

He jumped up like a troll and ran at her. He took her by the shoulders in his great hands and swung her round to face him. She cried out with pain and the girls in the bed-booth, listening, nudged each other and winked again, nodding and laughing.

But Sibbi was not laughing. His great teeth were so near to her face she thought he might tear her with them. 'Amleth,' she gasped, 'be gentle for Odin's sake. You should not be so rough with me.'

The women in the bed-booth clapped their hands over their mouths and laughed again, then put their ears to the wall so that they should have all the more to tell.

Sibbi broke away and stood trembling. 'Leave me be, Amleth, I

37

beg you. I did not do it. If the truth were told, Feng and his hench-men did it. He wears the crown now and lies in your mother's bed at night.'

Amleth began to beat his fists against his head. 'It cannot be,' he said. 'No man could put an end to Vendil. He was the god here. He was the sun and the thunder. He made the seed spring in the field-furrows. Without him the land is in darkness and the crops will not come. It cannot be. You are a liar and the daughter of a troll.'

Sibbi's teeth were chattering now with fear and all the warmth of her had turned to ice. But she dared to say, 'I may be the second, for all I know, but I am not the first, Amleth. All I can tell you is that Vendil's body lay in the hall for seven days while you were away, and we have much cause to remember it. Its stench filled the place from beer-cellar to gable-tower. It is not a thing we can forget. Then, on the eighth day, they put him onto the black boat and his two stallions with him and pushed it out, burning.'

Amleth made no effort to take her by the throat now but stood like a bullock after the pole-axe has fallen, still for a while, his long arms dangling; his mouth wide open. And at last he said, 'Vendil went away in fire? He has gone now, altogether gone?'

Sibbi nodded. 'It was a good burning,' she said. 'They tarred the boat freshly for it and the deck was laden with resin and pine-boughs. He went down half a mile off Hawkness, and on the tide next day only one piece of him came in. It was a finger from his right hand. I have kept it for you, wrapped in linen, in case you should want it. That is all there is left of Vendil now, my lord.'

Then Amleth gave a cry and ran from the bower, hitting against the door-posts with his great body as he passed through and shaking the chamber.

At last the girls came back again to their wool-teasing. They did not look directly at Sibbi but just hummed or sang quietly as they searched for their yarn among the straw.

Then the oldest woman said, 'You have let the fire go down, Sibbi. It must have flared fiercely while we were away.' She picked up a piece of charred stick that lay at the edge of the hearth and wagged it up and down a while, setting the girls off giggling again.

Suddenly Sibbi drew the blanket round her tightly and ran into the bed-booth; then they all laughed and began to tell each other what it must have been like.

Unferth the Lawspeaker was in the dark passage-way when Amleth ran past him crying out, 'Feng shall die with a stake through the heart. Vendil's son shall put an end to him. He shall not live another day.'

Unferth drew back into a nook in the wooden wall and let the prince run on without seeing him. Then he went down the seven stone steps to the war-room where Feng sat among the spears and shields drinking with his henchmen, Hake and Godgest, and said, 'He knows now. The young piglet knows that the old boar has gone.'

Feng nodded smiling. 'That will make him grunt,' he said. The two henchmen laughed. Unferth said, 'Aye, king, but now he grunts like the old boar himself and threatens to bury you.'

Feng said, 'Joch! Joch! It will pass, Lawspeaker! Should I shake in my shoes because a gelding squeals at me? Go, fetch him to me and we'll see who can outstare the other now.'

Then he took up his cup again and began to speak to Hake and Godgest about a herd of the royal swine that had strayed beyond their beechwood into Shadyvale.

Torfi was in the yard with Gautrek the Mild. They were playing knuckle bones and waiting to be called to the kitchen for their evening meal of sheep broth when Amleth ran out blindly towards them.

Gautrek rose and wrapped his arms about him and sat him down in the straw by the wall. 'There,' he said, 'there. This is no time to be screaming. There is no battle being fought that I have heard of.'

Amleth wrestled for his breath a while then cried out, 'Vendil is dead. They have killed the king.'

Torfi glanced at Gautrek then said gently, 'So, so. They must all die, the kings. It comes to them all.'

Amleth struck at him but Gautrek took his fist gently and held it, smiling down at him and nodding. He said, 'Would you rather have stayed and been stark too? Do you think they would have left you living once they had got Vendil down onto the ground? You did better to visit the Geat-king, though he did not want you in his service. Sometimes Odin arranges these things with keener craft than we give him credit for.'

Amleth groaned and said, 'This Feng, a stake through the heart will be too kind to him.'

Torfi nodded, 'Aye, too kind by half,' he said. 'But let us be kind for once in our lives, my prince. Let us make stakes for him and when we put them into him, let us remember to tell him how kind we are being.'

Amleth began to laugh now and his laughter was worse than his crying. 'Aye, aye,' he shouted, 'let us to the wood and cut stakes. There is no time to lose. Let us go now.'

He rose like a bullock after the first knock of the axe, swaying a while on his feet. His friends rose and supported him, then began to run with him away from Vendilsgarth.

Unferth stood in the dusk on the steps from Feng's chamber watching them go. Then he turned and hurried back to his master and said, 'The young boar has gone to sharpen his tusks on the oak-trees, Feng. When he comes back he may need some holding down.'

Feng the king laughed and said, 'We shall do that, Unferth. And we shall not call for help from you.'

Unferth, jealous at the heart that Hake and Godgest stood so high in the master's favour, said bitterly, 'You will need my help before the song is sung, Feng.'

Hake said, picking his teeth with a thorn, 'That will be the day, sheep-shanks.'

But Feng waved him to silence and said mockingly to Unferth, 'If you would be of use to me, then go now to the queen and warn her to be on her guard against the young boar. Tell her that my ears are everywhere, my eyes are everywhere. Tell her that I shall know if she speaks one word against me. And tell her that whatsoever the young boar speaks against me, she must tell me that thing.'

Godgest, drawing deep at his ale, wiped his thick mouth and said, 'Aye, but Gerutha is a queen, all said and done, Feng. You cannot send old Unferth hang-cock here to tell a queen what she shall do and what not.'

Feng glared at Godgest for a long while but the man glared back smiling so at last the king turned his gaze on Unferth and said, 'Tell the queen that in this world no one is safe. Tell her that the tongue of malice can bring a lion to his knees and can lay even a queen over the log. So tell her to be true to me and to no other. Go now.'

And when the old man had gone, Hake said, 'You mean this tale of Sibbi and old Katrina, do you not? And the thrall with the bag over his head?'

Feng slowly drew his dagger and began to pare the finger-nails of his left hand. He did not look up at Hake but he said quite clearly, 'Go to bed, you sot. King's business and queen's business is not for dogs like you to munch at.'

Hake rose and gripped the board. His neck was red with sudden anger. He said, 'You did not talk like that the night I scratched on the door to fetch old Vendil out.'

Then he saw Feng's eyes slowly rising to stare into his own and he wished he had not spoken. There was a long silence in that cold room. Even Godgest's thick fingers were shaking on his knee. And at last Feng said evenly, 'Sometimes in winter my hearing fails me with the cold. Go to bed now, Hake, and dream that you have many years before you yet.'

Hake bowed his head and stumbled from the room. When he had gone, Feng looked across the board at Godgest and said, 'Was there something you wished to say, henchman?'

Godgest took up his ale-can again and said quietly, 'Nothing much, master. When Hake has drunk too much his words puzzle me.'

Feng smiled at him, nodding. 'Which words puzzle you, Godgest?' he asked very gently.

41

The man rubbed his thick russet hair and said, 'When he spoke of scratching on Vendil's door, that puzzled me.'

Feng drew in his lips tightly. He said, 'Aye, that puzzled me too. I am glad that it puzzled you, my friend. Let us throw more logs upon the fire and pour ourselves another cup of ale. We do not puzzle one another, do we, side-man?'

Godgest smiled and got up to do as he was bid. 'I think we understand one another, Master,' he said.

When Unferth drew aside the hide curtain of the queen's chamber and stepped within he was blind for a while in the darkness and thought that there could not be anyone in the great bed. Then he saw that the queen's scarlet robe lay on the rush-covered floor and upon it Sibbi's shift of grey-striped linen. And when he raised his eyes he saw that the two lay with their arms about one another. They were not looking at him but were lying very still as though they were asleep. Yet he could hear their quick breathing. He even thought he could hear their hearts thudding together like the hooves of a galloping horse.

At another time he would have withdrawn from the chamber in silence; but now he was on king's business and so dared speak up. He said, 'It is cold tonight. You do wisely to share each other's warmth. I will throw another spruce branch on the fire.'

And when he had straightened from throwing on the branch, the queen had drawn up the coverlets of the bed and seemed to be lying in it alone. She said to him calmly, 'I am warm enough, lying alone. Did you think that the king lay with me here?'

Her eyes were so grey and cold that Unferth looked away from them and said, 'Nay, my lady, nay. I am just an old man whose sight plays him tricks at night. My eyes give me trouble.'

Gerutha smiled thinly at him. She said, 'We could cure that, old man, couldn't we? What have you to tell me? Speak out and let me go back to sleep.'

But the strength had gone from his legs and his voice. All he could bring himself to say was, 'My lord the king begs you to take

42

care for your safety, Gerutha. He says these times are dangerous.'

The queen yawned and said, 'All times are dangerous, especially to old men who have outstayed their welcome on the earth. Go back and tell Feng that I know of no one who would hurt me before they hurt him. Now leave me to sleep.'

She rolled back in the great bed and pulled up the blanket. He went out and drew the hide curtain behind him, trembling with anger. And even as he started down the passage-way he heard laughter in the queen's chamber. It was not Gerutha's voice, he was sure; but he was too afraid now to turn back and see what they were doing.

He shambled away to his own pallet at the end of the great hall where the horses were tethered, and there he lay with his fur-mantle up round his ears, whispering to himself, 'God, if I could only be away from this place! If I could only be young again and away.' Then he began to dream of bright places where the sun always shone and the sky was blue; places where the tall houses were made of white marble and there were doves and singing and red wine in cups of silver. Places where a man could speak out in liberty and never have to wonder if someone hid behind curtains listening to him and reporting what he had said.

All round him the kept-men were snoring in the straw or stumbling past him to make water between the horse-stalls. One of them went at it so fiercely he splashed Unferth who came back from his dreams of Rome and wiped his face with disgust. But he did not speak up against this man. He saw that it was the king's henchman, Hake, who seemed to be in a furious temper and was still wearing his short sword.

Amleth ran laughing madly into the wood, among the knee-high bushes, his breeches half-torn from his legs by the gorse spikes. Gautrek was three paces behind but could not reach out to grasp him. Torfi struggled along after them his twisted body making hard going of the run.

The dusk lay as heavily as chain hauberk on them all. The whitened boughs reached out to take the runners by leg or body or neck.

43

Below them the ground was so thick in mosses and pine needles that they made no sound. A listener in the wood could have heard only the breaking of sticks and the harsh sobbing of breath.

Then Amleth struck against a thick tree bole and fell off balance to the ground. Gautrek stumbled against him, then lay upon him to hold him there. Torfi came up groping and calling out, 'This is no time to cut stakes. We cannot see to cut stakes. We should have brought a torch.'

Amleth bit upward at Gautrek's hands, like a frightened savage beast. But his friend did not strike back at him; instead he waited for the prince's fury to wear itself out.

In Gerutha's chamber the two women lay, breast to breast, limb to limb, mouth to mouth. The fire had burned down again to white ashes and the air all about them was dark. They were not covered by sheepskins or hides yet it was as though they were enclosed by a strange almost silent whispering; as though they lay together in a thick wood of silent sounds. No man could have made his way through that wood though he took sword and axe with him. The chuckling that came from their throats was not of merriment. The shuddering that passed between them was not of cold. If all the words had gone from the world these two could have spoken messages to one another in that stifling wood through their limbs. One young, one old, they were of one flesh. Two branches of the same tree. Two waves of the same sea.

All that night they slept and woke in unison and the teaching went out of Gerutha's body into Sibbi's, then back again like a lesson that is rehearsed then taught again, then told back again.

And at last when the cock-crow sounded through the swinging shutters of the chamber, they fell apart and lay with their hair spread out and entangled upon the great bolster, only their lower legs now hooked about one another like the lower twigs of trees.

Gerutha reached out and took Sibbi's fingers in her own, letting them interlace. And at last she said low in her throat, 'Do you still remember the way through the wood, child?' Sibbi did not answer

44

with words but pressed the queen's fingers tightly and smiled a little, her dark-lidded eyes closed. Then Gerutha said, 'Now that you know the way through the wood, the labyrinth, could you take another there? Could you lead the Green Man there and make him King of the Wood?' Sibbi whispered, 'Yes, I have the power now, lady, though for the first time I should need to use the ball of wool to guide him to the centre of the maze.'

The queen said, 'The Green Man, is he afraid of the monster that waits at the centre, have you found out that yet?'

Sibbi rolled a little away on the broad bed and said, 'When he came back from Crabland, he was not ready. He was too heavy with the news of his father's death. He was a little boy again, weeping and unready to become the king.'

Gerutha nodded and said, 'Soon he will want to learn the steps of the dance, and you will teach him. Soon the king in him will rise like the ash-pole of a banner for he will want to trample Feng down. So all things will come together and you will guide him to the centre of the maze and show him how the monster is overcome.'

The girl said, 'Shall you put the sword into his hands, lady?'

The queen nodded again. 'At first it will be the small sword,' she whispered, 'but when Feng has gone it will be the great one. Now show me once again what is to be done, before they come to kindle the fire. I am of his blood, tell yourself that I am he and cast your spell over me, then go back to the bower.'

Feng, rolling and groaning in Vendil's wall-bed, woke suddenly drenched with sweat. He struck out at the kitchen-girl who lay beside him then dragged savagely at her tousled hair to wake her. 'Move your lazy bones, woman,' he said. 'Get me a jar of water from the cistern. I am dying. I feel that my throat has been cut, I feel that they have cut me open. I am full of pain. Hurry and bring me water for my parched mouth, you greasy bitch.'

The kitchen-thrall rubbed her eyes and yawned. To herself she grumbled, 'Ah, kings! Who would lie with kings if there was another way to keep out of the rain with a filled belly.'

45

She slid off the bed and went in the grey light to the rainwater butt with a clay pitcher in her hand.

Amleth woke when the cocks in the crew-yard at Vendilsgarth began to crow, but in the forest it was still night. The dusk lay heavily like wood-smoke between the trees. Torfi and Gautrek were sprawled on a mound of pine-needles, their arms wide, their mouths open and snoring.

Amleth got to his feet and took Torfi's wood-axe from the thong of his belt. Then he went quietly into the thickest of the trees.

In the centre there would be a holly-tree and this he would chop down and sharpen into a stake. And with that stake he would pin Feng to the ground as soon as the right moment came.

Then he and Gerutha would sit on the throne-chairs in Jutland and Vendil's ghost would never come to gibber at them in the dark passage-ways.

Two owls sat on a bough and gazed at him bleakly as he stumbled between the bushes; a large black bird was suddenly disturbed by his footfalls and fluttered away crying harshly among the upper branches.

And after a while Amleth heard Torfi and Gautrek crying out, 'Amleth, Amleth, where are you?' But he did not answer.

At last where the trees cleared to form a dark glade and the earth was bright green with water-mosses he knew that he had reached the centre of the wood. And there standing among high brown-tipped rushes was a woman in a grey cloak. At first he thought it was his mother; then he thought that it might be Sibbi. A great longing that he had not known before came over him and ran like mulled ale through his blood. He let fall the axe and putting out his arms ran in the murk towards the woman in the grey cloak. He was almost up to her when a gust of morning wind blew through the glade and swept the grey cloak aside. And then Amleth saw that Vendil was standing there growing above him all the while, his cloak flying, his eyes wide and dull grey like those of a fish. He was wearing his horned helmet and his mouth was wide open and black inside.

Amleth cried out, 'Do not stare at me like that, father. I am not afraid of you now. I have come to get revenge for you.'

But Vendil still grew up and up and then gave a deep groan that started below the ground at Amleth's feet. The earth shook for a while and suddenly Vendil began to lurch over, his arms above his head as though he wished to smother the prince.

Amleth tried to run back but the dead king came down onto him too fast. Amleth cried out for kindness but the dead king's hard fingers bore him down at shoulder and throat and then thrust him into the bright green mosses as though to stifle him.

And when Torfi and Gautrek found their young lord it took all their strength to lift the rotten oak-bole off him and to drag him clear of the marsh that had almost sucked him down.

Unferth woke suddenly as though a tree had fallen on him and remembered that he wished to be free of Vendilsgarth for ever. The horses were stamping in the straw, the kept-men were sprawled about sleeping until the thrall-women should come through the hall to shake them awake.

He rose and made his way out of the door. In the passage he heard footsteps and drew back from sight to let a kitchen-wench go past with a clay pitcher of water in her hand.

Then he slipped through the outer door and into the stack-yard. It was a cold morning but he did not dare go back to fetch his mantle of pine-marten's fur lest someone should see him.

He had reached the oak-stockade when from beyond the dunes he saw Torfi and Gautrek staggering along, bearing the prince with them, his arms about their necks as though he was drunk or dying.

At first Unferth thought to bend down behind the water-butt and to make his way on to the shore when they had gone by; but Torfi had seen him and called out, 'Come you, Unferth, and give a hand to get your master safely indoors. He is not well.'

The old man called back, 'I have been searching for you all night. Where have you been with the prince? Do you not know that the

47

king sent for him? Is this the respect you pay to Feng, Torfi Hook-back?'

Gautrek the Mild gave him such a look as would have steadied a charging steer and said, 'Take the prince's feet, sheep-shanks, and carry him to his chamber. He will talk with Feng another time when he has rested a while.'

Unferth bent and took Amleth's dragging feet. The old man groaned under the weight for the prince was not the lightest of men. In his heart he groaned yet again but this time because these fools had stopped him from escaping. It might be long enough before the coast was clear again and he could shake the stinking dust of Vendilsgarth off his feet. It might be never.

Outside the tall grey gates of Colonia a little man with a sparse red goat-beard stood between two mules. His woollen robe was so stained and ragged and his feet so caked with mud and dried blood that any man might be forgiven for thinking him a beggar. Yet his mules carried wrapped bundles on their backs and on one of his fingers he wore a thick gold ring. As he knocked on the tall gate he kept calling out in his high voice, 'Open up for me, you in there. I am Gilliberht of Fiesole and Lord Manuel Chrysostom is my patron. Do not keep me waiting, I have fine cloth to show the mayor of your palace.'

The keeper of the gate that morning was a Frank called Clothair who had passed a sleepless night with the toothache and had sunk his axe ten times in the gate-lintel to help the pain to pass. He looked down off the wall at the man with the two mules and said grimly, 'Pass on, stranger. Take the road northwards and do not trouble me. If I come down and open this gate for you I can promise you it will be the last gate you pass through.'

Gilliberht of Fiesole called back, 'This is not your lucky day, gate-keeper. When my patron Lord Manuel Chrysostom hears of this . . .'

But Clothair did not listen to him. He balanced his throwing-axe carefully and then drew back his arm as if to cast it.

The little man in the torn robe bent behind the mules then took

48

their halters and scuttled away. And when they were out of casting-distance he said to the sky, 'Oh, God! Oh, God! Strike the north with Your thunderbolts, I beg You. It is a place of darkness; and there is nothing here worth saving.'

Gerutha stirred in the great bed, hearing the men struggling up the winding stairway with their burden. She went to the chamber door and looked down on them, wrapped round with her scarlet robe, her long hair heavy on her shoulders. They were carrying the prince feet foremost up the steps and old Unferth had his back towards her. He was making more noise than the other two.

She called down to them, 'Bring my son into this chamber. Lay him on my bed. How bad are his wounds?'

Torfi said, 'He has no serious wounds, lady. He is sounder than I am; but a tree fell on him and took the strength from him. He will be whole again.'

Gerutha watched them edge him through the doorway then smoothed the bed for him to lie on. 'See, it is still warm,' she said. 'He will be in comfort here. Leave him with me, friends. I will send for you if he needs you.'

Outside that door old Unferth screwed up his nose and said, 'That place smells of women. These scents they use sicken me.'

Torfi gazed at him then smiled at his friend Gautrek. 'Get on downstairs, you old sheep,' he said to Unferth, putting his toe behind the man.

Gerutha looked down on the prince for a while then called into the bower for Sibbi who came yawning with a band of woven cloth about her waist. 'Look,' said the queen, 'he is back from the wood. His closest comrades say that a tree fell on him so we may be sure that he will bear the marks that a King of the Wood must have.'

They pulled the wooden hurdles across both doors so that they should not be disturbed, then they drew off the prince's ruined garments. Together they looked down on him, turning his limbs this way and that. Sibbi said, 'He has truly been into the wood and truly has the old king put his marks on him.'

The queen said in her gentlest voice, 'We must wash him and dress him afresh for this man will be our king before too long. We must honour him, Sibbi.'

The girl nodded and then the two women dragged over an iron kettle and set it to warm on the hearth-fire. Sibbi gave up her girdle of wool and the queen her scarlet robe to wash the prince clean of his journey's traces. And when it was almost done Gerutha said smiling, 'To see him now, so big, so much a man, I can hardly believe he came from me, a little seedling who is now a tree.'

Sibbi bent over him to dry his body. She said, screwing up her eyes as though she would have laughed, 'To see him so great, so hairy on his body like a bear—I can hardly believe he is still a virgin.'

Gerutha drew the sheepskin coverlet over him as he still slept. She said calmly, 'Each year is divided into its seasons or parts; like Odin's great year-beast, which had a lion's head, a goat's body and a serpent's tail. So is man's life divided; first the untried youth, as he is; then the King of the Wood, the great oak; and at last such a stumbling creature as old Unferth, who almost burst his heart carrying the prince's feet up the stairway.'

Sibbi said, 'I hope that I have gone under ground before Amleth comes to that.'

Gerutha took her by the hand and stroked her cheek. 'I hope that I may lie beside you, little one, rather than see the prince stumbling and gasping for his breath.'

Feng was still scratching at his head and rubbing the soles of his feet together, sitting on the wall-bed, when Unferth came in. He gazed at the old man without love. 'What do you want?' he said. 'I am a sick man, I cannot listen to your kitchen news this morning. My belly was cut open in a dream and my throat slit. I cannot bear to listen to your troubles.'

Unferth bowed his head and waited, then he answered, 'This is something you must hear, Feng, and it is not from the kitchen. Amleth has been to the wood and they have had to carry him back. He has marks on him.'

Feng grasped the edge of the wall-bed and said, 'What marks? Where are the marks? Are they the marks?'

The old man nodded slowly. 'They are the marks, lord. A man would say that old Vendil had put them there with his flint knife. There is the cut across the throat and the slash down the belly, just as the old ones used to mark the Green Men when I first came to Jutland. Amleth is the chosen one, lord, I would swear to that.'

Feng clenched his hands a time or two. He said, 'Yet I had the dream as though I was the chosen one. How can that be?'

Unferth grinned sadly. 'The prince has had more than a dream, lord. The women know it too, they have washed him and anointed him and now he lies on the great bed waiting for his senses to come back. I think we can look to see a different man when he talks to us again.'

Feng rose and walked about the narrow chamber, striking out at the wall-hangings. Hake and Godgest swaggered in yawning and said, 'What is it, Feng? Have the fleas been biting you in the night?'

Feng thought he would strike at Hake's grinning face but then he did not. He said, 'This Amleth plans to tumble me off the throne-chair. He lies as drunk and witless as the wine god on the great bed now with the queen anointing him and putting feast-clothes on him. When he awakes he will be the old Vendil come again. Is that not cause enough for a man to tear his beard out?'

Godgest said, 'You are angry because she has never let you lie in the great bed, in Vendil's bed. That is the truth. Her nymphs have never tended you; you, a king, have had to choose from the kitchen-thralls and sheep-tenders. That makes you angry.'

Feng glared at Godgest wishing he could strike him down with a thunderbolt. But then he swallowed his pride and said, 'You two, my sworn henchmen, you owe me something, surely? I have clothed and fed you and have never asked for anything in return. Now I ask you to go quickly to the great bed while he is still asleep and put a cord about his neck. No blood must be spilled on the great bed but if you pull the thong tight enough it will do. He will never wake to be a king.'

But Hake and Godgest shook their heads smiling at one another.

'If there was a time for that,' said Hake, 'it has gone by now. As we came from the hall we met his side-men, Torfi Dwarf and Gautrek the Mild. They were going to watch at the foot of the stairs for him with their faces painted black as though for war.'

Feng beat with his fists at his thighs in fury. 'Are you afraid of those two?' he yelled. 'What weapons do they carry?'

Godgest said drily, 'Six-foot ash stakes, sharpened more keenly than these swords you gave us when we took service under you, Feng. A brave king like you might care to end pinned to the wall by one of those but Hake and I are kept-men, not kings. Why do you not swallow fern-seed and become invisible? Then you could slip past them and put the cord round Amleth's neck yourself?'

Unferth was about to laugh at this, then he saw that the king's eyes were on him so he set his face back into its solemn lines. Feng glared at him a little while longer then said fiercely, 'What do you advise, you old fool? Do I not keep you in food and shelter for the advice you are supposed to give me? Give me advice then or the cord shall go round your dried stick of a neck before this morning is out.'

In a way the old man would have welcomed this if it could have been done without pain. There was little enough to live on for, in Vendilsgarth, this place of damp salty winds and stinking fish for every meal. He thought of the fish, and the sea where they shoaled, then he said to Feng, 'My lord, your only way is to leave this place for a while. Go along the coast in your longship and see what the gods have for you there. Then, when you come back, things here will have sorted themselves out a little. Who knows, perhaps this Amleth may lean too far over the castle wall and break his neck falling down into the moat. I was looking at it yesterday, there is no water in it now. It is quite dry. A man could fall down there among the swine . . .'

But Feng had risen and waved him to silence again. 'Be quiet, you old goat,' he said. 'You run on like a water-conduit. I will order my own life and it has come to me that the thing to do now is for us to take the longship along the coast a little way. Who knows what the

52

gods might offer? Up towards Crabland we might find some lord-less warman who would be willing to poleaxe a bullock in return for a sack of meal.'

Hake and Godgest nodded. 'The air is heavy here,' said Hake. 'It would be good for us all to stand up in the clean wind for a few days.'

Unferth folded his hands together and bowed his head gently. He was thinking that as soon as the longship had pushed off he would make up a bundle of things, anything he could find outside the treasure-chests, and get away towards the south. Life among the Franks could not be worse than it was in Jutland; Franks were Christmen he had heard. This Kristni had taught his followers to be gentle to one another, to turn the other cheek when the one was struck. So he would go among such fools and see how many cheeks he could strike. They might make him a great lord among them when they saw what he carried in his bundle. He was smiling in his heart at this thought when Feng grasped him hard by the shoulder and made his teeth chatter against one another.

'While I am away, old goat,' the king said, 'you will not stir from this place. If I hear that you have set a foot outside the stockade, I will hang you over the wall for a day and a night by the heels. And if you should think to rob my chests and go with a bundle into Frankland, then think again, for I have cousins down there who would wait for you and catch you. They count the family-blood we share higher than this Kristni the priests make them pray to.'

Unferth put on a forgiving smile and said, 'My dear lord, have I not taken the oath of fealty to you on my bended knees? Am I not your oldest, most trusted counsellor?'

Feng was drawing on his leather-breeches that would keep out the sea-cold. Over his shoulder he said, 'I trust no one, old goat, least of all you. See to it that you obey me and start now; I want you to hide yourself in her chamber, under the straw, and listen to all she says to him and he says to her. When I come back I want to know all. Do this for me and perhaps I shall reward you. It may be that what you tell me will prove that Gerutha is a faithless woman to her husband.

53

Then, surely, the gods will visit her by night and carry her off. Then I shall need a new queen to lie on the great bed with.'

Feng was pulling the ivory comb through his beard now, grunting when it tangled and going red in the face. He said between these grunts, 'Up in Scania there is a princess who will one day be a queen. Gudrid, or Gudrud, I forget which, Skerja's daughter. A woman who talks with birds and can turn water into wine. That's the sort of queen I want. Maybe I will send you up there in a longship with offerings for her father. Would you like that, old goat? Would that please you and bring the red back to your dead old cheeks?'

Unferth bowed, wishing he could strike the king down into the rushes and tread on his great loud mouth. He said, 'The gods know, I do not deserve such a generous master. While you are away I shall pray for your safe return every hour of the day.'

Feng turned away and let the stale air from himself. The henchmen laughed at this kingly wit. Feng said, 'Spend your time listening for me not praying for me, old goat. No god will pay heed to your prayers. So be about it now and see to it that you tell no one what I have spoken this morning.'

Torfi and Gautrek sat at the foot of the stone stairs with their ash-spears across their knees, letting no one pass. To speed the time Torfi asked Gautrek this riddle: 'A creature came where many wise men were sitting in the market-place. It had one eye, two ears and two feet. It had twelve hundred heads, two hands, arms and shoulders, but only one neck. What was its name?'

Gautrek said, 'If you were as able in other things, you would be a rich man now and not a yard-thrall. I do not know, what is it?'

Torfi said, 'A one-eyed onion-seller.'

But Gautrek was not listening to him; his head was cocked on one side as though he heard something else. He said, 'I think we have rats in the boards above the rafters. I think I heard one slither across on its belly just then. What did you say the answer was?'

Unferth was delighted with himself at having made his way above the hall rafters and through the loose wattle-wall into the queen's chamber without being seen or heard. Now he lay in the corner nearest the great bed with a heap of straw upon him. He did not dare part the straw in case the queen should see him but he could hear the prince's deep breathing very clearly and knew that everything said in that room would reach his ears.

He was praying silently that Feng's longship would strike on a sand-shoal a mile off-shore and that the whole ship's company would have to sit out there, in sight of land, until death clenched them about the bowels. He thought that in justice this was the least Odin could do for him after all the torment he had been through at Vendilsgarth over the years.

Then he stopped praying because from the great bed Amleth had begun to cry out. He was saying, 'Mother, mother, where are you? Come to me, mother.'

Unferth heard the door-curtain slide past on its iron rings and then the queen's footsteps across the oak boards. Then he heard her say so sweetly, 'There, there, my bird, my eagle! There, there, my king.'

'Mother, I have been dreaming in the darkness.'

'Lie still, my king, the dream is over now. Look, you are all fresh and clean. And look at the fine clothes you wear!'

Unferth hardly dared to breathe while they were talking in case he should miss something that Feng would want to know about. He held his breath so long that he almost choked out loud. Then at the thought of this his heart began to flutter. What the queen would do to him if she found him under the straw, he did not know. But it would be something bad, something a man could not bear, he was sure. Then they were talking again so he put aside his fears and listened like a blackbird, his head leaned sideways in the dry straw.

'Such fine clothes call for a sword to set them off, mother. It is the woman's place to give the sword. Is there no sword?'

Unferth's ear-drums almost burst with the blood that beat on them as he listened in the heavy silence for the answer. Then it came: 'Feng bears the great sword, your father's sword, the kingly sword. One day very soon it will be yours, my bird. Until that day, you shall carry the short sword that was my grandfather's, old Rorek's sword. It will see you through until you can take hold of the greater sword.'

Unferth heard her feet on the boards and then the opening and shutting of a dower-chest. Then the feet came across the room once more but faster now and the prince cried out, 'Old Rorek's sword! Hey? This is a pretty enough weapon, mother.'

Unferth heard the mattress-straw creaking as Gerutha sat beside the prince. She was saying, 'What a pretty sword, Amleth. How well it suits you, my eagle. Look, if I pull the sheath away you see it has a tip of red coral. And further down still there are two garnets set into it near the guard. Such a sword is worth a kingdom, my bird. You must see, in using it, that the jewels are not harmed for that would take away the worth of such a weapon. My grandfather used to say that he would sooner lose two fingers from his hand than the two stones from his sword.'

Unferth wished he could have pushed the straw aside to see this heirloom. His old limbs shook at the thought of such a sword. It had been many years since he had seen what they were talking of.

Then the prince said, 'Cover it up again, mother. It makes my eyes flash with fire. My heart beats in my throat to see it.'

Gerutha said laughing, 'It is only the winter sun shining on the jewels, my bird. You will become used to that, when you wear it proudly as a prince should. See, I will show you again.'

Then in the midst of her playing Unferth heard the prince say sternly, 'Leave it be, mother. It is mine now, leave it be. There is something else I wish to speak about.'

Unferth opened his mouth so wide that he half-swallowed a piece of straw and had to smother a cough. Then he heard the prince say, 'You have lain with Feng with your lips on his.'

'My bird, my eagle, there are customs a queen may not break.'

'Who suffers if they break them?'

'The people suffer, my bird. Corn does not grow then.'

'What if the king does not love the people? What if he wishes them to die? What if he hates the taste of bread?'

Unferth tasted the dry straw; to him it was no less sweet than any bread he had eaten at Vendilsgarth. He thought: This youth is not the fool men make him out to be. The bread here stinks of fish and rusted iron.

Then the queen said, 'You are talking in your dream still, Amleth. You are saying things that a man does not say, a prince does not say. There are some words a prince may not speak.'

Amleth said, 'Do you mean that some words are not clean, mother? Do you mean that they should be washed with brine?'

His voice came to Unferth so unknowing and guileless that the old man wished he could slap his thin thigh and laugh with this youth.

Then the queen answered, 'Let us look at the sword again, my bird. Let us finger the two jewels then pull back the sheath and see the bright coral gleaming under our hands.'

After a while Amleth said, 'Why, mother, it gleams like blood. It must have come from the deepest sea, where the sunlight never reaches it to fade its colour. Where did it come from, mother?'

Unferth could hear no words in answer. To himself he whispered wisely, 'Nay, but I guess where it will be going to.'

Then Gerutha said breathlessly, 'Amleth, my king, my king, my king, oh my king!'

And Amleth seemed to draw in his wind slowly before he said: 'My queen. My queen. Yes, my queen!'

And after that he sounded like a Lawspeaker standing on the Thing-rock. He said: 'In the rutting season, Gerutha, stallions fight for the mares. They back up to one another and kick their rivals' brains out. Then the mares join with that stallion who triumphs. Is that not the truth?'

Queen Gerutha lying flat on the bed with her eyes closed said in a whisper, 'Yes, my eagle. Do not trouble me with these foolish thoughts.'

Then the prince said, 'You have coupled with such a beast, do you deny it? Feng kicked Vendil's brains out; and now you have wiped out all memory of your proper king. Can you wonder if I, Vendil's

57

son, wish to set the balance straight? What I shall do is for my father, to avenge him. And for you, to bring you to your senses. Do you agree to that?'

Unferth, loving this prince for his hatred against Feng, opened his mouth again to shout a silent agreement. A straw sprang into his throat. For a moment he clutched wildly at it, held his breath like a diver deep below the sea then, being a human man, no more, he coughed.

Feng's longship swept round Gannet's Ness as proudly as any in Jutland. Yet just as she made the caracole a puff of salt wind caught Feng in the nostril and he coughed. The longship swung wide and headed towards Crabland. And before he could get the steerboard round again, the long low shape of a black-painted wargalley streaked out towards them, showing no pennant and hoisting no sail.

Hake, who was known locally as a baresark but who never went in at evens, beat his head on the deck and cried out, 'Thorspiss, we've bought it now. To go salt-treading with such a blunder-ass, that I should never have done.'

His side-mate, Godgest, cried out from the golden prow, 'God save us, but I've seen some cow-handed madmen in my day down at Micklegarth among the Romans—but never one like this.'

He was the warman of the longship whose task was to time the rowers, to drop anchor-stone and to arrange all fighting. But now he gazed round the shock-headed thralls at the oars, then back to the steerboard where Feng and Hake stood like boys with a bellyful of crab-apples. Then he flung his own sword far into the grey sea and called, 'For god's love, thralls, let us have no heroes aboard. When the black galley boards us, keep a smile on your faces even if they pull your nose off.'

Feng said bravely, 'Why, I only coughed. What is there in that? And me a king?'

Hake slipped his sword quietly over the side then walked away from his king. Half-way up among the oarsmen he said, 'If you don't know, I cannot tell you at this stage, Feng. But when I sail abroad again, if the gods give me leave, I'll go with a shipmaster who does not cough. What we have in front of us would make me afraid to cough lest I dirtied my breeches.'

It was low in the water with a wolfshead prow and thirty rowers on either side. Not more than four black strakes showed above the salt and over that the round shields lay in a row, lapping one another, red against white against blue against yellow; hawk against wolf against bear against snake.

It came at them like an arrow from a Turk's horn-bow; too fast to slip away from. Hake said, grinding his teeth to grit, 'Curse on you Feng for coughing now.'

Godgest leaned over the gold prow and waved to the oncoming galley as though they were friends of his and he was glad to greet them once more. A hot trickle ran down his left leg. He wished to god that Feng had died in the night from that rough kitchen-wench.

Then the black galley ran alongside, taking off two inches of the king's soft oak and drawing up the longship with a sickening shudder. Feng fell onto his knees with the shock. Hake was hard put to to keep his vomit behind his teeth. Godgest was still smiling and waving and wetting himself. They were all smiling, even the oarsmen, and that was sign of something for such men had nothing to gain or to lose whatever the outcome. They were beyond punishment or reward.

Then horns blew like the day of atonement, shrill and thin and as clear as autumn ale. 'Keep down,' yelled Hake to all the men. And as they ducked a shower of arrows came over roaring like hornets and into the salt on the far side.

The horns squealed again like new gelded pigs. One oarsman-thrall who had never been in action before glanced up just as the second arrow-flight came over. There was nothing to be done for him. Hake tipped him clear for the fishes on the steerboard-side then began to call out, 'Come aboard, my friends. Welcome aboard! Our ship is yours. We come from Vendilsgarth; where do you hail from?'

The first man aboard stood half as tall as the mast. He was dressed in black wolfskins and wore gold all along both arms. In his right hand he carried an iron sword inlaid with silver, as long as a man's leg; on his grizzled head he wore a helmet that you could have milked a cow into for size. It had a bristling boar's head at the fore-peak and two eagle's claws cast in gold on its sides. The flap that fell behind the neck was of chain-links bronze set against steel. There was no other helmet like that outside Jerusalem or Rome.

Godgest was the first to recognize it. He stood up, risking his life, and bawled out, 'Greetings, King Beowulf of the Geats! Greetings, Cock of the North!'

King Beowulf halted and sniffed about him. 'I have stood on sweeter middens than this,' he said. No one challenged him. So then he said, 'I have made water against stouter masts than this and have watched them crumble.' And still no one challenged him. So he turned then to Feng in the after-end and said, 'Are you not the sausage-skin that was left behind when they took the meat out of Vendil the king? Are you not the boneless wonder that lies against the Jute-queen weeping through the night?'

Feng saw this man's thick arms and the gorse-growth of red hair upon his body—so thick that a mere man could not have stepped over it. And Feng saw that this man had thin nostrils like a wolf's which smelled out what other men had in mind. Feng had no wish to offend such a sea-king and to have that length of bright iron go through his belly, albeit inlaid with silver.

He fell to his knees on the after-deck thinking he would deal with his oarsmen later on the way home and baring his head, cried out, 'Yes, lord, I am the sausage-skin, the boneless wonder, as you say. Now, since there is no quarrel between us, may I rise again and greet you aboard my unworthy vessel?'

King Beowulf of the Geats stared at him long, sucking in his thin lips till they vanished inside his mouth, leaving only his stiff beard to be seen. Then he said in a flat voice, 'I have been out a week waiting for some fool to take this channel. I cannot be generous to all the world, you know, Jute. A man must make his living.'

Then he turned to the three captains who had followed him aboard. 'We will take every third rower,' he said, 'provided they are sound between the legs. I want no geldings, mind. And then unstep the mast and see what they have down below. Take it all even if it is only iron. Leave them one cask of voyage ale and no more.'

Then he put his long sword under his left arm, turned and went towards Feng with his right hand out. 'Greetings, my brother,' he said, smiling and showing his long teeth. 'We kings do not meet often enough on the water.'

Feng reached out for the Geat-king's hand and missed it first time. Then he tried again and wished he had missed it a second for it seemed that his bones had suddenly dissolved to a jelly.

He said with what smile would come, 'Greetings, King Beowulf. It is a pleasure to meet another man.'

The king of the Geats gazed above Feng's head and said smiling, 'Aye, it is always a pleasure to meet a man.' Then he looked round the decks as though he was searching for one. Suddenly he lowered his eyes and said directly to the Jute-king, 'Your young Amleth will be such a man if he is allowed to grow to his full size.'

Feng hung his head sideways and smiled sickly, 'Aye, aye, king,' he said as though in a secret pain, 'and that is something I would wish to speak with you about. He is a great trial to his mother the queen, and to me.'

As Unferth coughed Amleth started from the bed with mouth and eyes wide open like a man drowning. His weakness left him. In his mind there was only Feng, Feng alone in the world. He brushed Gerutha aside from the broad bed and was over the boards before a man could count three. He stood above the piled straw in the corner where the sound had come from. He sniffed the air like a hound above a badger's sett. Below him the pale yellow mound of straw seemed to heave. Amleth drew in his breath and held it. He moved about that mound on tipped toes. He poised the new sword in his right hand, its point towards the boards, then waited.

No second cough came. It was as though the straw was suffering not to cough, not to breathe aloud, as though it had a sort of life in it.

Amleth stepped round the edge of the pile and listened. Then his sharp eye saw two straw-stalks fall apart lower along the heap as though a small mouse had shifted underneath them.

'Hah!' he shouted raw-voiced and slashed down.

'Oh, oh, oh!' screamed the straw, thrusting upwards at the deepest point, in the dark corner.

'Hah!' cried Amleth, slashing down there as well.

Then the straw flung itself all over the room, much of it clotted together with deep red. Amleth turned away and wiped the wet blade down the coverlet where his mother lay, her hands over her ears.

'There, there, little bird,' he said, bending to her ear. 'It was only a rat. Only a rat!'

Downstairs Torfi was asking Gautrek the Mild another riddle. But Gautrek could not answer it and held out his right hand in protest. Suddenly his palm was wet with red. He looked up straightway and said, 'When it rains red through the roof in Vendilsgarth, what does that signify, my riddling friend? That's a new one for you.'

Torfi got up stiffly from the stone steps. 'It signifies that we should go upstairs and see who is dead,' he said. 'And that is not new.'

When they pulled the straw away and saw that it was not Feng who lay there Torfi and Gautrek stood about, waiting to be told where to dig a hole for the bled white carcass.

At first Gerutha tore at her hair in disappointment, then she began to cry out that old men had a right to live their few remaining days in peace. Amleth led her to the women's bower, his face all white and stiff, and told her to see to her woman's affairs and not meddle in his. She went as docile as a tame mare and did not look back into the spattered room.

Then Amleth went to his henchmen and said, 'This is on my head, on my hands, and not on yours. Now you have seen what has been done, I consider that the manslaying has been properly declared and I shall make no more noise about it. I advise you two to do the same. Go down to the hall and broach a fresh barrel of the autumn ale. What else is to be done, I shall do and you will not know of it. So, if Feng should question you, you can speak up honestly and tell him that all rests with me. If I wanted your help, I should ask for it; but since I don't, then obey me and leave this place. There is no more to be said of it.'

He spoke so evenly, looking them in the eye, that they turned away and left him. When he had heard their footsteps shuffling off into the rush-strewn hall, he went to the bower-door and called for Sibbi.

She came, white-faced, having heard what had happened. Yet she smiled when he asked her, 'Are you a good cook, woman?'

And when she nodded that she was, he said, 'Then away with you to the kitchen. Get out the big iron pot and make up the fire. I have a few joints of meat to seethe, just as one seethes pork. See that the kitchen-thralls are sent away. I have no wish to be taunted for my poor cooking later on.'

The two longships, grappled together with iron hooks, bobbed about offshore. King Beowulf and Feng sat on a sea-chest talking, their closest henchmen a few yards away, sitting on the deck with their swords across their knees, keeping silent and pretending not to listen to what was being said.

Feng did most of the talking, but from time to time the Geat-king looked over his shoulder and called out to his porters, 'Have you collected all? Are you sure of that? Now break open all the chests and see what is there. Nay, pay no attention to this king; he is a good-natured fellow and is busy with his own affairs at the moment.'

Feng said, 'Thus you see, Beowulf, that this Amleth grows to be a spear in my side. What way might there be to draw out that spear and break its shaft?'

The Geat-king looked at him narrowly then said, 'I can see how the young man troubles you. There is yet much of the animal, the

63

woodland beast, about him. He is much as I was when young—strong, a little stupid, stubborn. It takes such men many years to grow up in their understanding, though they are fully-grown in body at an early age. Most of the heroes I have met, up and down the world, have been so.'

Feng watched his sea-chests being smashed open and bit at his knuckles. Yet he put on a smile and said, 'I see that you understand men, Beowulf. Few kings understand them better than you, my friend.'

The Geat stroked his great hand down Feng's cheek as gently as a woman, though the hand itself would have made a bear stand back. He said, 'Yes, I have watched many kings in my day and I think I can read them as the scholars in Rome read their books. And I can read that you wish me to put an end to this Amleth for you in return for my taking a few little things from your ship. Well, you must understand that I do this not as a sea-wolf, a pirate-robber, but merely for my pleasure. In my hall in Scania I have a treasure room so high-stacked with such trinkets that I shall never in my lifetime again look on those which are closest the floor. They lie too deep. So you will understand that I do not need your poor things. And I surely would not bring myself to kill a prince for that which means so little to me, would I, Feng?'

The King of Jutland was very miserable to hear these words for he had no treasure-room and the things that Beowulf was taking from him were of great value in his life. Yet there was little he dared say. He smiled stiffly as though the next thing would be tears.

Then King Beowulf rose on the deck and stretched his arms to the sky, yawning like a chasm. He said in a while, 'This Amleth came to me on Crabland, wishing to join my warband and forage up and down the world. I had no use for such an untried colt. The men I take with me must be trusted and old in experience of arms and raiding.'

He strode across the deck to look at a gold inlaid cup that one of his sailors had taken from a chest. He held it up in the light and turned it in his fingers. Then he said, 'Do not put that with the other rubbish. I will have that in the after-deck cabin and will drink from that myself.'

Feng twisted his hands in misery again. 'Oh, my lord,' he said, 'that cup has been in my family for five generations. It came from Antioch and is of untold worth.'

The Geat-king smiled and nodded towards him. 'Aye,' he said, 'it is a pretty cup. I must take care that no one steals it from me.'

Then he came back towards Feng again and said in a harder voice, 'If this Amleth is still of the mind to join my warband then tell him to bring a longship and meet me in the mouth of the Humber a month from today. Tell him that the Duke of Britain, the one men call Arthur the Bear, wishes to form a company of Geats and Jutish-men to drive out some Picts that are making a nuisance of themselves in his land. Tell him that he will be in good company and will gain great fame in such a war.'

Feng looked up at him in torment. 'My lord,' he said, 'this is not what I want of you—that you should lead Amleth to fame in Britain. I want him dead, but far away from home so that the people shall not suspect me.'

The Geat-king blew through his nostrils as though there was a bad smell near him. Then he said, 'Have no fear, he would go alone to Britain. I shall not go near that place again. When I was last there in their city called Caer Leon I made merry with the queen they call Gwenhwyvar Golden-hair while this Arthur was fighting off a few shiploads of our own folk down in the south of that land, at a place called Dubglas or Bassas, I forget which. Nay, I shall not go there again for they have long memories, these Romans; they would hang me up by the neck on a pole and geld me. And that I have no wish to be present at, having seen them at it when I was there. For Romans, a most uncivil folk, I would say. Nay, I shall not go!'

Feng watched the last of his treasures being stowed aboard the black pirate-ship. He wrung his hands and said, 'Then in Odin's name what are you advising me?'

King Beowulf walked across to the side and began to climb down into his own craft. He said over his shoulder, 'Send him there, you donkey. But before you do, send this Duke Arthur a letter telling him that Amleth is my son, and that if he wishes to get his revenge, then he can take it on this Jute-prince when he lands in the Humber. Is that not good enough for you?'

He did not wait for an answer, but dropped aboard and straightway shouted orders that the grappling-irons should be unhooked.

As the low black ship scudded away with swift beats of the oars, Feng gritted his teeth and punched at the gunwales with his clenched fist. Then he said to Hake who stood by him, 'Well, at least this thievish Geat has put an idea into my mind. At least we now know how we can be rid of Amleth.'

Hake picked his nose thoughtfully and said, 'Aye, but how shall we send such a letter?'

Feng almost struck him in his fury. 'How?' he said. 'How? Why, by a fast ship, that's how.'

Hake shrugged his shoulders and said patiently, 'That I can understand since as yet we have no birds in Vendilsgarth who can carry messages in their beaks. But what I meant was, who will write this letter? This Arthur is a Roman. He cannot read our runes, doubtless; so who will write to him with a pen on sheepskin in the Roman runes?'

Feng's anger calmed. He stared at Hake with wide eyes. 'Aye, that is to the point, old friend,' he said. 'I know of no man in Jutland who can set down the Roman runes. Doubtless a man would have to journey as far away as Colonia to find such a writer and that would be two months' journeying.'

Godgest took the helm on the way back towards Vendilsgarth, for now Feng was deep in thought and could not be trusted to rein in the longship away from the rocks that guarded the channel down to the haven.

In the kitchens Sibbi had little taste for the work Amleth gave her. Yet she was amazed that a man could fall to nothing so easily in the great iron pot. Unferth's old bones were thin and brittle. They broke readily under the cleaver and then fell to white dust in the roaring

66

log-fire. But the rest after seething in the boiling water was not unlike swine-flesh, though it seemed tough and its smell was not good. A thrall who blundered into the kitchens just as they finished their task screwed up his nose and said, 'Odin, but what are you cooking there, lady?'

Sibbi said, 'I am teaching the prince to seethe swine-flesh.'

The thrall said, 'I have never smelled such swine-flesh. That swine must have been rooting about some old battle-field for his fodder.'

Amleth turned to him, the cleaver still in his hand, and said without a smile, 'Come, lay your arm on this block, fellow, I can see that your finger-nails need trimming.'

The man ran away then and so Amleth ladled the meat into a wicker basket and carried it from the kitchen. When Sibbi went to help him he said, 'No, you have done enough, my friend. I can manage the rest alone.'

Three paces along the passageway from the queen's chamber was the privy used by Gerutha and the bower-women in the night. At Vendilsgarth the rule was strictly kept that no women of the upper floor must go down through the hall, among the kept-men and the thralls, after dark. This privy was set in an angle within the watch-tower of the castle and had a broad seat of grey slate with a round hole in the middle. The vent which led down from it was wide and came out onto a stone chute that fed into the moat. In times of rain-fall the moat swallowed all; but in times of drought offal lay about so long that Vendil had given the swineherds leave to drive their beasts down there into the dry ditch to forage and to clear all away.

Amleth took his basket into the privy and sitting on the slate seat rolled up his sleeves and drew out pieces of the seethed flesh. He counted them as he let them slither down the vent and they came to twenty-four. Each piece fell into the moat with a thud, and after each thud the prince waited to hear the chumping of the pigs' jaws. And when all the counting and the chumping was done Amleth went into the queen's chamber, put the sodden basket on the blazing hearth-fire to burn, then washed his hands and arms in the bronze bowl that stood on the chest beside the great bed.

67

As he dried his arms the queen came in and said, 'What have you done with him? Where is he?'

Amleth looked through her eyes to the wall behind her and said, 'Who? Where is who?'

Gerutha said, 'Do not be foolish, my love. Feng will want to know. He was Feng's closest counsellor so Feng will want to know.'

Amleth thought for a while then said, 'Feng will be told the truth though he will not believe it. Men like Feng always cry out for ghosts and trolls and mysteries. Tell them the plain truth and they do not believe it.'

Gerutha went to him and took his face between her long thin hands. 'Oh, my bird,' she said, 'I am afraid that if you tell him the truth he will have you killed. Let us say that Unferth went away from Vendilsgarth, that he could not bear to stay here any longer.'

Amleth bent and kissed his mother gently on the lips. Then he smiled and said, 'Well, that would be true too, mother. Aye, that would be true; when I last heard his voice he did not sound at all happy here.'

At dusk that day Torfi and Gautrek the Mild ran into the hall and told Amleth that Feng's longship had come into haven, but that all the sea-chests had been broken into and even the ballast from under the mast-stepping gone. They said that the ship rolled about as though it was an empty walnut shell.

Amleth smiled and said, 'Then Feng must have met someone up along the coast. He has come back with less than he took out and that is bad for a king.'

Gautrek said, 'It will not help his temper, brother.'

Amleth said, 'Pish, pish to his temper. Before he has been back long he will have even more to be sorry about.'

And when Feng strode into the hall with Hake and Godgest behind him carrying knives, he found Amleth sitting on the throne-chair with Torfi and Gautrek the Mild on either side of him, holding spears. And Amleth had old Rorek's sword unsheathed and lying across his thighs and was dressed in fine clothes, with a scarlet coat

68

and lace down the front, and striped stockings of blue and yellow. Feng stopped short and glared at him then said, 'Why do you sit on my chair, Amleth?'

Amleth looked at the tips of his fingers and said, 'Because it is the only chair in this castle that fits my backside since I have grown so much.'

Feng did his best not to let his anger show. He said, 'But this is a king's chair, my son. It is for a king not for a prince, you understand.'

Amleth said, 'Have they not told you that I am the King of the Wood now? That is a king, is it not, uncle?'

Feng began to stride about, pulling at his beard and at the warrior-plaits that hung above each ear. 'Aye, aye,' he said, making his mouth smile, 'but not a true king, my son. King of the Wood, well, it is not the same. King of the Wood is leader of the revels, the maze-dances, but it is not war-leader or counsellor, let us say.'

Then he thought for a while and said, 'Where is my counsellor? Where is old Unferth? He should be here to greet me.'

Torfi laughed across at Gautrek the Mild, 'Aye, old Unferth sheep-shanks,' he said. 'He was a strange old fellow, that Unferth.'

Gautrek said back to his comrade, 'Aye, and we shall miss him in this black castle when the long nights come again.'

Feng stopped pacing. 'Where is Unferth?' he said. 'I demand to know where he is.'

Amleth signalled to his henchmen to be silent then very slowly he said to his uncle, 'It will be heavy tidings for you to bear, my lord. And pray god that what happened to him may never happen to you.'

Now Feng came close to the throne-chair and leaned so far towards Amleth that their foreheads almost touched. 'Where is he?' he said grimly.

Amleth suddenly gave a little butt with his head like a playful young ram that sent the king back half a pace holding his nose. Then he said through his big horse's teeth, 'He was such a thin old man, Feng. He went up to the women's privy, slipped down through the hole, and the pigs in the dry moat ate him.'

Feng and his henchmen drew back and glared at the prince in silence. At first no words would come to the king's lips but at length he frothed a little and then whispered hoarsely, 'You dare to say that this happened to my faithful old friend, Unferth? You dare to say that?'

Amleth nodded, 'Aye, I dare to say it,' he answered, 'because that is what happened. I tell you, I shall not eat bacon for the next year.'

Then he rose from the chair and went forward with his henchmen close behind him. Feng gave way like a thrall and so did Hake and Godgest. And when the prince had left the hall, the passage-ways echoed loud with his laughter. Feng rushed to the chair and sat on it as though claiming it again. 'We shall not need to send him to Britain,' he said, 'he is so mad that the people of Jutland will beg us to kill him ourselves, so that they can sleep safely in their beds at night.'

Hake said quietly, 'You have spoken wisely, Feng. All that we need now is for this prince to show everyone how mad he is. The people must see it and hear it for themselves then our way will be clear.'

Feng nodded and pulled at his beard again. 'Aye, aye,' he said. 'We must set our traps carefully. You two shall help me in this. Together we will show Jutland such a fool that they will put him to death themselves if we do not knock him on the head.'

Then Godgest said carefully, 'That will hardly be enough, my lord. We must think further than that. We must find ways to get rid of Gerutha and her daughter, Sibbi, if we want to enjoy the kingdom we have worked so hard for.'

Feng rose and struck at the throne-chair. He said, 'Nay, not Gerutha, not yet. That can come later, after I have put a son into her so that Feng's line can stay on this chair when I am gone. But first that must be done, even if you two must hold her down while I do it.'

Hake nodded, picturing the scene, laughing at what he saw in his head. He said, 'But Sibbi, she is different. She could be got at, Feng?'

The king nodded and grinned with a broad mouth. 'Aye, oh aye.'

he said. 'That we must do before we knock him on the head. We must set them together, then come on them swiftly while they are at it. The folk would not tolerate them at that game. It is the oldest sin, men say. They would have her over the log and the scalding brine in her before a cock could crow thrice. Aye, they would cure her of that for all time.'

Amleth was sitting on a stile talking with a barley-raker called Giso whose folk had come from the flat-lands in Linnuis many lives before, where the best barley in the world was grown. And this Giso was saying, 'What you need is black river-silt lying between chalk wolds for good barley-heads. You folk here in Jutland think it has to be a woman-dragging through the soil; but I tell you, prince, it is nothing of the sort. Keep your women where they belong, in the kitchen or the bed; but never think they bring good barley. That comes from the black earth clenched within the chalk. There is no more to be said.'

Amleth slapped the man on the shoulder and laughed in the new sunshine. 'This magic they speak of, Giso,' he said. 'This magic of the Barley Queen and the Green Man?'

Giso slapped Amleth on the shoulders this time and almost tumbled him from the stile. 'Horse-piss,' he said. 'If you will forgive the word, horse-piss, prince.'

Amleth nodded and said, 'I always thought so, Giso. But who am I to tell these folk how their crops grow? Who am I?'

Just then Torfi appeared over the gorse-bush by the stile and said, 'Who are you? You are a walking deadman unless you watch your step, Amleth.'

The Prince turned and saw who it was. Then he put his sword back. He said, 'What news then, Torfi?'

The dwarf said, 'Feng is out to destroy you. I hung below the window-ledge when they were talking and I have heard several things.'

Then he made a certain sign to Giso who was not slow to take the hint and to start running; and when he had gone Torfi said, 'First,

71

they want you to seem mad before all the people. And next they want to catch you with Sibbi.'

Amleth stared at him and said, 'I think I am mad, Torfi, otherwise I wouldn't be listening to this sort of talk. But what is this about Sibbi? She is a pretty young girl and clean and comely. If she were of noble kin, I would even marry her, come the time I wanted to settle.'

Torfi scratched at his dark head and said, 'Prince, I am a simple fellow and cannot explain many things in this crafty world. So do not press me. All I say is: pretend to be mad, if you wish. But don't let them catch you on top of Sibbi. Do you understand, my lord?'

Amleth nodded his shock-head. 'I understand, best of friends,' he said. 'I swear this oath; if they catch me as you have said, then may I suffer Unferth's end and get fed to the moat-swine.'

Torfi clapped him on the shoulder with an effort. 'That's the way, my lord,' he said. 'We'll have them yet.'

The next morning the henchmen, Hake and Godgest, came below Amleth's window and knocked on it with a spear-shaft. 'Get up, get up, you layabed,' they called. 'We have a horse for you here and the new sun of Spring calls all men to ride forth. If you call yourself a man, come with us along the beaches now and let the folk see what manner of prince they have.'

Amleth put on his dirtiest farm-smock and an old straw hat, then tucked a dagger under his woollen vest and went out to meet them. The two henchmen rode red ponies with white flashes down the mask. The horse they led for him was so old it could scarcely lift one hoof behind the other. He saw well enough what was going on when a line of dark heads appeared above the stockade. All the Vendils-garth folk were out to see him ride forth.

So he said to Hake, 'Just hold this raging stallion's head a moment, then I will mount as a warrior-king should.'

Hake bowed his head as though to an emperor. The people began to nudge one another and to fall off the stockade. Amleth shouted

72

out, 'Death to all traitors!' Then he gave a great leap and landed on the nag's back, his face towards the tail.

An old man called Gorm fell off the stockade then and died on the ground laughing before anyone could reach him.

Amleth drove his heels into the nag's sides and said, 'Come, henchmen, let's be away.'

Gerutha watched her son go, arsy-tarsy, through the gate towards the shore and wept that he should so belittle himself.

But down on the beach Godgest called out to the prince who rode backwards, 'Hey, Amleth, what do you think of the flour they grind down here?' He pointed to the sand.

The prince slipped off the old horse and took up a handful of the sand. Very gravely he said, 'This is not the smoothest grinding I have seen.' Then he put a little of it into his mouth and said, 'This is not properly ground, friend Godgest. It has not had the miller's stones on it; whoever ground it used the surf to do it, and that does not make for good flour. Here, taste it yourself and see if you agree with me.'

Before Godgest could avoid him Amleth had him down on the beach and was shoving the salt sand into his throat. Behind Vendils-garth Dunes the folk stood up to watch this strange thing. Most of them cheered to see Vendil's son holding down Feng's henchman so easily with one hand.

Afterwards with Godgest spitting sandgrains out and coughing all the way they came to an old reach where a wrecked longship from Scania lay rotting. Hake pointed out the great rudder and said, 'Now, my prince, did you ever see such a huge knife in your days? I never did.'

Amleth rode round and round the rudder. Then in a loud voice he said, 'That is the knife for cutting up moat-swine. If poor Unferth had only had that knife he would be alive today.'

Then he ran at Hake and dragged him from his pony. 'Come down, warrior,' he said, 'and kneel with me to pray for poor Un-ferth in Valhalla.'

And when he had got Hake by his side, Amleth leant over and

73

thrust the man's head so hard against the oaken rudder that his nose spread across his face and the blood ran out of his head all across his chest.

Behind them, in the dunes, the people cried out for their prince.

Now Hake and Godgest wondered what next they should do. One of them was still choking with salt sand, and the other could hardly see for the size that his nose had swollen.

But at this moment Feng rode up and called out, 'Dear son, I bring word from Vendilsgarth. The lady Sibbi needs an escort through the wood. Who better than a prince to protect her there?'

Amleth nodded and said, 'Yes, lord, I will go. But I beg you, see to these good friends of ours, who are not now as well as they were when we set off riding.'

As the prince rode back through the dunes, Giso Barley rose and waved to him. 'At it, warrior,' he called. 'You'll have them by the sweetbreads after all!' Then all the people cheered, and the prince rode on to where Sibbi waited for him by the stockade gate.

Torfi and Gautrek the Mild watched the prince lead the girl into Vendils Wood, and when they had gone from sight, hand in hand, Torfi said, 'Come on, brother, from the way the lass is walking I would say that they'll be down at the first glade they come to and I don't want Feng's snuffling hounds to be on the scent before we can reach them.'

Sibbi had on a long russet gown trimmed with white fur at neck and wrists, embroidered about in fine silver thread to show the shapes of dragons and serpents winding about the bodice. The cloth was so delicate that even the slightest breath of wind held it against her body. About her narrow waist she wore a girdle of plaited yellow hide, at each end of which was set a silver acorn. On her small feet, shoes of blue-dyed deerskin fastened above the ankle with scarlet cords. Her thick hair of burnished bronze hung in one great plait

74

down to her hips as she walked. On each of her fingers she wore a broad gold ring set with agate and on her thumbs silver rings set with jet from Whitby to ward away toothache.

Into the girl's hair Gerutha the queen had set such plants as butter-bur, cockscomb and reed-grass, so that she looked like a wood-nymph as she walked.

Amleth, towering high above her, his rough sheepskin cape about his great shoulders and his shock-hair tousled by the winds, seemed like some god of the woodland too. When he had stabled the old horse he had drawn off his hide breeches and now walked shaggy-legged and shoeless. Had he had hooves instead of feet even Pan would have envied him.

They did not follow the sheep-tracks or the swine-paths but breasted the new boughs and reeds like gods going their own way. Sometimes the girl paused and pointed to the freshly-springing buds on the boughs, smiling and touching them gently with her finger-tips. Amleth drew her hand away and told her that they were tender as yet and must not be broken before they came to their full growth. Once as the wood grew darker she stopped and pointed to where a red fungus reared itself proudly in the shade beneath a hawthorn. Amleth drew her away again, saying that such things were poison-ous to man and to woman. At last below a tangle of beechlings, the two proud walkers came to where a cluster of cuckoo-pint grew in the damp black earth. Sibbi stopped, her arm now about the prince's body. 'Look, Amleth,' she said, dragging at his belt to bring him closer. 'See how the hard spike thrusts up through the opening pale sheath. See how royal this purple flower is, pushing its way like a king. See, it will not be denied—and who should deny such a brave pintle-bloom? See how the gentle sheath parts to let it come through. This is the emblem for a prince to wear in his hair as I wear my garland now.'

Amleth bent closer and stared at the flowers. He said, 'They call them Lords and Ladies, though I have never known why.' He began to draw away then but she held onto him closely, laughing gaily up at his solemn face. 'Oh, my prince,' said Sibbi. 'You are as blind as a

75

puppy. Come, come, there is a green bank behind the beechlings. There I will teach you why the flowers are named so.'

He let her drag him along between the boughs but when she flung herself down and drew the knot of her girdle loose he made no move to go too close to her, remembering Torfi's warning.

She said, 'See, this gown is made to fall apart when the girdle is loosed. Do you not like that, my prince?'

Amleth looked and then said, 'I do not think it is wise to wear no shift beneath such a flimsy robe. The winds are still biting keenly. You could take a chill, dressing so.'

She rolled nearer him and said almost into his mouth, 'I am too warm to be chilled by our silly winds, my lord. Where is the sword? Where is the coral tip? I could explain how the flowers got their name more easily if you put the sword haft into my hand.'

Amleth's heart was troubled then because he had forgotten to bring the sword with him into the wood and suddenly he wondered if the girl had spoken an omen and if he might soon need it. But she went on laughing near him and seemed to have forgotten the sword. He said, 'Take care, Sibbi, you will hurt yourself with such wrestling.'

But though her mouth and eyes were wide open she did not speak; and then the prince seemed not to be where he had been but in another place far away, as far away as a journey in dreams. And yet he had travelled quietly and smoothly and in all kingly comfort, as though the way had been prepared for him by a loving servant who had given long and tender thought to all that would be wanted.

And as he looked up he saw the intricate tracery of boughs above his head, all turning and twisting and coiling over him, like a myriad serpents moulded in smooth silver and in ancient rough green bronze. They were like the curling dragon-mouthed runes that scholars drew in the broad margins of books, their tongues shooting back and forth, their mouths gaping wide then shutting tight.

Amleth thought only one thing: that he was not upon Sibbi as the warning had run. It was she who was on him so there could be nothing to fear now.

And then all thoughts of fear or revenge or of anything went from him in a great eagle-soaring towards the sky. At that moment Feng's henchmen could have put the point into him and he would not have known.

A spear's cast away Torfi turned to Gautrek the Mild and whispered, 'Now the fool brings his doom on his own head and no mistake. If they come upon him now, he'll have no sight to see them, and no strength to rise and meet them.'

Gautrek drew his dagger and said grimly, 'And they are coming. I can hear their feet on the rotten sticks behind us. Shall we stand and keep them from him until his senses return, brother?'

But Torfi shook his head. 'You are already an outlaw, Gautrek,' he answered. 'Another manslaying, even for the prince, and they will bury you to the neck in sea-sand. He must save himself if Feng is to be satisfied. Here, perhaps the gods have given us their word in this nest of gadflies.'

Swarming in the last rays of the sun upon a bank of nettles were a thousand flies. Torfi bent and snatched up a handful of rotting straw and scattered it at the swarm. They rose, buzzing angrily, many of them still bearing strands of the straw on their bodies. Then a sudden breath of wind caught the swarm and swept it between the trees towards the green bank.

Amleth opened his mouth like a drowning man gasping for air. A swarm of gadflies passed over him, showering small pieces of straw across his face. He spluttered and gasped again, pushing Sibbi away with his hands so as to use them in cleaning his face. She rolled helpless from him down the bank then sat under a bush and drew her robe about her crossly.

Amleth was standing now, beating away the gadflies, when Hake and Godgest burst through the beechlings, their drawn swords in their right hands.

They saw the prince striking at flies and Sibbi picking the buds from a wild-rose. They turned to one another amazed. Hake was the first to speak; he said, 'I ask pardon, prince, for coming towards you with the sword, but we heard you cursing and we did not know what was happening. Our only thought was to protect you.'

Amleth flung his sheepskin over his head and ran down the mound. 'Then drive away these flies,' he called solemnly. 'Beat them off with your swords since you have them out.'

Torfi and Gautrek the Mild crouched back in the gorse and watched the prince go homewards through the woods, with Sibbi trailing three paces behind him, her bright robe now torn and draggled at the hem. On the mound, Hake and Godgest still beat at the flies, their fierce faces black with anger.

Then Torfi punched Gautrek on the chest and whispered, 'May Odin help us both, when we have such need, brother!'

Gautrek the Mild plucked a red berry and bit it between his sharp white teeth. He said, 'I shall not punch you in return, little one, for if I did there would be nothing left of you for the gadflies to make a meal of!'

Then they too went laughing back to the stack-yard.

When Feng had heard this meagre news from his henchmen he said, 'So, it seems he is too wise for us after all. I cannot understand it; he, a son of old Vendil! There can be little of the old man's blood in him if he can go with a woman into the wood and spend his strength catching flies. I shall never understand the young men of this day. They seem to lack the heart that we old ones had when we were youths.'

Hake said, 'You must do as the Geat-king advised you, now. Send him to Britain and we will see that he does not come back, Feng.'

When Sibbi reached the women's bower, Gerutha was waiting for her by the hearth-stone. She said, 'Is my son a man now, Sibbi?'

The girl sighed and rubbed her stomach and then sank onto a pile of calf-skins. 'Oh, my queen,' she said with scarcely enough breath to send her words on their way, 'he is a man. I will tell you that he is that and more. He is the rightful son of old Vendil, my lady; he is three men.'

The queen smiled and kneeled beside her, drawing the girl to her breast in great love. 'I am glad in the heart to learn this, Sibbi,' she said. 'We must have a true man to be king over this Jutland-midden if the people are to prosper.'

Sibbi let herself slide down onto the pallet. She said wearily, 'They will prosper with this King of the Wood, that I can tell you. He is like a god, my lady; he is like the thunder-storm that does not know its own power. He is the bolt that strikes deep without meaning to hurt. It is one of the wonders of god that he should be so powerful—and yet not know it.'

Gerutha rose and said, white-faced, 'We must not call him a god, for then the other lesser gods might envy him and strike him down as they struck Balder down in my grandmother's time. The greatest we must call him now is a hero.'

Sibbi rolled gently over onto her front, the palms of her pretty hands upright in the fire-glow. She smiled into the prickly cow-hide. 'Aye,' she whispered as she fell into sleep, 'we'll call him a hero. We'll surely call him that. I am the first opponent who has met his attack and I should know if anyone does.'

Feng sent Godgest to fetch the prince to his chamber and there, in company with the sullen henchmen, he said, 'My dear son, recently I have been keeping an eye on you, and it seems to me that you have behaved in every way as a true prince and a future king should.'

Amleth gazed at a carved dragon on the head of the king's throne-chair and held his great head on one side modestly. 'I have not set out to please anyone,' he said. 'I have only acted as I felt I needed.'

Feng smiled and then nodded to Hake and Godgest proudly. They nodded back rather more curtly as kept-men do. The king said, 'So much the more creditable for you. Not knowing that eyes were upon you, your deeds, being the more natural, carry greater weight in my heart.'

Amleth bowed his head a little thinking what a fool this man was:

79

how unlike Vendil his dead father who could look at a wolf or a mouse and know what it was thinking.

He said, 'If I have pleased you I give thanks to the many gods. To please the king is all that I desire.'

Feng poured out a horn of ale with his own shaking hands and offered it first to Amleth. He said, 'You have pleased me so much, my son—and I must confess that I regard you as my own closest kin —that I now intend to do for you in return what you wish the dearest.'

Amleth wondered what this meant but he did not let his bewilderment show on his face. He only said, 'My lord, I am listening.'

Feng said, 'Some time ago, you wished to join King Beowulf's warband and to forage abroad with him in the longships.'

Amleth nodded, 'That is true, my lord. I went to Crabland to offer my services to him, but he chose—as any king has the right to —to refuse them.'

Feng nodded to his henchmen and smiled gently. 'Well,' he said to the prince, 'While I have been away from Vendilsgarth on your behalf, as a father should for his son, I have bearded the Geat-king once more and this time have persuaded him to accept you and to put you in the way of gaining kingly fame in preparation for the time when you will rightfully sit on this throne-chair after I am gone.'

Amleth said, 'I know that your ship came back empty with its sea-chests broken open, Feng.'

The king smiled down at his feet more ruefully this time and said, 'King Beowulf is a hard man. He asks a high price for his favours: yet no price is too high for me, to get for a son I love the thing he desires. I owe that at least to dear Vendil's memory if not to the deep love I bear you.'

Amleth said, 'Yes, my father would have paid for me to go off journeying. You are very kind, my lord, and I thank you.'

Feng waved his hand. 'Think little of it, my son,' he said. 'It is my great pleasure to give you all that a noble prince should have.' The two henchmen smiled and nodded.

Amleth said, 'Am I to sail to Crabland and meet Beowulf, then?'

Feng's eyes clouded a little. He said quickly, 'No, my prince, our arrangement was not that. The Geat-king has certain calls to make which would only tire you. So he begs that, a month from now, you take our soundest longship and meet him where he lies at anchor in the mouth of the Humber.'

Amleth said, 'It is a long time and a long distance away, my lord.'

Feng said, 'Pah! Pah! my son! You must do one thing, and that is to obey a king's wishes. There are scores of princes up and down the North who would wait longer and travel further for this chance. You are indeed a lucky youth if I may say so.'

Amleth smiled and bowed his knee then. 'Aye, you may say so, my lord,' he said. 'You may say so.'

He paused a while then went on, 'And when we cleave up the Humber into Britain among the Romans what then, my lord?'

King Feng bared his old ground-down teeth. 'You might well ask what then, dear son,' he said. 'But I can tell you that you will load your ship with far greater treasures than I ever gave to the Geat-king for your apprenticeship. Indeed, he has promised to take you under his broad wing and to see you have such adventures that most vikings, princes or not, would give their ears and more to have.'

Amleth fingered his two great red ears and said, 'They are precious things, ears, my lord. I would scarcely wish to lose mine even for the king in Micklegarth, for all his treasures and his daughters.'

Godgest looked slyly towards Hake at this but Feng met this smile and doused it with his own damp glare. He said, 'You go to an even greater king than that puppet of Micklegarth, my son, and one whose only daughter is already betrothed to the King of the Welsh among the mountains. But what Duke Arthur will offer you will be of great splendour. You shall ride, beside King Beowulf in the Roman Duke's company of Comrades, his *Kymry*: that much is already promised. And with this Arthur the Bear you shall go against all manner of foes, from Chichester up to Edinburgh. Against West Saxons and Picts. And what treasures, what heirlooms, no man knows! But you will know, my son. Aye, you will know, and they will be yours. I shall claim no part of them when you return here. No, not the smallest part.'

Amleth said, 'And will you also fit me and my men out for this voyage?'

Feng answered, 'I promise that upon your father's great sword.'

Amleth gazed at that sword. 'May I take that sword of Vendil's to lay on its blade even greater glory?'

Now Feng drew back a little. 'My son, my dearest,' he said sadly, 'how can I give this precious sword to you until you take it, as is your right, from my dead hand? You know as well as I do that the King of Jutland must always carry this sword: and when he stops carrying it, then he stops being King of Jutland. But this I vow to you, you shall have another, the best in my armoury, that is as long, as sharp and as rich. Now, will that not content you, my own?'

Amleth nodded lightly. 'Aye, that will content me, Feng,' he said. 'As long as I can take Gautrek the Mild and Torfi with me on this journey.'

Feng laid his head on one side and smiled sadly. 'Oh, my son,' he said, 'What hard choices you give me. Look, you may certainly take Gautrek; he is an outlaw and by the time you sail back his outlawry will be over and he will be a free man to live in Vendilsgarth again. Besides he is a great fighter and will protect you, my own.'

Amleth frowned. 'What of my dear friend Torfi?' he said. 'Is he not as brave and as nimble with his weapons?'

Feng said, drumming the chair-arms with his thick fingers, 'My son, do not misunderstand me when I remind you that Torfi, though the bravest and craftiest of lions, is a dwarf. I know that this affliction is not his fault and indeed came on him by his courage in war. But, I ask you, is he the most comely of henchmen for a Jute-prince to take among these splendid Romans?'

Amleth's brow-furrows became even deeper and his great horse-teeth began to show between his lips. He said, 'Who are these famous Romans if they need two shiploads of Northmen to help them fight such enemies as Picts and Saxons?'

Feng looked at Godgest and Hake for help but suddenly both of them had become most interested in a grey sparrow that was fluttering, trapped, among the hall-beams.

So he turned back to Amleth and said, 'My son, my son, allow me, the king, your father, a little wisdom, I beg you. Your friend Torfi is needed here badly. When you are gone and I travel about to see to our kingdom, as I must, who then will there be whom I can trust to guard the safety of your mother, Gerutha, and all her helpless women?'

Amleth smiled in his heart as he thought of the helplessness of Sibbi. But he nodded obediently all the same. He only said, 'If Torfi stays, I shall give him a twelfth part of any treasure I might gain, Feng. And for your part, if he conducts himself well, I demand that he be made a Jarl and is no longer required to live like a thrall in the stables. Is that agreed?'

Feng nodded and tugged at his beard. 'You are Vendil's son,' he said. 'You drive a hard bargain. But yes, for your dear sake, I will agree though the price is a high one.'

So Amleth bowed his head and his knee once more and then went off to tell Torfi and Gautrek what had happened.

Torfi shrugged his crooked shoulder and said smiling, 'I am content, Amleth, as long as you watch your steps while you are away.' Then he turned to Gautrek the Mild and said, 'But if you let one of these Picts or Saxons get behind him, do not return, whatever your treasure, for I will cut your throat, though you are my blood-brother.'

Gautrek said, 'If you so much as hint that I would shut my eyes while watching our Amleth, then I will let even you, little hound, reach up and cut my throat. And before that I will let you take the kitchen-cleaver and hack off my right hand to show Jutland that it had lost its cunning and was not worth saving.'

He turned away, then turned back and said smiling, 'What is more, little Torfi, you may feed me to the swine in the moat! And I cannot think of anything worse than that, can you, Amleth?'

But the prince did not answer. He was too troubled.

Down in the hall Feng spoke to his two henchmen in whispers now. He said, 'All goes well. But Odin alone knows where we shall find a scribe who can write a letter for us in Roman runes to tell Duke Arthur that when Amleth lands on Humberside his throat must be cut.'

Hake shrugged his shoulders and said, 'Patience, patience, Feng. We have time. We have a whole month before us. We have the Barley Feast and the Maze Dance to be got over before that fool sails. Something will turn up, I promise you.'

Godgest nodded wisely. 'Aye, something will turn up,' he said. 'Just put your trust in Odin, Feng. When has he let you down?'

On Frigga's Night when the moon was roundest and most silver all the free-folk together with the able-bodied thralls, both men and women, gathered at the maze which lay on the opposite side of the castle from Vendil's Wood, four long bowshots away, past Crow Spinney and the winding brown peat-stream which men had always called Adon's Weeping.

Many of the oldest folk of Jutland still named the maze Demeter's Dancing-floor but none of them could remember why. It lay on top of a chalk wold in sight of three rivers meeting and was tucked away in a shallow basin twenty paces in width. It had always been there, yet it was the rule in Vendilsgarth that every three years seven girls who had not known men should go out in the moonlight with ancient antler-picks and trim the turf that formed the maze-pattern, to make the many circles and twists and turns clearer for the dancers. Since such girls must needs be children and since their tools were clumsy and the light they worked by often dimmed by sea-frets, the maze had taken on many serpentine whirls and whorls which it had not had when the First Folk came up from the Middle Sea and fashioned it in imitation of the great bull-run their forefathers had known at Cnossus. In Vendilsgarth castle, set in a stone niche beside the queen's privy on a slate shelf stood the Maze Relics. One was a tall wine-jar of red clay on whose belly the maze pattern had been deeply scratched and then filled in with lamp-black; the second was a green bronze coin which had the maze on one face and the horns of a great bull on the other; the third was a broken grey tablet covered with small runes that looked like a thorn bush. In the time of Vendil's own father a Greek slave-trader from Syracuse had stayed overnight in the castle and had professed to read this tablet. He said that the writing meant: 'Daedalus of Crete claims a free passage to Britain in return for making this maze.'

The Vendilsfolk remembered that this Greek had been such a liar in so many ways that few believed his reading of the runes; and when he told Vendil's fierce old father that the mazes were based on an ancient plan of Troy City, the barons in the hall began to throw bones at him and might have put an end to his travels; but the Greek, whose name was Saurus, called for order and told them all that they, the distant children of Achaea whose forefathers had fought beside Agamemnon beneath the Trojan walls, should not behave so, should not disgrace ancestors who had gone to war in great chariots and had worn golden helmets—and then the barons had given up throwing beef-bones and began instead to fill the Greek's belly with their finest ale.

Before he had left the next day, this Saurus told the barons that their great days were not yet over; that in time they would return to the southlands and hack out new kingdoms as far away as Libya, where Athene herself came from. And when the Greek had gone on his way with a score of slaves tied by the neck behind his mule, some of the barons dragged out their old ships from haven and began to ask each other the best way to Libya. But few of them ever went, and those few were either waylaid by wandering Finns and became slaves, or left their heads on the Saxon stockades among the marsh-lands beside the Oder.

All the same the Maze Relics of Vendilsgarth were held in esteem especially by the bower-women who always made a habit of bending the knee a little as they passed the stone niche on the way to the privy. So the relics received more homage than any others in that stark fortress.

On Frigga's Night in Jutland kings and queens did no more than serve out, with their own hands, the strongest barley beer to all the dancers. Then they sat back in their chairs to watch the dancing. The king would address the queen as Moon and she would speak back to him as Saturn.

At Vendilsgarth this year Torfi was chosen as the Hornman and crouched in the moonlight at the centre of the maze. His body was bound round with bull's hide and on his head he wore the stone antlers of a great red deer, which had been dredged up beyond all memory in the peat stream, Adon's Weeping.

The first part of the dance was not pretty but it caused more laughter among the thralls and bower-women than anything else that happened in the year on that grim coast, where there was commonly so little to laugh about. The main dancers were the Prince, the Princess and the Merry Followers. This year Amleth was the Prince and as custom demanded wore only a stiff hood of straw which rested on his shoulders and blindfolded him. In his right hand he carried a blunt old lath of yellowing whalebone which they called The Sword. And this year Sibbi had been named the Princess and was dressed in a gown of green that came down to her bare feet. The bower-women had spun a triple-plaited length of red worsted, one end of which Sibbi held wrapped round her right wrist, and the other end of which was tied to a part of the Prince's body. Facing the blindfold Prince across the twisting maze, it was her task to guide him towards the centre, where the Hornman waited for him, by twitching the strong wool here and there, by loosening the rein or tightening it as the occasion demanded, and by tugging the hooded dancer quickly along those paths of the maze that were straight. Some years, excited by old grudges and the strong barley beer, Princesses had not been gentlest in their guidance; and each time the chosen Prince cried out, or fell from the raised maze-path into the chalk-runnels beside it, the Merry Followers, who were always chosen by the queen from among her older bower-women, laid about his buttocks with birch-switches until he was on his way towards the Hornman again, and going silently as a hero should.

But this year was the kindest men remembered and there was little laughter for the thralls. Sibbi moved quietly here and there, drawing gently on the wool, never once letting the Prince fall beneath the birch-switches, until at last he set his great feet firmly onto the centre, felt round for the Hornman and then struck him three times on the back with the whalebone sword crying out, 'So die, monster, die, and bring us a good year!'

Then off came the antlers and the straw hood and then began the courtship dance of the Partridges. Led by Sibbi with Amleth close behind her came the other dancers, always the woman before the man, bent forward, their bodies swaying, their arms outspread like wings, moving three paces at a time along the paths, then pausing and shuddering, then three paces more, until the dance was over and the couples had been to the centre and out again to the ale-booth, where they lay about under the pine torches, breathless and weary, too full of the good ale to care whether what they had done would bring forth its harvest in the coming months.

By Yuletide many of the women who had danced that night would miss the winter-feasting, being laid up in the straw. Yet at the next Maze Dance, they would have forgotten what they suffered and would be ready once again to stretch out their arms and shiver like partridges shaking their feathers after rain.

Now this year when the dancing was at its height and the dancers knew nothing but what they danced, a strange thing happened. Suddenly, into the torchlight on the wold stepped a small man with a sparse red goat-beard, leading two starved and stumbling mules behind him. His lashless eyes glared wide with fury at what he saw and in a shrill voice, his arms raised high, he cried out, 'I am Gilliberht of Fiesole and Lord Manuel Chrysostom is my patron. O you people of darkness, listen and obey me! Have done with these godless heathen ways! Fall to your wicked knees straightway and follow me in the Supplication of Forgiveness!'

King Feng was the first to see and hear this strange man. He turned to where the henchmen were standing just behind the throne-chair and nodded to them. Hake and Godgest put down their ale-cups, rose silently and came behind the man in the tattered robe.

It was Godgest who switched him away by the thin beard into the dark shadow of the pine-woods and Hake who drew out the sword, waiting for his comrade to bend the man's head over so that it could be done at one stroke.

And when Gilliberht understood what it was they were about to do to him he cried out again, 'For the love of God, have you lost your senses? Did you not hear who I am?'

Godgest said, 'For Odin's sake, keep still, man. How can we do it cleanly if you will keep jumping about?' He took another grip on the beard and spat with disgust to find that pieces of it came out into his hand.

Gilliberht kept shouting, 'When the Lord Manuel Chrysostom hears of this . . . Oh, when he hears of this . . .'

Then all at once it seemed to Gilliberht that his patron had never existed and that Puteoli was a city in a dream that lay beyond India. Then he called out, 'Mercy, my lords! Mercy! I have come to make you a present of my two mules. Is this the way you treat a friend?'

Hake had made two attempts to use his sword but was now so drunk with the good ale that he had the blade entangled in his feast-sleeve. This gave Godgest time to swing Gilliberht out of the sweep and say, 'Hold, friend Hake, he wishes to say something, this bent little stick of a man.'

And indeed Gilliberht was saying much, much more than he had ever said at one time in his life before; he was on his knees telling them how much he loved the north and its folk, their gods, their customs, their food and drink; and how he meant to travel south-wards again one day and explain to these stubborn Romans and Greeks that all their centuries they had made the mistake of living wrongly, praying wrongly, doing everything wrongly.

Godgest listened to him a while, his shaggy head on one side, then he said, 'Aye, aye, but this about the two mules. Get back to that, friend.'

88

Gilliberht said, 'Yes, yes, they are yours, dear friend. One for you and one for your companion here.'

Hake said, feeling his sword-edge, 'But they are outworn brutes only fit for feeding to the swine.'

Gilliberht wrung his hands, and said, 'I assure you, sir, they are worth more than they seem. On their backs they carry rolls of the finest cloth from Frankland. Cloth that a king would envy to wear, my lords.'

Godgest flung him onto the turf and put his foot under the man's chin to keep him there. He said, 'Swear by your gods that these gifts are for Godgest and Hake and no other.'

Gilliberht said with some difficulty, 'I swear that the cloth is for Godgest and Hake or may I die.'

Hake bent over him and put the point of his blade into the man's mouth. He began to be sick with terror now. Hake took the point away and gazed down at him with interest. 'Are you a Christman, stranger?' he asked. Gilliberht flung himself about on the turf, shaking his head with violence. 'No, never! Never, my lord,' he cried. 'Look, give me pen and paper and I will write it down for you that I have never been a Christman. That is all a lie. Fetch me pen and paper.'

Godgest held Hake back with his arm then and said gently, 'This pen and paper. . . . Do you mean that you can write the Roman runes then?'

Gilliberht almost swallowed his tongue at last seeing some faint light of mercy glimmering through this horrid darkness. 'Yes, yes,' he yelled. 'Of all the scribes, I am the most able. I can write such letters that even the greatest of emperors will listen to my words.'

Godgest kicked him in the throat to quieten him a while, then smiled and said to Hake, 'You see, Odin has heard our prayer, comrade. Here we have one who will write a letter to this Duke Arthur for Amleth to take with him to Britain.'

He turned again to Gilliberht and said, 'Did you understand what I said to my friend, cow-patch?'

Gilliberht said, 'Yes, my lord. I have picked up the language of the

89

north in my journeying. I will write the letter you say. I will write even to the Caesar in Constantinople if you wish.'

Hake said, 'We do not wish. He is no friend of ours. Do what you are asked and no more.'

Godgest said, 'Do not poke the sword into him any more, comrade, or he will not remember how this writing goes. He is not a bad little fellow, though too much like Unferth perhaps. All the same when Feng knows that he can write he will let us keep the cloth and so we shall all have done well out of this Maze Dance.'

He bent and picked Gilliberht up under one arm then carried him gibbering quietly to where the king and queen sat on their throne-chairs. He flung the man at Feng's feet and said, 'I have brought you a scribe. Hake and I have trained him well at the woodside. This blood is nothing; it will wipe off and show him to be as good as new below it. He ran into a thorn-bush before we could stop him. You know what these scribes are when they see a sword come out.'

Feng nodded. 'Aye, I know,' he said. 'What did he give you for his life?'

Hake said blank-eyed, 'Give us, king? What has such a shrivelled stick got to give anyone, my lord?'

Gilliberht knew better than to speak now. He heard Feng say, 'Very well, take him down to the garth and I will join you when the dance is done.'

All the way down, across Godgest's arm, Gilliberht tried to recall the Curse on Patrons he had learned as a novitiate at Arles. But his wits were so jumbled he could not set one word against the next, for them to come out as sense.

Now the dancing was over. The queen Gerutha sat in the booth that had been set up for her with Amleth at her feet, his face and furred chest glistening with sweat, his great legs and feet caked with dirt. Beside him Sibbi leaned, her back against the queen's knees. Torfi and Gautrek the Mild stood by the booth door, leaning on their spears, more than half drunk. They were all laughing now as though the Maze Dance had released them from a smothering darkness; as though what they had done would bring the sun back again and let the new rain steam in the field-furrows to warm the barley shoots, to bring everything up green and stiff and sprouting.

Torfi said wryly, 'Those blows across my arse with the whalebone, Amleth. You strike shrewdly for a lad, I'll not sit down for two days in comfort.'

The queen said, 'He is a lad no longer, is he, Sibbi?'

The green girl pushed a wisp of damp golden hair from her eyes and smiled. 'I will swear an oath on that, my lady,' she said. 'How you Barley Queens went at it until dawn in the old days, I do not know. The men could not have been like the heroes we have today.'

Queen Gerutha pulled at her hair sharply and said, 'Those days are not so long gone. Do you think I am a crone, then? We had our ways then, just as we have them now. I could do the Partridge Dance still if there was a man to do it with.'

Amleth looked up at her backwards and grinned. 'Come, mother,' he said, 'I will go round with you; Torfi and Gautrek can beat their staves together to give us the pacing-time.'

Sibbi sucked in her breath sharply, staring at the queen. Torfi stepped forward a pace and said, 'Nay, nay, my prince, enough is enough. The barley will grow without that.' He said no more but his eyes started and his jaw was working.

Queen Gerutha smoothed her son's wet hair. 'You hear what is said, my prince,' she whispered. 'We must not go against the word of the folk. Besides, I spoke only to taunt Sibbi; she understands me, being a woman herself.'

Amleth said, 'Aye, a woman among women. And if she had her rights she should be a queen, mother. She should be my queen.'

Gerutha glanced sharply at the girl then said to Amleth gently, 'Soon you are to go voyaging to Britain. The Romans there do not know you so you will show them that you are of old Vendil's true blood. If they call their Duke the Bear of Britain, then they must soon learn to call you the Bear of the North. They must find that you have fangs and claws, Amleth. Then perhaps they will set you up as king in one of their many kingdoms over there.'

Amleth said, 'Much will depend on what my overlord, King Beowulf, lets me do, mother. I must bow the knee to him and take his hand. It will be his to say what I do.'

Gerutha frowned. 'When you land in Britain,' she said, 'you and this Beowulf will be equals, not lord and man, my son. When you come to know the Geat-king better you will find that there is something wrong with him that will cancel your oath of fealty.'

Torfi and Gautrek nodded to one another. Amleth said like a child, 'What is it, mother? I like to know about these kings.'

Gerutha pinched Sibbi's arm and the two smiled, face to face. Then the queen said, 'This Geat-king came to our Maze Dance one year when I was the Riadne Nymph with the wool and was chosen as the Searcher with the bone sword. I can tell you that he went from the Maze centre in shame. I will say no more.'

Amleth thought a while and said, 'When I am in Britain then I will keep my eyes open for a kingdom there. It should not take longer than a year to set myself up in such a place. This Duke of Britain has a daughter, so it should not be hard.' He looked down at Sibbi as he spoke. She met his eyes and smiled back at him. 'That would not offend me, my lord,' she whispered. 'A stallion goes to more than one mare—though he always chooses his favourite and I know who that would be.'

Amleth took her hand gently in his great paw. He nodded, 'Aye, Sibbi, you know,' he said. 'And I know. And I will promise you this, that one year from now, just at the Maze Dance, I shall come back to Jutland for you to make you a queen in Britain.'

Gerutha said a little sternly, 'And will that be all you come back for, my son?'

Amleth stroked her thigh and said, 'Nay, mother. There will be one or two other things. My uncle Feng may need to be spoken to a little sharply by then, and as a king in Britain, I should have the sharper words to speak.'

Torfi came forward and said, 'Amleth, my lord, this needs some thought. It should not be decided so quickly. Look, let me advise you—when you have been away a year let the message come across to Vendilsgarth that you have been killed in some foray. Then when Feng least expects it land here shaggy and bristling and surprise him. He will think it is old Vendil come again!'

Amleth nodded. 'Aye,' he said, 'it would give me pleasure to see Feng on his knees slobbering. We will do that, old Torfi. It would make a good revenge for a start.'

Gautrek said, 'What do you mean, brother, for a start? Is there more to come?'

Amleth ran his fingers up and down his long chin. He said slowly, 'Aye, there would be more to come, Gautrek. Much more to come; but I will not say what is in my mind yet. A prince must have some secrets.' Then all at once he swung round towards his mother and said, 'While I am away, watch over yourself and Sibbi. Torfi, you will not come with me to Britain—you will stay here in the castle and see that my two women are not harmed. Do you promise this?'

Torfi said, 'It was in my mind to ride at your side to gain your kingdom, Amleth. But if I must stay in Vendilsgarth, then stay I must. And may Loki crack my neck-bone in the night if I leave the queen and Sibbi unprotected.'

Amleth got up and went to him. He put his arm round Torfi's neck and drew the rough hairy face towards his lips. 'You are my brother,' he said. 'No man ever loved a brother as I love you, Torfi Dwarf.'

Then he turned back to Gerutha. 'Mother,' he said, 'I have work for you and Sibbi too. While I am away, weave a great woollen hanging for the feast-hall—a cloth that falls from roof-timbers to the straw and weighs so heavily that it could bear down men. Can you do that?'

The queen smiled. She said, 'If it is what you want, my bird. It will keep us all busy, all of the bower-women. What pictures would you like stitched onto it? That must be Sibbi's job, she is very clever at guiding the needle, aren't you, girl?'

Sibbi stared back at her openly and said, 'I know how to get it into a hole and out again without pricking my finger. What pictures do you want, Amleth?'

The prince frowned a while. 'Let it be the story of Vendil, King of the Wood,' he said. 'Show him hanging on the tree then coming down refreshed. Then show him at the Maze Dance with scales on his body and a great beak like a bird. Then show him standing in moonlight by his door while two men come at him from the darkness with axes. Will you do that?'

Sibbi nodded. 'Are there to be women in the pictures?' she asked.

Amleth said, 'No women, sweeting. But you can have all your will with the men, that should keep your needle from going too slowly with weariness.'

The girl smiled. 'They shall be men,' she said. 'When the hangings are hung, everyone shall agree that they are men.'

Amleth nodded. 'I do not want these hangings up on the beams until I return. Let all the folk be wondering at them when I come in.'

Then to Torfi he said, 'And you, dear friend, while these women are stitching away you will need something to busy yourself with.'

Torfi grinned and said, 'I could always go to the bower and let them fashion these men in my likeness, Amleth.'

The prince slapped him on the behind. 'Nay, nay, monster,' he said, 'they have seen men before. They will not need reminding. I have another task for you: before I come back see that five score stakes are cut, of ash, holly and oak. Each one to stand as tall as I do and each one to have such a spike as would run through a galloping horse. Harden the points in the fire and then hide them away where Feng will not find them. Will you set your hand to this, friend?'

Torfi turned to Gautrek the Mild. 'He is truly mad,' he said, 'but one must humour a madman.'

Gautrek said, 'You are the lucky one, Torfi. Think of me, voyaging with such a madman!'

In Feng's chamber Gilliberht sat shivering at the table, a goosequill in his fingers, a small sheet of scraped sheepskin before him. He had made his ink from lamp-black mixed with a little glue from cow-hooves. In the torchlight the three fierce men stood over him like vultures watching all he did. Their eyes glared so much, Gilliberht thought they must be madmen.

'What shall I write, master?' he asked.

Feng scratched his thick beard and winked his little red eyes. He said, 'Set down my name first and say that I am King in Jutland. Say that Vendil was my brother and that I now have his Barley Queen for my own queen.'

Gilliberht began to shuffle. He said whispering, 'Lord, when the kings of the South write to one another, they begin with the honours and titles of the man they write to.'

Hake glared at him as though he was about to snatch him from the stool and put his foot on the scribe's neck but King Feng pushed his henchmen away and said, 'Let us have the letter according to the southern custom, Gilliberht. A king should show that he is not a beast, so write your finest runes, for I shall be watching you.'

Gilliberht's courage came back a little then. He dipped his quill in the ink and on the table-top wrote the word, Dung. 'Is that how you spell your name in the Roman runes, lord?' he asked innocently.

Feng bent over the word and made little movements of his lips. Then he turned to Hake and Godgest and said, 'Smell at this rune, my dogs, and tell me your opinions. It is better to have three noses at work on a job like this.'

The two henchmen came over and gazed at the marks in the wood. Then Hake said, 'This looks to be how a name should be written.' Godgest nodded too and said, 'Aye, in my opinion this scribe is a man of some small learning, Feng.'

The king nodded then and said, 'However much learning these fellows have picked up it is as well for them to be kept in order by kings and warriors. I think he will do, this fellow.'

He went back to his chair and took up his iron cup. 'Now, little Gilliberht,' he said, 'set down what I shall say. But first put in the honours and titles after the Roman fashion.'

Gilliberht's heart was much lighter than it had been though his face was as serious as before. He began to write, then after a while stopped and said, 'I have laid it out as follows, lord: *To Arthur the*

Bear, by Romans named Artorius, Count of Britain, Dux Bellorum, Pendragonsson, Duke in the Military Zone, on whom rest God's Peace. Is that as you wish, lord?'

Feng glanced at his henchmen, then said, 'Aye, it is exactly as I would have put it myself, fellow. If the Roman had been of the true religion, I would have said "Odin" and not "God", but there is no wisdom in offending him before we even start.'

Gilliberht bowed his head. 'You are indeed as wise as men say, lord,' he whispered. 'Now, your own titles, King Feng.'

Feng bit at the iron lip of his cup a while then said, 'It ill becomes a man to brag and boast in such matters. Set me down simply as the King in Jutland, Ring-giver to Danes, Steerer of a thousand Long-ships. That should satisfy him.'

Hake who was trying to count how many ships the king could call on began to laugh behind his hand. Godgest put his elbow into the man's rib to silence him. Gilliberht scratched on.

And when the pen was still again, Feng said, 'The message is a short one, fellow. It is this: I, Feng, send to you my stepson Amleth in the charge of my henchmen, Godgest and Hake. I beg you, see that this Amleth is killed on landing. In return I will see that no Jut-landers of my wide kingdom harry your shores during my life-time.'

Gilliberht wrote on patiently, pausing a little when he got to the words 'this Amleth', and when his quill had come to rest he turned and said, 'Will you now set your name at the foot of the letter, lord?'

Feng said, 'First, bring it to me so that I can see if you have put down my words as I spoke them.'

When he had the parchment in his hands he turned it this way and that so that Gilliberht should know that here was a king who could not be tricked by Roman runes. Then he looked up sharply and said, 'Do you take me for a fool, scribe?'

Gilliberht felt his old fear rushing back. 'Lord?' he said. 'What have I done wrong?'

Feng said, 'I have eyes as sharp as a weasel's, fellow. Show me where the name "Amleth" comes.'

96

Gilliberht pointed out the name. Feng ran his finger along the lines and said, 'Ah, but see, the name does not show itself the second time that I spoke it. How do you account for that, you treacherous little sucking pig?'

Gilliberht's heart almost jumped out of his mouth but he kept his voice even and said, 'My dear lord, you commanded me to write as the southern kings do, and that I have done. A Roman king would not set down the name "Amleth" twice; the second time he would say "the Prince" as I have done.'

Feng pushed the letter back at him, laughing now. 'Ah,' he said, 'it is just as I thought; you scribes need watching. I only wanted to show you that you are dealing with a king who has eyes in his head.'

Gilliberht sighed. 'Have I done right then, lord?' he asked.

Feng nodded then belched. 'Aye, right, little pig,' he said. 'I should have put it that way myself but I wished to test you.'

Gilliberht said gently, 'Then, lord, will you set your name down at the letter's foot?'

Feng said largely, 'I will do better than that, fellow. I will give this Arthur the picture of my own thumb and you may write my name beside it. We of the North have no great liking for these little quill spears.'

He dipped his thumb into the ink then pressed it down on the parchment. Then with a broad sweep of his thumb-nail he made a mark like a sword slash across the sheet. 'There,' he said, 'if this Arthur has eyes in his head he will see that it is signed by a warrior-king whose deeds speak louder than words.'

Gilliberht bowed his head. 'Arthur will understand, lord,' he said. 'Now may I go on my way in peace, great one?'

King Feng screwed up his red eyes and gazed down into his iron cup. He said, 'Give the letter to Godgest. He will deliver it to the British king.'

And when Godgest had folded up the sheet and had pushed it into his belt, Feng said, 'Now you two, leave me a while with the scribe. I wish to ask him something about life in other places. A king must learn what he can about the world or he is not fit to be a king.'

And when the two had gone out, Feng got up from his chair and took Gilliberht by the beard and said, 'Now, little piglet, what is in the bundles on your mules' backs?'

Gilliberht would have fallen to his knees but the king kept him hung up by the beard. He said, 'Rolls of fine cloth, lord. A present for you, great one. Your henchmen asked me for the cloth but I told them again and again that it was a kingly gift, no less. That is why they beat me and left me as you saw. It was for you, my lord, that I took their blows.'

Feng let him go then and said, 'Your beard does not grow very strongly in your head. You should rub horse dung into it to make it grow, fellow. That is what they do in Scania.'

Gilliberht nodded and smiled with joy. 'Yes, lord,' he said, 'I will do that. Advice from a king is always worth following. Thank you, my lord.'

Feng said, 'When you get to Scania, Dung-beard, tell them I told you how to grow hair on your face.'

Gilliberht said, 'But, lord, I can follow your advice without going to Scania. It was in my mind to journey back towards Colonia again and to see what sort of harvest is growing in Frankland.'

Feng spat upon the rushes. He said, 'No, you will go to Scania, Dung-beard. They have harvests there—the fish they fetch out of the sea. When you are not scribing for the king there you shall help gutting the fish for him. In that way you will come in time to learn more than they could teach you in Frankland, where the sunshine makes men lazy and good-for-nothing. Our northern life is hard to such folk, but if a man can learn to stand it, it teaches him much. It is worth losing a couple of fingers in the gutting-sheds to learn what the North can teach, scribe.'

Gilliberht edged towards the door, wondering if he might break away and find his escape along the winding dark passages of Vendils-garth before the red-eyed king could lay hands on him again. But Feng was already shouting out in his loud bull's voice, cutting off his freedom.

'Hey, Hake! Hey, Godgest! Fetch the little slave then! Throw him into the next smack that goes north. I owe King Beowulf a last gift and this shall be it. Odin has served us all a good turn, sending the poor fool here to Vendilsgarth.'

The night before Amleth set course for Britain he spent in Vendil's Wood, wearing the antlers and a wreath of mistletoe about his neck. The only tunic he wore was of untanned hide such as the King of the Wood must always wear in his vigils.

This coat Amleth wore was far older than Vendil himself. It had come from Uppsala Grove and had been bound first to a hanging man by a priestess of the Cimbri. That was in the distant time of the Ynglings, and in Vendilsgarth no man recalled whether it was dedicated to Freyr or to his sister Freyja, the bull or the cow. Some said that it was of neither but of a stallion who was nameless. This was because the belt of the tunic was a thick and knotted thong, fibrous and stretched beyond its first length by the many kingly wearers of Jutland. Old crones in the castle-garth told how in the ancient days a widow-woman had mourned her husband, she being still young, when a farmer's boy had run in with what he had cut in good humour from a recently dead stallion, crying:

> Here can you see
> A good strong vingull
> Chopped off from
> the father of horses.
> For you, lusty wench,
> this staff will be
> brisk enough
> where liveliness matters.

The old garth-women swore that this vingull took life as required, and allowed the young widow to console herself when she needed consolation. At other times she wrapped it in a fine linen cloth with herbs and onions about it to preserve its strength and flexibility. For long it was a family god; and at certain feast-times the young widow would even entertain her women friends with it, until at last its force became a byeword in Uppsala, and many stark-faced women of all ages came in Maytime to test its powers. How it came to Jutland no-one knew.

But what concerned Amleth more closely was the bull-calf's horn that the bower-women had bound to him with tight wool and damp thongs, the secret knots in the small of his back where he could not undo them. Its purpose was to shield the king in him from beast and briar, and to stop up his barley-force if wood-hags tried to draw it from him in the night.

Even after three days and nights of fasting the prince found this horn a penance and the tight-drawn belt about his middle a torment. At times as he drew towards the centre of the wood where old Vendil's oak had been, Amleth must needs lean hard upon his staff to keep the sense upright in his head. And when he reached the place, he straddled the fallen oak-bole and set his feet hard and firm into the overturned earth like a man stamping down a writhing serpent. And there he stood in the dusk waiting for a sign.

This sign came so slowly, so gradually, that for a while the prince was not sure that he would be visited. Then his feet, set to the ankle in the loamy soil, lost all their feeling as feet and their toes began to grow outwards and down like roots. Amleth stood quite still, feeling his legs set hard and the warmth drain from his belly into the earth. Now the hide coat hardened on him as stiff and rough as bark and the horn at his thighs sprang out and forward rustling with leaves. Slowly he raised his arms towards his head and touched the antlers there. They had already grown beyond his reaching but he felt the buds and leaves upon their lower tines and as he started to lower his arms again, he felt that they too had stiffened, that his fingers had lengthened and now were like great branches, each one.

He had time to bellow out but once in triumph before his mouth set and filled with lichen. His roar rushed through the dark wood as the vast sighing of the night wind among great trees. Now all feeling went from him save that he was rising and rising, until at last he sensed the distant light from the east and then he knew that he stood tallest of all the oaks in the wood.

Once before dawn reached Jutland a stranger dressed in golden mail came through the wood, his sword drawn, and rested against the prince's feet, weary from journeying. Two beasts with hide like wicker leapt out on him from the bushes and tore at him with their beaks.

Once two men strode grimly past the prince, holding spears and shields, calling, 'Amleth, Amleth, where are you?' Then they went on and the beasts crouched behind the bushes nodding and smiling, their white eyes glimmering.

A great oak at his side whispered through its leaves, 'Let us rise, my lord, and march on Vendilsgarth and tread it flat.' The other oaks round about took up the plea: 'Let the wood move, king, and possess the land again. King of the Wood, Green Man, we wait your command. Now that you have come among us, let us avenge Vendil. Let us stamp down all men. Let us take back our kingdom, even to the sea's edge. We wait, lord, we who are your oldest kin, your fondest subjects.'

For long with the slow green blood moving in him Amleth stood undecided among his tall host. Then from the moss about his bole three women in black hoods called out into the wood, 'Stand fast, seed of Vendil, this is not the time yet. There will come a time, but this is not the time. If you move now you will destroy the Green Woman who clings to you. Be still, know tree-patience, wait, wait, wait.'

Then Amleth was aware of the full-berried mistletoe that clung to his leeward side away from the damp sea-fret and the wolf-winds; and it was gripping fast to him, sucking at his inner sap with tender probing roots. He felt the sap leaving him gently, going into the mistletoe, feeding the Green Woman to make her golden berries grow plumper and more round.

He called out to her, the wind hissing in his leaves, 'Sibbi, Sibbi!' And then the last of the green sap sank down and down and the dawn came as white as polished iron and he was standing again with his feet in the soil, leaning hard upon the staff and gasping. Three black crows fluttered away from him. Two badgers sniffing behind a bush over a dead hare turned away and went to seek their own darkness.

Then Hake and Godgest came tramping back over the leaf-mould, their shields upon their backs, their spears below their arms, blowing on their cold hands and saying, 'We have looked for you all night, my lord. Come now, they have dragged the longship out and tarred it for the voyage. We must take the morning wind in our new sail, Amleth, if we are to prosper.' They spoke furious with impatience.

He nodded to them smiling and drew his chilled feet from the earth to go with them. Now he moved more easily than before with the bull's horn gone from him and the vingull-girdle slack about his waist.

All morning against an east wind thralls worked to set up a pavilion of red cloth fringed with gold on a low mound that overlooked the shore. And when the pole was up and the ropes staked hard into the ground, before the entrance to the tent, King Feng with his own hands drove in the wrought-iron standard, taller than a tall man, crowned at its head by a raging stag chiselled from bronze.

And when this had been done, he said aloud, 'This is a king's place now. Let none enter here but kingly folk.'

Then he stood aside, took up his own great ceremonial whetstone with the heads of bearded kings at either end and kneeled in the sand with his head bowed, waiting.

At the oaken runway by the shore the longship also waited, its prow deep-carved with serpents and dragon-heads, thirty-eight rowers about its length wrapped in sheepskin against the wind, shields ready set along the gunwales, the ash-mast in its stepping, the tent-posts raised. No finer king's ship than this would be seen nearer than Bornholm. A king of Sicily would have envied it.

Amleth came down at last from the castle wearing only a blanket about him. The bower-women had washed his body and cut his hair for the journey. Behind him came the queen carrying his sword and dressed in her feast-robe of green to signify the richness of the year and red to signify the blood that men must shed to enjoy such richness.

And at her heels came men with the cart of gilded oak on which lay the prince's war-gear: above all stood the bronze helmet plated with silver and set with red garnets, that had come from Vendel in Uppland in the time of King Njord of Sweden. This was a great heirloom. It was like a bold face frowning, with its long cheek-pieces and its lowering silver eyebrows. It would protect a kingly warrior from chin to neck-nape. Its hind-pieces would touch the wearer's shoulder-blades, so forked out were they and long. Its nose-piece was like the long curved beak of the hawk and pointed at the end. Its crest was the boar's head, most sacred of crests. And the name of this war-helm was Hildisvin the Battle-Swine.

This helmet lay upon a coat of iron mail that would come down to a tall man's knees and even lower. Each link of this chain-web was as round as a bower-maiden's ring-finger and no greater. And this war-mesh was called Fenrir's Better; because in the world's young days Loki Evil-Tongue sired a wolf called Fenrir, so fierce that only Tyr-Warmonger dared feed him, which caused Odin such anger that he had chains made by dwarfs to keep this wolf in. And each chain Fenrir snapped, so that Odin was forced to put on his wisdom-cap and have forged a special chain, wrought of the earth's most secret things—the roots of a mountain, the breath of a fish, the sound of a prowling cat. When this chain was made, wolf Fenrir agreed to wear it provided only that a god would place his hand between his jaws as a hostage. Of all the gods only Tyr-Warmonger would dare do this; and so Fenrir was bound, the chain held, and all gods but Tyr-Warmonger laughed loudly, for he had lost his hand. And this mail-shirt was of that ancient chain, no less.

Now behind both helmet and shirt on the cart stood Amleth's shield. All men who saw it wanted it, for it had a skin of solid gold upon the wooden frame. It had come from Götland last of all, but earlier than that some Roman king had held it on his arm, for in its centre-boss there was the face of a man with curled hair beneath his crown, and below this face such a war-horse with claws instead of hooves that only the Great Caesar should have had this shield for his. And round the boss, in circle after circle, right to the outer rim, were patterns of roses, curling apple-boughs, the sea-waves, and at last war-ships. Who could conceive a finer shield should not be on this earth but in Valhalla, among the ale-trestles, taking rings from all the world's dead kings.

Then, apart from such treasures, there lay a gold-filigree collar from Alleberg in Västergötland, covered with the little masks of all the woodland creatures. This Amleth would wear at a king's feast in Britain. And beside the collar was a great silver dish bearing the imperial stamp of Anastasius of Byzantium, the great Roman who had died but recently. And so that such a dish should not be disgraced when a prince ate from it in Britain, there were two spoons of silver, marked with the Greekland runes of *Saulos* and *Paulos*.

And clasping all these lay Amleth's warrior-belt, named Thor; the gold buckle of this weighed a pound, dead-weight, and was chiselled into the shape of a hundred serpents biting one another. Such a buckle was never seen before, and will never be seen again, for it was longer than a woman's hand from wrist to finger-tip. The Serpent of Ragnarok did not enclose the world more strongly than this buckle and belt held in the heirlooms on that war-cart.

So the prince strode before all these rich things, on his way to the bright pavilion, looking neither to left nor to right, a man whose body and blood held the deep secret that came from his dead father. He walked as heavily as a lion, his head nodding as he went, his light hollow eyes looking ahead but seeing all that lay to the side as well. As he passed Feng who knelt holding the whetstone beside the tent-door, the king shuddered to feel Amleth's shadow fall across his back. It lay like a weight of ice upon him for a while as the prince halted to look down on him, musing, half-smiling. Then Amleth came out of his short dream and passed inside and Feng felt the great load gone from him. He rose then and followed Queen Gerutha within, where they were to dress the voyager. The war-cart stayed outside, in charge of the gear-steward whose task it was to pass the heirlooms through the flap as they were called for.

Now the prince stood naked before the king and the queen. They looked at all parts of his body and then the king said in the old words: 'This tree is sound at the outgoing.' And the queen replied: 'May Thor keep it as sound for the homecoming.'

Then first they pulled on the warrior's under-drawers, with the iron-mesh at the crotch that would guard the king in him. Then over his body they drew the thick vestment of white wool woven from the fleece of a virgin lamb. On top of this they put the padded shirt of brown linen, stuffed with pine-needles between the two layers of strong cloth. Then Amleth himself bent and dragged on the tight-fitted cow-skin breeches that reached from his arm-pits to his ankles, the brown and white hair outside. Bending, the king himself put on the prince's long horse-hide boots, with the cross-straps that wound round his legs to the knee.

And when this was done the queen poured out a draft of voyage-ale into a great aurochs-horn bound at the lip with silver. She drank from it first, holding her clenched fist over it in the sign of Thor's hammer, and saying, 'Fare forward, blood of my blood, and come back a king.'

Next Feng sipped from the horn, his clenched fist above his head, saying, 'If I wish you ill on this voyage, may the Hammer fall as this does.' He beat himself upon the head, then shuddered as he passed the horn to Amleth. The prince gazed down into it; it was more than half-full. He drained it at one pull then said as all voyagers must say: 'I will fare as far as Odin takes me, and should I come back a king, the honour is yours. While I am a-viking may the Hammer fall on the oak-strakes and tumble me into the salt-maw if I think ill, dream ill or act ill towards my own folk on land.'

As Amleth spoke these words he held the horn so that the first and second fingers of his right hand crossed and so freed him of his oath. Feng saw this below the fringe of hair that fell over his bowed head and smiled with the secret knowledge.

Then Amleth flung the horn upon the ground and the two men stamped it to pieces so that it should not be used for vow-swearing again. They trod like wild swine who come upon an adder in the fern, in the fury of fear.

And when this was done Feng drew the mail-shirt Fenrir's Better down over the prince's body; Gerutha latched the bright collar round his neck; and then, lifting it as though it were a new-born child, Amleth placed the war-helm Battle-Swine upon his head and face, shutting the cheek-latchets like two stark gates, pulling down the hawk-beaked nasal and settling the boar's crest firmly onto the woollen pad about his fresh-cropped hair.

Then he stood like a stranger before them, like a stallion, the cold harsh scent of iron and leather coming off him now, his light eyes glaring like a ghost's out of the shadowy helmet. Gerutha felt a shudder pass down her upper body and rest at her lowermost belly; Feng shared the same shudder, but for him it went on down his legs and into the soles of his feet, which seemed to shrink and draw him up on tiptoe, like a thrall facing the spear that will be his death however much he plead.

Then the prince said, 'The sword, mother. Give me the sword.'

As she held out the golden belt and the great sword Quern-biter in its sheath, Gerutha smiled thinly above it as though she was thinking of dire things that might happen even now in the coloured pavilion. Feng saw that smile and came near to wetting himself. But then the moment passed and the queen bent and buckled on the girdle and the girdle-iron. Feng saw that the Peace-thong of the sword was tied, and it could not be dragged out suddenly; then he smiled and placed his hands upon the warrior's shoulders.

'You are a giant, my son,' he said, the sweat making runnels from his nostrils into his beard. 'All Britain shall bend the knee to you.'

Amleth glared out of the dark helmet at him then said harshly, 'Raise the tent-flap for me, uncle.' He spoke as curtly as a lord to a thrall. Feng almost ran to do his bidding. Then, when the king stood outside, Amleth leaned a little way towards his mother and whispered, 'See that what I have commanded is done, my lady. And see that my woman, Sibbi, knows I thought about her before I set forth. If I have put that in her which will become a king, see that it comes into the world whole, see that it is known as Vendil and is kept safe for me to hold in my arms when I return.'

Then he stepped out of the pavilion. None of the folk waiting on

106

the shore had seen such a man since the old king's first viking. The rowers who had been cursing in the wind while his gear was put on now turned and punched one another on the chest in joy to be led by such a great beast. The bower-women who lacked husbands or lovers whispered to each other, 'Oh God, such a man! Such a strong boar! And to think that the Maze-nymph has had this on her while we have come no nearer than washing his shirts.'

The horns blew from the headland and the sea-birds terrified at the fierce din rose shrieking as the prince strode down to the longship a head and a half taller than any man there. He spoke to no man. He walked like a troll among men. Three paces behind him with his dagger drawn walked Gautrek the Mild, wearing his horse-hide helmet and his great-shouldered sheepskin coat. Torfi stood on the mound beside the queen, his own spear held high. If the prince should see it, well and good; if he did not, then Torfi Dwarf knew that Amleth was his brother still and was content.

Feng went a little way towards the oak runnel down which the men would roll the longship soon. He did not go right down to the shore lest Amleth might suddenly turn and butcher him before all the folk. Yet his face was sadly smiling, as befitted an uncle whose nephew was going to his death.

Godgest and Hake strolled behind Gautrek, so far behind that he could have no fear that they would rush him at the last moment. They both smiled and even waved to the castle-folk who stood in a line along the dunes.

Then the longship was sent faring, the men jumped in, Amleth stood at the steerboard looking ahead and not back towards the folk.

And as they settled the long oars into a steady pull, they passed a broad-bellied smack with a brown sail that lay at anchor-stone, waiting for the right wind to drive it up towards Scania.

In the bottom of this boat, his wrists and ankles bound with twine, lay Gilliberht whose patron had once been Lord Manuel Chrysostom. He heard the horns and the folk shouting their farewells, he heard the skipper of his own craft cry, 'Odin, but these are men, not such as we are. These are of gods' own blood and bone!'

107

Gilliberht rolled over miserably into the netting and the scraps of half-rotten herring that they would use for bait further north. And to himself he said, 'No, no, no! They are savages! They are dead men, if there is a true God in Heaven! May they rot! May they rot! May they rot!'

The smack-master rolled him over and kicked him gently in the mouth. 'Nay, friend,' he said, 'do not fall to your prayers at such a glad time as this. No one is going to hurt you, little old one. There, let me sit you up to see the prince go by.'

II

Britain

ARTHUR sat in a long booth at Barrow Haven in Lindissi listening to an elderly woman in a grey gown, who would keep jumping up from her oak chair to shake her forefinger in his face. Sometimes he would look away through the small square window-holes, but outside there was only the grey Humber river and the slimy brown salt-flats of the Haven. So he would sigh and stare back again at the horny nail and the knobbly joints and would listen to the whining Celtic voice.

He was fifty-four now. The teeth on the right side of his mouth had gone in a sudden sword sweep outside Caerwent. He could hardly see from his left eye by reason of a blow from a lance butt as his opponent, one of Cerdic's few riders, swept past him. Arthur regretted this blow more than any other of his life, because he had drawn his own horse back and had thought the man had missed him entirely. Yet it had turned out a grave wound, one which had kept him on his back in darkness for a month before the doctors knew for certain whether he would hold his sanity or not. The loss of this eye made all hard; the cutting of meat, the judging of a target with the bow, measuring the distance of his saddle.

Arthur mourned far less the loss of his hair, the rheumatism in his left hand which made shield-holding intolerable, his jumped-up right hip from a horse-fall at the third Battle of Bassas against Kentishmen.

It was a warm day and the horse-flies had come through the window-hole from the midden just beside the booth door. One of them kept settling on his damp brow, fascinated by the Bear of Britain it seemed. It was driving Arthur mad. He said to the woman in grey, 'For God's sweet sake, queen, give me the solid substance of your woes and I will do what may be done to set things right. But let us have no more delays with all this wailing and finger-shaking. I have a ship to meet and cannot be here for ever.'

The woman in grey stood back and pursed her pale lips at him. She screwed up her mouth at one side and said, 'Nay, nay, War Duke, you cannot be here for ever and that's for sure. Rely on me, there is one who will be coming before long to see to that unless you change your ways forthrightly, I'll be bound. When a queen comes for justice from a mere duke and when that woman's king is an old blind man up in the chalk Wolds of Lindissi who cannot raise spoon to mouth without help, then Britain has fallen on bad times. Why we ever let the true Romans go, God alone knows. We did wrong, every one of us.'

Arthur said as patiently as he could manage, 'We did no wrong, lady. The Romans went without our yea or nay. They went in your grandfather's time, what is more. When they went, we were a life-time away from seeing any of them. So I beg you let us have no more of Romans. If there are any Romans left, we are they. There are no others. Not even in Rome. That mould is broken now. I beg you, proceed and let me know what troubles you.'

He stood up from the throne chair and leaned by the window-hole, his thin elbows in their iron mail against the hard grey Lindissi stone. The queen came up behind him and struck him on the back with her iron house-key but he only said, 'Go on, woman, go on.'

'Very well,' she said, 'then I will go on and much may you like it when you have heard.'

The duke was thinking: If I were a young man again I would be far away from this damp island of gulls and sheep-shit. I would ride with Belisarius against the Goths, or against the Carthaginians. Or, Jesus Christ knows, against anyone from whom I might gain a simple bag of gold—enough to feed a gentleman and his horse for a week without this constant raving up and down the land, tax-raising, wall-raising, army-raising.

He stopped then and thought: By God, I can raise anything, except the one thing that matters!

And this made him smile gently at himself. He turned round still pleasant and said, 'Please let me know your complaint, lady, and then I must go. Be assured, I will attend to it.'

Queen Cedda of Lindissi almost spat in his face in her fury. 'I'll tell you my complaint, sir,' she said. 'My blind husband, Caedbaed, and I put our young niece out to foster with your fine Anglian nephew, Medraut, here on Humberside . . .'

Arthur nodded. 'Aye,' he said, 'a pleasant little lass she is, with her blue eyes and yellow hair. I recall her well. She had a corn-doll she named Blodwaen, or some such . . .'

The Queen of Lindissi struck him sharply on the cheek with her iron key. 'Corn-doll!' she hissed. 'The little lass is pregnant and only fourteen. That's what we get from such as your splendid nephew, who swore to care for her as her father. Unless she falls from a horse, she'll spawn her Anglian bastard before Christmas. And what does the Bear of Britain say to that, I'd like to know?'

Arthur rubbed his cheek where she had struck him and gazed at her evenly like a man who is used to being struck, without anger. He said at last, 'This is all very well, lady, but do not forget that I know the girl well enough. She is one of those who are forever scratching at the inner leg and lifting the shift before visiting lords. She did it before me the first time I came to your house in Caistor. It seems that at last she has picked the wrong man—and now you come complaining. Do you think that being War Duke of this land is nothing but mating men with young lasses? Do you think that I am some sort of farmer and this land a stud-stable?'

There was a harsh red weal across his cheek where the key had struck. The Queen of Lindissi suddenly found that her legs were shaking and wondered if she had gone too far, hitting at the Bear himself. She said with lowered eyes, 'Lord, when all the kings in Britain joined to elect you as their general in the field, putting aside all rank, they also agreed to follow your counsel without question in other matters that had to do with the government of the land. This is such a matter. My niece Elene may have the itch, may be too forward when there are men about, but do not forget your own sainted mother Ygerne was not famous for her coldness in this respect, and do not forget that such women often make the best mothers and the best queens. Why, myself, in my greener days, can remember when I . . .'

Arthur wiped his damp forehead wearily. 'Yes, yes, Cedda,' he said with a faint smile. 'We all remember. We have all enjoyed your hospitality from time to time. It has never been in question. But you are asking me to punish some man of Medraut's for putting a child into the girl when for all we know she probably was the one at fault in the affair.'

Queen Cedda reached up and with her own stole wiped the Bear's face of its sweat. 'Nay, nay, Bear,' she said, smiling, 'I never said the man should be punished. Who am I to suggest that what passes between a man and a woman is a case for whipping? If it were so few of us would go about with a whole back. Nay, what I ask is that the man be persuaded either to wed the lass or to take her into his house as his properly announced concubine. Is that punishment, Bear? Nay, in my opinion it is merely common decency and no more.'

Arthur went back to his chair and sat down heavily. His maimed leg was giving him more pain than ever; he tried to remember what it had been like to run and jump, without this dragging lump of lead beside him, but he could not, any more than he could recall what it was like to be hopeful of the future, or to be brave in battle, or anxious-hot to get to a woman's bed. All those things were as old as the Romans, long past, forgotten now. He said, 'Very well, Cedda, if it were anyone else I would tell them to ride to Lindum or Ebura-cum and lay their distress before the magistrate there—but I have a soft spot for you, if only because of the feastings we have held together. Who is the man?'

Queen Cedda of Lindissi smiled and said, 'Aye, we have played the only game an hour or two, and a day or two, in our time, Bear. And with blind old Caedbaed at the other end of the hall! God, what a thing youth is, Arthur! What risks a woman takes then!'

Arthur rapped at the chair arm and blew his breath out noisily. 'Who is the man concerned, Cedda?' he said. 'Make haste, the

Jutish longship will be down at the mooring before long and I am sworn to meet the man who sails in her.'

Queen Cedda nodded. 'Very well, Bear,' she said, 'it was Medraut. It was the Anglian king himself. Elene swore it after the Bishop at Lindum had thrashed the confession out of her. I'll say this for the lass, she would have shielded him. She wept bitter tears when we made her tell.'

Arthur punched hard at the chair arm. 'Jesus Christ,' he said without passion, 'but why must all the world conspire against me? Have I not troubles enough without some little beanpole of a girl flinging herself flat on her back under Medraut of all men?'

Queen Cedda clucked, and said, 'Aye, aye, Arthur. I know the Anglian king is your own nephew, but . . .'

Arthur gritted his teeth like a boar. 'God's belly!' he said. 'The man is not the king of the Angles, you silly woman. He is no more an Angle than you are, you fool. His father was King Lot of Orkney and Lothian. He is no more than my lieutenant here along the Angle-coast, to see that these incomers stay eastward of Ermine Street. No more than that.'

Queen Cedda smiled. 'Ah, well, have it your own way, Arthur,' she said, 'but I wish my man, blind Caedbaed, had a quarter the power and riches this Medraut holds. That comes of his being your nephew, no doubt. Aye, aye, the ways of warlords these days! They override the true kings.'

Arthur said dryly, 'Lady, we warlords as you choose to call us, ride or march every day of our lives as the old Legions did. Many of us get more iron in the belly than good meals. We lie hard at nights under a leaking tent roof not under thatch. We possess just as much as will sit in the palm of our hands, no more. We are not farmerly-kings to stroll round our boundaries gently and then return to the villa for a warm meal and a soft bed each evening. As for Medraut being my nephew, hear this: his mother had a sister, a woman with hair so golden that in my foolish days of youth I called her "White Tresses", Gwenhwyvar, or as these Angles here call her, Wander. I took her to wife and so her sister's son, this Medraut, became my

115

nephew—by marriage, not by blood. Can you take that in, old one?'

Queen Cedda pursed her lips and nodded. 'Aye, and much more,' she said. 'And what I know is that warlords stick together in thick or thin, blood or not. If I ever get justice for poor little Elene, then I shall know that the spirit of old Rome is not dead in Britain whatever men say.'

Suddenly Arthur sprang from his chair, his thin face bunched. 'By God and all the Seraphs,' he cried, 'it is folk like you who are dragging down this poor land. It is you who give her a bad name in the world, prating of injustice, old Rome and what not! Then, by God, I will show you that there is justice wherever the Bear treads.'

He limped to the door, flung it open and shouted to the man outside, 'Go, fellow, and fetch the lord Medraut here straightway.'

The guard leaned on his javelin and said yawning, 'The lord Medraut has gone down to the farriery to get his black horse shod, Bear.'

Arthur shouted now: 'Then, by Jesus, fetch him away from the farriery and tell him that his captain sends for him.'

The man bowed his head and went off. At the door he saw two of the other Kymry sitting in the dust, playing dice. He said, 'By God, but the Bear is about to break both of Medraut's legs today! I have never seen him so put out.'

One of the men looked up and laughed. 'Good,' he said. 'Call me when the leg-breaking begins. I have a mind to see that Pictish bastard crippled.' Then they went on with their game.

And after a while, Medraut came into the room where Arthur and Queen Cedda sat on their chairs. He was a wide-shouldered man, very thick in the body and with hair so flaming red that no-one would have guessed the black Pict blood in him. He stood over a head taller than Arthur and seemed to remember this as he swaggered in and leaned on the Bear's oaken chair-back. He said, 'So, you have sent for me, uncle?'

Arthur snorted. 'For the love of God, don't call me uncle,' he said savagely. 'You are my own age but for a year or two.'

116

Medraut bowed and said, 'Aye, that is true but I have kept my hair and my eyes and my legs—and that makes me feel much younger, uncle. At any rate, you sent for me?'

The Bear of Britain screwed up his mouth. 'Aye,' he said, 'I sent to you with gentle words—before King Caedbaed sends for you with the gelding-irons. Is the matter clear to you?'

Medraut smiled broadly across at Queen Cedda who looked away. He said, 'It is this matter of the child Elene? She is pregnant, I hear.'

Arthur said coldly, 'Aye, the girl is pregnant. When will you take her into your house and give her your name?'

Medraut came from behind the chair and began to play with the fringes on Queen Cedda's mantle. He said, 'Aye, when? That is the question, Uncle. This lass will clamber over any pigsty wall if she knows the pigman is mucking-out there, regardless of the mire she treads in. So I must give her a name and a house, hey?'

Queen Cedda sucked in her breath but did not dare speak out now. Arthur sat with his chin on his hand and stared Medraut in the eye. And when he saw the warlord's gaze waver he said, 'Aye, it is my decree that you shall take the woman Elene into your charge and care, Medraut Lotsson. If we warmen cannot be trusted with a woman's little thing then we cannot be trusted with the ruling of a king's army. It is no more difficult than that. Are you content?'

Medraut gritted his teeth so hard that Queen Cedda thought the ends of them would break and fall onto his red beard. But they were of harder stone than that. Instead, he bowed until his boar-crest almost touched the knee of Arthur. Then, his head still low, but his light grey eyes looking upwards into the Bear's, he said, 'Aye, lord, I am content enough. Tell me to take any stray bitch into my house and it shall be done. Tell me to give my name to a sow in farrow and it shall be done. I am content.'

Arthur stood up. He said, 'See that it is done soon, Medraut, I beg you.' Then he passed across the room, limping like a wounded wolf and out towards the jetty at the Haven.

The guards playing dice did not halt their game as the Bear

passed. But one said to the other: 'It seems there was no leg-breaking today. I heard no howling from the Pict.'

The other said: 'When this Arthur breaks a leg, it often happens that the man does not know until the next day. He may look like a fool, but ask yourself, comrade, would the Kings of Britain choose a fool to lead all the armies in the field?'

In the chamber Queen Cedda rose from her chair to go back to Caistor in her litter. Medraut did not speak until she was near the door then he said, 'Woman, you came to the Bear behind my back. All the way home, among the Wolds, to your draughty palace of driftwood, see that I am not behind your back. And in the coming winter see that I am not behind your blind husband's back, hey?'

Queen Cedda turned on him by the door and said, 'Stinking fish, Pictman. Go back to Orkney and sit on your midden there. If ever I see that you are behind me I shall call for the duke and he will put you away, red-beard.'

She turned her back on him then altogether he made a great show of dragging at his dagger. Then she went out into the yard to sit in her waiting litter.

Medraut stood watching her. Then all at once he drew his dagger and struck it to the guard into the soft architraves of the booth-door. 'By Mabon and Belatucader!' he groaned. 'I will find the answer to this Arthur one day. I will find it before long.'

One of the guards, playing dice, rose and went to him. 'Give me leave to draw the dagger out, lord,' he said. Medraut nodded and then turned away when the blade was back in his hand.

The guard said, 'It strikes home hard when these Lindissi kings come lording it over the men who fight in the field, my lord.'

Medraut turned and glared at him out of grey eyes that had no lashes. He said, 'Get back to your dice, cow-dropping. Who are you to speak of kings to me.'

At almost the same hour that Amleth's longship drew alongside the wooden jetty at Barrow Haven the smack bearing Gilliberht put back into the muddy creek of Vendilsgarth. Three times the captain had tried to round Crabland and each time his look-out man had sighted a black-sailed roving vessel lying low in the water like a sea-snake, waiting for unwary travellers to come through the Gut.

It was more than the captain's right hand was worth to let Feng's smack and captive be taken and now the shipman vented his fury on all about him, like a bear with a sore head. Gilliberht as usual came in for most of the curses and kicks.

'You are a bad omen, you bald-headed sniveller,' shouted the captain, striking the thin-shanked, thin-shirted, shivering fellow across the wind-chapped face. 'This is the last time I will put to sea with a book-reading Christman. It is as bad as carrying pigs aboard. Nay, it is worse: you can at least kill and eat them if the fodder runs out but, Thor knows, you'd make a right bony dish for a man to break his teeth on.'

He would have beaten Gilliberht some more, but just then the watcher on the dunes came down and told the captain that Gerutha had sent for the scholar to be taken up to the castle.

'Old Feng's hunting a wolf to the south in Bogland,' he said, 'and I think the queen feels the lack of a man.'

The captain laughed. 'A man!' he said. 'She might just as well take a dry stick into her hand as take this one. He has no more about him than would make a meal for a sparrowhawk. Now if she wants a real man why doesn't she send for me?'

The watcher said, 'You had better ask the lady herself, tarry-arse. If you dare. As for me, I don't know what passes in a woman's head, any more than I know what a milch-cow might be thinking. I don't even know what my own woman dreams about, much less a Barley Queen. Come on, you shivering scarecrow, you.'

Gilliberht was glad to be on dry land again, after rolling and tossing about for a week drenched to the skin off the Jutland coast.

When he stood before Gerutha's chair he was not so sure that she looked gentler than the sea. Her hair was unbound and flowed like a shaggy mat into the red fox-fur cape about her shoulders. She wore no rings or bracelets: only a robe of blue wool, held to her by a hide thong knotted above her hips. Gilliberht noticed that her bare legs

119

were covered with fine golden hairs even beyond the knee. His own legs were as bald as his head and nowhere near as strong-looking as this woman's.

She fixed him with a grey-eyed gaze and said, 'Well, paunch, have you seen enough or would you like me to untie the girdle and show you more?'

The bower-maids at the back of the hall giggled at this and paused a while at their spindles and looms.

Gilliberht flushed and said, 'Oh, great lady, I beg your pardon if my eyes wandered. You are so comely.'

Queen Gerutha tightened her mouth and glared at him starkly. She said, 'I have always wondered what you Christmen scholars were like but Feng sent you away before I could find out. Now you are back, so I may learn for myself. Queens must know all. Come here, fellow.'

Gilliberht went forward afraid and stood on the lowest step of her throne-platform. She said sharply, 'Don't be a fool, man, come up to me, I cannot reach you there.'

His bowels turned to water as he mounted the steps. She said with a twisted smile, 'You are a dry old stick, your ham-joints creak as you walk. Let us see how you Christmen differ from others. Stand closer.'

When she put her hard cold hand upon him he drew back at first with the shock of it, being held by a woman, and a queen at that. But she gripped him and twisted him without mercy. 'Did I give you leave to go, fool?' she said. Then over her shoulder she called to the bower-maids, 'If all Christmen are like him then they can be of little use in this world. A dog would stand up more bravely.'

Tears of shame stood in Gilliberht's eyes. He said five Aves and tried to think of the Passion. Then the lady gave him a sharp tug towards her. 'Don't pull away, you mannikin,' she said, half-frowning, half-laughing. 'Anyone would think you had never stood before a queen in your poor life.'

This was true. The nearest he had been before was to have a cattle-drover's young daughter on his knees at the confessional, but she had cried out and run away before he could find out anything about her.

But before a queen, such a woman as this, all was terrifying. He began to shake from head to foot. He thought she meant to kill him. In the House at Fiesole he had heard the brothers say that this could bring death on a man. So he said, 'Have pity, lady, have pity.'

She answered, 'It might be possible. Though, Freyja knows, the reward would be a little one. Yet a queen must know all things, come closer.'

With her left hand she untied the thong girdle knot so that the heavy blue wool of the wrapper fell aside as she edged forward in the oak chair. Her sandalled feet were wide apart on the dais.

'Oh, my lady; oh, my god,' said Gilliberht the tears on his cheeks, trying to fall to his knees but being prevented.

He began to shiver again. It was not that it was cold. Indeed, it was warmer than he had known for days on the salt, wind-whipped sea. Warmer than he had ever known, standing so close to this queen whose long hair smelled of musk.

She called to the bower-maids, 'Let there be no laziness at the looms. Be about your business with quick fingers, you wicked creatures!' Yet though her voice was harsh, her lips and eyes were smiling, and Gilliberht's heart began to thump like a pony's hooves. All thoughts of God went from his head. No thoughts were left there, only those of fear and shame.

Then all at once standing so close to a queen he began to feel like a god himself. He even thought that he was flying through the air, higher than ordinary men, like a bird.

But his journey was not far. And then he fell to the ground and the queen let him go from her grip as though she despised him.

She called back to her maids, 'Fetch me my black robe. This one is soiled.'

She pushed at Gilliberht with her foot, rolling him down the steps. 'Christmen,' she said from curling lips. 'What manner of thing are you? What place can you fill in this life? I had thought better of you, but now I know why you lock yourselves away from women in your

Houses. Get up from your knees, little one, and do not drip your tears all over my floor. Go back to the captain and let him take you away where some fool of a king might have use for you. I have none.'

When he could rise and walk away, Gilliberht of Fiesole was glad to go, with the bower-maids mocking his stumbling steps and laughing at his hanging head, although he must run the risk of meeting the black-sailed sea-rover again, off Crabland.

He thought: 'Better a bloody-handed pirate than this she-animal with the pitiless grey eyes. At least he would not shame me before my god. At least he would let me render up my soul like a hero, and not grovel in the rushes like a thrashed dog.'

Amleth leaped over the side to make a good show, ignoring the salt water that splashed his chain shirt. Gautrek came over closely after him, holding his halberd aloft to show all men that he guarded his prince's back.

As he strode up the wooden-slatted cat-walk over the mud, Amleth thought: 'Now my mother will be dreaming of me as she prays for my safety here among the Romans. She will have no thought but of me. I must do her credit.'

Gautrek whispered, 'See, the Romans are lined up to greet you, brother. Can the little bent man in the middle be their Bear? I thought he would be a giant from the way men tell of him.'

Amleth said, 'Men always talk of kings as though they were gods or trolls. Yes, that is Arthur; see, the man on his right hand bears the banner of the black bear; the one on the left carries high the bird-banner. That bird is the chough into which they say that their king's spirit will go when he dies. It is a lesser bird than our great goshawks and ravens.'

On either side of the Jutish party along the dun-coloured river bank spirals of dark smoke rose from low thatched hovels. When the wind changed and blew upstream it brought on it the thick stench of the midden-heaps that lay outside each cluster of hutments. Amleth pinched his nostrils in tightly to keep out the smell. He said in a low voice, 'These Romans—these liars! Their land is not so well kept as our own. Yet they would have us think its streets were paved with golden tiles.'

Behind him Hake and Godgest smiled. Hake said aloud, 'Perhaps it will not offend you for long, my prince.' He held Gilliberht's letter in his right hand.

Amleth half-turned and began to answer him but just then a herald who stood before the dark-cloaked Romans stepped out and called into a leather horn, 'Here stands the Bear of Britain, and by his side the Count of the Saxon Shore, Medraut, son of King Lot of Orkney and Lothian. And beside them stand Kei the Leader of Harryings, long in wrath, heavy of vengeance, whose sign is the Moon; together with Bedwyr, Swiftest of Men, the Counsellor, whose sign is the Lightning. They greet you, my lords of Jutland, as do their followers, Gwythyr son of Greidawl, Gwyn son of Nudd, Fflewdwr Fflam Wledig, Rhuawn Bebyr son of Dorath, Celyn and Conyn the sons of Caw, Llary son of Casnar Wledig, Sberin son of Fflergant King of Llydaw, Drudwas son of Tryffin . . .'

His voice went on as the ship's party made its way up towards where the Romans stood. Gautrek, now close on Amleth's heels, dropped his head and said, 'We did wrong in not bringing a herald, Amleth! These Romans seem to make a great thing of it.'

Amleth smiled but held his head erect. He said, 'When Jutlanders run ashore on another man's coast they need no herald, brother. They are seen to be men with swords in their hands and that is all anyone needs to know.'

All the same he wished that he had had his mother embroider him a banner showing a black raven or a green oak tree. His iron standard with the leaping stag seemed most stark among all the coloured cloths on the shore-top.

Godgest behind the prince said, 'Amleth, little one, these Romans also carry swords. How do you think we shall come out of it if they rush us?' He winked at Hake as he spoke. Hake shook Gilliberht's letter back at him in mockery of the prince.

Amleth did not answer him but, setting foot on hard land now, strode past the herald and straight towards the Bear of Britain.

123

Arthur whispered to Kei on his right hand, 'He looks tall, this Dane. Can you manage him if things go amiss?'

Kei had been watching Amleth every inch of the way. He whispered back, 'Aye, Arthur, his mail is torn under the left armpit I see. That is where I shall go in.'

Medraut chuckled aloud. He said, 'Why, Kei, my poor fellow, this Dane would shovel you into the hole in his helmet and munch you up without noticing he had eaten anything. Then he would do the same for Bedwyr One Hand, here.'

Arthur said grimly, 'Have your spear at hand, Bedwyr. Medraut is trying to make fools of us but it is just possible that the god speaks through his mockery.'

Bedwyr nodded and then quietly lowered the iron pile of his ash-pike so that it could be thrust upward at Amleth if he started a run-in upon the Bear.

Queen Cedda's litter was halted further up the shore and was standing on its carved lion-legs in the rushes. Her slaves were lying about, joking and whisking the flies away. The Queen of Lindissi had her curtains drawn back and was staring out. She said, 'By Mithras! That Dane is a tall youth. So is the man behind him with the halberd. They stand two heads higher than any of the Kymry.'

An old slave called Eri, who was allowed more liberties than the others because at his birth Cedda's father, a herdsman-king, had assisted too much like a farmer and had lamed the child for ever, shaded his eyes and stared down towards the shore. 'Two of the Danes are offering a paper to the Bear, Cedda,' he growled. 'We might do better if we came to see him in a longship up Humber-river instead of wold-ways along Caistor Road.'

Queen Cedda's face was stark with fury. She said, 'It is always the way, strangers may thrive while kith and kin must go on their knees for a crust from the Bear.'

But then Eri held up his hand and said, 'Nay, nay, Cedda! Something is happening that we would not like. See, the Bear has read the letter, and now Kei and Bedwyr have dragged the two Danes away. Listen, you can just hear them shouting out.'

Cedda smiled again, then she drew her mantle about her shoulders and said, 'Get the men to take up my litter, Eri. Perhaps it is not so well to come asking favours in a longship, after all. Let us be away.'

Kei and Bedwyr came back from the reeds, blood up their breeches to the thigh, wiping their weapons. Amleth and Gautrek stood back to back, on guard, now too far from the longship to reach it before Roman arrows reached them. But Arthur the Bear stepped forward gently, smiling, the paper still in his right hand and said, 'It is done, my lord, as the letter from the king your uncle commands.'

Amleth cried out, 'Come no nearer, I warn you.' He put out the long sword, Quern-biter, and Arthur halted, but still smiling said, 'You do not read Latin, my lord?'

Geutrek the Mild answered for the prince, saying, 'We find no need to read anything. In the north we are for doing, not for reading. Keep back.'

Bedwyr leaned on his long spear and said pleasantly, 'No man may reason with a woman out of bed, an adder in the bracken, or a Dane on the shore. We have obeyed their king's letter, so they can like it or lump it. Let them go back to their ship now if that is what they want.'

Amleth cried out, 'Feng would never ask for Hake and Godgest to be killed, one-arm. They were his henchmen.Is this your Roman justice?'

Duke Arthur shrugged his shoulders, the chain-mesh creaked against the hide shirt. He said, very tired, 'Your uncle's letter says this: "I, Feng, send to you my stepson, Amleth, in the charge of my henchmen, Godgest and Hake. I beg you, see that these two are killed on landing." He makes a promise then, which I will not burden your brain with understanding. In any case, being a Jutlander, he is unlikely to keep it.'

Amleth said, 'Feng loved these men. He set great price on them.'

The Bear of Britain half turned away from him, then thought again and said, 'I loved my first son, Anir; but when he plotted against me with the Saxon Cerdic I struck him down, nevertheless. As for the price of these two rogues, you shall have their worth in gold when we come to one of the city-treasuries. Now, is that Roman justice?'

Amleth considered a while then said, 'All things are strange here. The King of the Geats was to meet me on Humber-river, yet his longship is not here. Have you killed him, too?'

Kei, whose eyes were small and black and set close together, whose neck was thick and red above his mesh-shirt, glowered and blew through his wide nostrils. 'Pack him off to his ship, Arthur,' he growled. 'He asks more questions than the Five Kings of the West. We cannot use such a fool here.'

Gautrek the Mild called back, 'Step over here, Bull-neck, and I will use you and with a vengeance.'

Amleth signed to him to be quiet, then said, 'If you mean so well by us, where is Beowulf the Geat then?'

Arthur sighed deeply and said, 'Jesus Christ only knows the answer to that, my friend. He comes when he wishes and goes back when the tides turn his ship about. No doubt he is up in the Whitelands now, ridding the north of snow dragons.'

He spoke with such good humour that Amleth smiled though the heavy cheek-pieces of his helmet hid that smile from all men. He said, 'I half believe that you mean well, Duke.'

The Bear of Britain flung Feng's letter to Bedwyr, who caught it in his one hand, his spear-butt thrust into the shore mud. Then Arthur turned to a fair-haired youth who stood immediately behind him, wearing a purple tunic and carrying no weapons, and drew him forth by the hand.

'Amleth,' he said gently, 'this is my second son, Lacheu, who is dearer to me than my right hand. He shall come and stand before you now. You have nothing to fear from this boy, he is not armed. If you think that we mean ill by you, then do with my son Lacheu as your nature compels you. This, too, is Roman justice.'

126

The young boy went forward, trying not to soil his gilded sandals in the Humber mud, and stood before Amleth. A gentle perfume came from his golden hair. Amleth saw through the holes in his helmet that the boy's eyes were very blue and as clear as forest pools in summer. The boy put out his white hand and touched Amleth's iron shirt, stroking it as one would stroke a fierce hound to make him quiet. Amleth had not seen such a pretty boy in his life before, he was more like a fairy prince from under the hill where the ancient gold is stored. Only the most brutish of beasts could harm such a boy, and even they would be ashamed afterwards.

Amleth slowly put up his sword, Quern-biter, and said to the boy, 'Greetings, Lacheu. I hope that we shall be friends.'

The boy smiled but did not answer. Arthur called out, 'He is from Cornwall, Dane, and speaks only the old language they use there. But he shall be your friend, and you shall teach him north-talk as the time passes by. Now are you content?'

Amleth nodded, then swung back the flaps of his helmet and smiled. The Celts stared at his fierce blank face and his ashen hair with admiration. He said, 'Aye, well content, Arthur. Now what am I to do with my ship, and what will you do with the bodies of my uncle's henchmen?'

Arthur wiped his streaming forehead. 'Send your ship home,' he said wearily. 'You can always fetch it back when you need it again. As for the dead men, they will sink into the ooze here, unless wolves and dogs find them first. They are not worth a mound burial as far as I can judge.'

That night the three score cavalry of Arthur lay at a villa under the wolds just north of Pontus on the way to Lindum. Medraut came in to the atrium where Arthur was drinking wine with the owner, an Angle who had taken the name Maximus and who worked hard at running his household as he had heard the Romans had done. His wine was so thin and sour that Arthur found it as much as he could do to keep it down and wished to God that these incomers would stick to brewing the drinks they knew how to make—sharp ale or sweet mead—and forget that the vine had ever been brought north to Britain.

Medraut did not wait to greet the man but signalled him abruptly to leave the room. When he had gone Medraut said, 'I have just left the Dane. He is laughing his great head off with Kei and Bedwyr, he must be simple-minded.'

Arthur sank into his chair. He said, 'Is that any reason for your ill-manners to our host Maximus? Our one-night stay here will eat up all his harvest this year.'

Medraut winked and laughed. 'You worry too much, uncle,' he said. 'This Maximus, whatever his name is, is a rogue. He has paid no taxes at Lindum for three years. We are only collecting our rightful dues. I have a more important matter to discuss with you. This matter of the child, Elene.'

The Bear of Britain sipped at his sour wine silently and waited. Medraut sensed that he must tread carefully. He said, 'I wish only to be just to her.'

Arthur said quietly, 'I am sure you do, so you will take her into your household and give her a name as I have judged.'

Medraut shook his red head. 'Bear,' he said, 'you judged too hastily, you judged to please Cedda and that blind old king in Lindissi. You did not consider what would be best for Elene herself. Consider, Arthur, if I name her as my own woman she may bear a brat who will one day think he should be king in Orkney. My brother Gavin would have the boy's throat cut before he would allow that.'

Arthur nodded. 'Or he might cut Gavin's throat, which would be no great loss to Christendom as far as I know,' he said.

Medraut poured himself a beaker of wine, tasted it, then spat it out again and set the cup back on the table. 'Look, Arthur,' he said, 'I have put the case badly, I am no magistrate, I am a warman like yourself, I will start again.'

Arthur nodded; with a flushed face, Medraut said, 'Consider this, we are on patrol through the Civil Zone. At any time a messenger may ride in with news of trouble down at Tribuit, or up at Celidon, or across at Caerwent. We do not know what Cerdic is about. He may well be moving north out of Wessex with more men in his host than we have ever set eyes on before.'

Arthur nodded and sipped at the sour wine. 'It is always possible,' he said. 'But we are paid soldiers, we live from day to day, we are not priests who forecast the future.'

Medraut began to wave his hands about. 'Consider,' he said, more loudly, 'when we ride, we ride. To take the girl Elene with us would be an anchor-stone on our speed. Besides, once I had given her my name, think what a prize she would be if Cerdic got hold of her—as might well happen in a running battle. So, what is the answer—to leave her up here, among untrustworthy Lindissi-folk, who might take her as a hostage and screw another twenty-miles strip of territory out of us before we got her back?'

Arthur smiled grimly. 'It seems that you went in further than you thought when you made light of the girl,' he said. 'A captain should always consider these things before he commits himself.'

Medraut banged with clenched fist on the arm of his lord's chair. 'It is you who committed himself in passing such a judgement,' he said. 'I tell you this, Arthur, I am now considering what is best for Britain . . .'

'As well as what is best for Elene?' said Arthur. 'You have much on your mind, Medraut. How do you propose to solve your problem?'

Medraut eased himself into a chair and ground his teeth with impatience. 'How the Western Kings ever came to elect you as the Duke of Battles, only the Virgin will ever know,' he said. 'Look, the answer is simple; this Dane, Amleth, has some notion of finding himself a British princess to marry while he is here. He has said as much to Kei and Bedwyr already. So, you can give him Elene and when we get to Lindum the Bishop there can marry the two of them.'

He leaned back in triumph then. Arthur regarded him coldly, then said, 'Elene is noble, being the niece of King Caedbaed, but she is not a princess, even in Lindissi where, God knows, everything that isn't a sheep seems to hold a title.'

Medraut bent forward. 'In the sacred name, Arthur,' he said, 'must I lead you like a blind man up every step? You could adopt her, nominally, which would make her your daughter, a princess. This Dane will sail away when he has seen his fill of battles and has collected a few trophies, then who will be the wiser?'

Arthur was growing very tired again, his leg was hurting so much that he could scarcely speak. He said with an effort, 'You never look farther than the end of your —' He paused then and put down his hand to still a sudden shooting pain that came up almost to his rib-cage. Medraut was glaring at him. Arthur said—'nose.' Then he drew in a deep breath and said, 'What if this Dane asks about the kingdom that his princess is heir to? What then?'

Medraut began to whistle like a blackbird and even took another sip at the tart wine. He said, 'Old Cunneglassus of Powys has named you the heir to his five thousand acres of barren moorland that they call a kingdom. The old man is likely to die before winter, or even before the summer has gone, unless he learns to eat less and to keep out of damp beds. So, there is the kingdom you need. I will fetch the girl in straightway so that you can adopt her.'

Arthur was screwed up in his chair, enduring too much pain to answer. When his senses returned to him Medraut was back again, pushing Elene before him. She was a delicately-featured girl with bright yellow hair, although her skin was darker than that of Celts and her nose more aquiline. She had put a red flower behind her right ear and looked very pretty in her blue robe, though she had torn it at the hem climbing over the villa wall to see a litter of piglets that Maximus was proudly showing to the Kymry and not one of which would still be about the next day, had he but known.

Arthur said to Elene, 'Queen Cedda tells me that you have been a sinful girl.'

Elene drew in her lips tightly and glanced up at Medraut, as though asking him what she should say to the Duke. Medraut just smiled down at her and patted her on the shoulder.

She took courage from this and said, 'I am as God made me, my lord.'

Arthur smiled stiffly. 'I would say that you are as man made you, at the moment. Tell me, do you find such things pleasurable?'

Elene lowered her head a little, but still stared the Duke in the eye from under her brows. She said, 'You have the right to whip me or to put me in prison, Duke, but you have no right to ask me that.'

The Bear of Britain smiled sadly. 'Tell me, Elene,' he said, 'if I were your father, would that give me the right to ask such a question?'

Elene raised her head defiantly. 'Yes,' she said. 'A Roman father would have that right, but you are not my father.'

Arthur said, 'Come here and kneel before me, child.'

When she hesitated, Medraut pushed her forward and even made her kneel on the broken tiles of the atrium. Arthur placed his hands upon her shoulders then, kissing her in the middle of the forehead, said gravely, 'In the presence of a witness, I, Arthur son of Uther Pendragon, declare that I adopt you, Elene, as my daughter with the style of Princess of Powys.'

Elene stared up at him for a moment then burst into tears. He raised her to her feet then sat her on his good knee with some effort.

'There, little one,' he said, 'do not cry. Though I now have the right, I shall not ask the question. But I will ask you something else; this Dane-prince Amleth is a great warrior among his folk in Jutland. Would you be a faithful wife to him, do you think?'

Elene looked up at Medraut then said, 'I am betrothed already to my lord here.'

Medraut shook his head smiling. 'Not now, Princess Elene,' he said. 'Now you are your own woman again, being kin to Arthur the Duke.'

Elene stared him in the eye for a while, then said softly, but with great dignity, 'It is not my custom to offer myself twice, my lord. Yes, father, I would be a faithful wife to the Prince of Jutland if he asked me.'

Arthur stroked her golden hair and then kissed her again lightly on the nape of the neck. 'He will ask you, daughter,' he said. 'Yes, I can assure you he will ask you. So you will be married in good time, as we pass through Lindum where your centurion of a forefather must have been stationed, once upon a time.'

Kei and Bedwyr had taken the tall Danes to their hearts. In a corner of the great barn they sat together in the straw, talking about their lives, their wounds, their battles, their weapons. Lacheu was their princely cup-bearer and brought them the good mead which he had found in a cellar, hidden away by Maximus when he heard that the Kymry were approaching.

The Romans had admired Amleth's war-gear and had heard the names of his weapons. Kei said, 'Old Arthur has nothing better; his lance, Ron, would fall apart if this Quern-biter of yours got to work on it.'

Bedwyr said, 'How do you compare the Bear's sword, Caliburn, with this Quern-biter, brother?'

Kei said, 'Much the same—even though the Bear swears that a mere-woman fashioned his with spells and put it in his hand. I would think that a Barley Queen is no less than a mere-woman, hey, Amleth?'

Amleth said in the Anglian tongue they were using, 'Barley Queens are the most ancient sort of womankind, friend. They hold their secrets direct from Mother Earth. Sword-iron comes from the earth and so must carry magic in it. I have yet to hear of iron that came out of water.'

Bedwyr smiled; he said, 'Your own King Beowulf showed us one when he was here last. He swore that he picked it up from the bed of a lake when he killed Grendel's mother under the green-scummed mere.'

Gautrek broke in and said, 'If you believe Beowulf, you will believe anyone, friend. In our land, men cutting peat in the marshes often strike on buried swords and gear of many sorts. That is how Beowulf Bigmouth got his sword, if you ask me, and I would tell him so were he in this barn now.'

Kei snorted and looked grim for a while. 'This mead is stronger than we think,' he said. 'So is this Beowulf. He is no friend of mine

132

after his betrayal of our Duke's wife; but he is no man to despise. In the feast-wrestling at Holderness, the first time he called at our shore, he laid me on my bed for a week and then went on to floor three of the champions of Gwynedd.'

Bedwyr said, 'You brood too much on that, comrade. You were sick at the time his longship put in to haven.'

Kei glared darkly and said, 'If he ever puts in again, they can fetch me off my death-bed and I will pay him back.' Then he bent towards the Danes and said in a low voice, 'If the truth were known, this boy Lacheu is his son. The lad's birth came nine months after Beowulf meddled with the first Gwenhwyvar while Arthur was down at Bassas against the Saxons.'

Gautrek scratched his flat nose. 'He is a pretty lad,' he said. 'Though I do not see him standing in the thick of battle. Rather I see the harp in his hand and his back clothed in flowery silk.'

Amleth waved this aside. 'What do you say about the first Gwenhwyvar, Kei?' he asked. 'Are there more than one?'

Kei glanced about the barn for a moment, then said, 'It is a title, my lord, rather than a name. Arthur is an old man now, but there was a time when he was much like his father, Uther Pendragon, son of the Emperor Constantine. If Uther wanted a woman he took her.'

Bedwyr placed his hand on Kei's shoulder to silence him, but the strong mead would not be denied and Kei had drunk as much as four men could hold already. He pushed Bedwyr's hand away and said, 'Uther Pendragon fathered Arthur on the wife of Duke Gorlois of Tintagel and Dimilioc; all the world knows it. There is no secret about it. Thank God he was decent enough to hack Gorlois' head off just before he did it or our Arthur would have been a full-bastard instead of only half a bastard.'

Then Bedwyr rose and struck Kei across the mouth. The Danes watched silently with wide eyes, marvelling at the manners of these Romans. They expected Kei to leap up and strike back at Bedwyr; but he merely bowed his head in acknowledgement of the blow and said calmly 'When Gwenhwyvach struck her sister Gwenhwyvar, the blow was harder, comrade.'

133

Bedwyr sat down again, half-smiling, and said, 'It is thirty years since we first rode into battle together, Kei; and in all that time you have not changed. I doubt whether it is in my power to teach you anything now—yet I must try. That is my right.'

Kei nodded carelessly, 'Aye, comrade,' he said nodding, 'it is your right. And it is my right to answer our guests when they ask questions. I am the Duke's Steward and my task is to see that his visitors are entertained.'

He turned back to the Danes and said, 'Among our people, this name Gwenhwyvar means little more than a royal harlot, friends. We are a dark-haired folk in the south-west, much like you Danes in general. It is the old Greek blood in us, no doubt; but it is not comely in a woman. So they dye their hair to gold, which is what the name Gwenhwyvar indicates. Though I would not have you think that these women are of the streets. They are more like the Vestals in old Rome, they are of noble blood. When Arthur wants the other sort, he takes such as Indeg and Garwen and Gwyl to his bed, to name but three!'

Suddenly Bedwyr broke in and said in a loud voice, 'And the name of his shield is Prydwen, which has the icon of the Virgin painted within it, Amleth.'

The prince was about to ask why Bedwyr had thought to say this when he heard footsteps behind their stools and turned to see the Bear himself coming towards them, leading a golden-haired young girl by the hand.

The Danes rose clumsily in their war-gear when they saw Kei and Bedwyr stand before the Duke.

Arthur signed for them to sit again, then he pushed the girl gently towards Amleth and said, 'My lord of Jutland, this is my daughter, the Princess Elene. She was brought up in the house of King Caedbaed of Lindissi, which is an ancient kingdom. Later she was the ward of my nephew, Medraut. And now, as a token of my regard for you, I offer her into your safe-keeping while you are in this land. Will you take on the duty of protecting her?'

Amleth glanced round at Gautrek, then at Kei and Bedwyr. Their faces showed no yea or nay, but were grave and silent. Their eyes stared at nothing, the eyes of men who kept their own counsel.

Something in the young girl reminded the prince of Sibbi when they were children together, though this Roman was darker-hued and more restless in her movements. But her hands were so fragile and flower-like and her lips so proud and her chin so haughty and her hair so golden. She only stood as high as his breast, but her bearing and gaze were those of a queen.

Amleth looked into the eyes of Arthur and nodded with a smile. 'Aye, Bear,' he said, 'I will take care of this princess. My sword and shield are hers for the time being.'

Then he kneeled in the straw before the little girl and bowed his great head like a well-trained war horse. When she put her hand upon his neck to accept this homage he felt that it was warm and a little moist. It sent a strange shuddering thrill through him that he had only known from two women before in his life.

It was going to be a hot summer. The air shimmered above the straight military road that lay beyond Pontus towards Lindum Colonia. The white dust rose from under the hooves of the Bear's cavalry as they cantered southwards. They made a good showing with their banners and their lances held high. The sunlight glinted on their mail-shirts and their boar's head helmets.

Arthur rode at the front on a white horse with Lacheu on a black pony at his left hand and Medraut on a heavily-built charger at his right. Kei and Bedwyr came immediately after, riding abreast on matching chestnuts. As a sign of courtesy, the Danes were next in the cavalcade; Gautrek on a raw-boned roan with staring eyes and enormous hooves, and Amleth on the biggest mount they could find for him in Pontus, a dappled grey that could have drawn a war-cart on its own, without trace-horses.

On the great saddle before him sat Elene, plaiting flowers into the charger's long mane. She was as gay as a spring lark under the blue sky, riding before her knight. When Arthur had said she must go in a litter as a noblewoman should, she had whispered a very indecent word in his ear and had ended up with, 'You may be the Duke of Britain, old one, but the Jutlander is my husband—and from now on he is the man I shall obey.'

Arthur stared at her solemnly. 'He is not your husband yet, Elene,' he said. 'Not until we can persuade him to kneel before the Bishop in Lindum; and not even then, until we can persuade the Bishop to wed a heathen Dane.'

Elene began to play with the hanging buckle of the Bear's war-belt. She said, 'I will persuade my prince to kneel, have no fear, Arthur. Tell me, who is the Bishop now?'

Arthur said, 'Not the one who thrashed the confession out of you, little one. He is off on a pilgrimage, you will be pleased to know. Old Dubricius of Silchester is in Lindum, I hear.'

Elene put her arms round the Bear's waist and held him close, although his armour was harsh to her body. She said, 'Then our problem is solved, father. He first put the crown on your own head when you were only a boy, so he will do what you tell him to do, heathen or not. What is better, he is an Archbishop, not a mere Bishop—so my knight and I will be firmly joined as noble folk should be.'

Arthur slapped her lightly on the behind. 'I have small doubt of that, my girl,' he said, 'Archbishop, Bishop—or nothing.'

The road south was straight for mile after mile and, apart from the places where liontooth and elder had pushed their way up towards the light and had disturbed the facing-stones, was as smooth as when the Ninth Legion had marched along it up to the fortress at Eburacum. All his life Amleth had heard of the great roads that Romans had made through the world, and he had pictured them to be like Jutland sheep-tracks only rather broader, of course. Now he was riding along one and it seemed to him one of the wonders of the world. He turned to Gautrek and cried out, 'Why, man, three laden wagons could go abreast down this road!'

Gautrek was thinking about Torfi the Dwarf in Vendilsgarth and said, 'Aye, oh aye, that they could.' Then he was silent again. Roads did not interest him greatly.

136

Elene reached back and placed her hand on Amleth's thigh as he rode. Then she leaned sideways and smiled up at him so that he should see her pretty lips and white teeth. 'Gautrek is a strange man, guardian,' she said. 'I think he does not like us Romans.'

Amleth smelled the sweet scent of her golden hair. It was like having a spring flower on the saddle before you always. His heart was very light. He said laughing, 'Gautrek is my blood-brother, princess. In his own land he is greatly feared by men and is a famous outlaw. In battle, he strips off his mesh shirt and runs at the enemy unclothed.'

Elene turned and stared at Gautrek smiling and biting her forefinger. She said, 'Would he show me how he does it, my prince? There are woods further along the road where no one else would see. We shall be resting there before the ride into Lindum.'

Amleth shook his head. 'It is not a thing that he does to amuse folk,' he said. 'After men have seen it, they die.'

Elene turned her face up towards him and answered, 'I am not a man so perhaps I should not die.'

Amleth put on a serious look and said, 'Let us talk of other things, princess. It would make Gautrek angry if he heard us speaking of battle-things. They are for men alone, and among men, for warriors alone.'

Now Elene lay across his thighs as though she were in a cradle and reached upwards to play with the cheek-flaps of his helmet. She said, 'What shall we talk about then, my guardian? Let it be of anything you wish, and I will talk with you. We Romans speak openly of all things because we seek the truth. So do not be ashamed but ask me what you will.'

Amleth waited a while, then said, 'Very well, lady. Since you are a princess and a daughter of the Bear himself, tell me where lies the kingdom that you are heir to?'

Elene stopped smiling and rose stiffly from his knees to sit upright in the saddle. At last she said, 'That is hardly a polite question, knight. I expected you to ask something else. Women are not interested in kingdoms; they are for men to bother their heads about.'

Amleth said solidly, 'Am I not a man, lady?'

Elene began to chew the stem of a flower from the horse's mane. She said quietly but just so that he should hear, 'I have only your word for that. There are some things that must be proven by more than a word.'

Amleth did not answer but began to whistle then, through the face-hole of his helmet, but Kei turned in his saddle and stared at him so strangely that he stopped. Then he realised that the Kymry were riding in silence, sitting quite upright in the saddle and staring ahead as though they were on parade on the Field of Mars in Rome herself under the gaze of the Emperor.

He wondered why, then he saw that they had run into what seemed like a long straggling settlement. On the left-hand side of the great road the moorland was covered with scattered dwellings, some of them of rough-hewn wood, roofed with boughs which still held their browning leaves, others of turf, others of hides slung over poles. Smouldering fires burned here and there among the hovels. Light-haired men in rough blue tunics, with axes in their hands, stood at the roadside staring at the Kymry and shouting out in a strange harsh tongue. Beside them stood shaggy-haired women in coloured blankets, many of them, even the youngest ones, with babies at their uncovered breasts. All seemed to glare with their light eyes like wild beasts to see the Bear's banners going by.

Elene said, 'Hold in your breath, Amleth. It is possible to take the plague from them. They are Frisians who come over in little boats no bigger than wash-tubs and live along the road here on slugs and roots that they grub out of the earth. Most of them have never slept under a tiled roof in their lives. They are unclean folk, their women bear litters of children three times a year and eat them if they cannot find worms and roots to gnaw on.'

Amleth whispered, 'Why do they stay on that side of the road?'

The girl said, 'They are afraid of the road. They think it was made by our god and that if they tread across it they will waste away and die.'

Amleth said, 'Poor cattle! Most of them are already so wasted they will die in any case. To risk the seas and then to live like wild swine, rooting for acorns, that is no sort of life for a man.'

Elene shrugged her thin shoulders but did not answer then. Half a mile along the road she said, 'Brutes are brutes and Romans are Romans. These incomers are used to living on ditch-frogs and crab-apples. When they break into our orchards and steal our Roman plums and peaches, they either spit them out again or are sick on the ground like dogs.'

Amleth thought a while, then said, 'These peaches—what are they? We have not such things in Jutland.'

The girl pinched him quite sharply. 'I think that you are almost a Frisian yourself, prince,' she said. 'You have something of the same look in your eyes.' She was laughing as she spoke but he glared down at her so starkly that she began to fondle him and to tell him that she was teasing him. And then suddenly pointed away to their right, where a red-tiled house with a white wall stood well off the road, backed by long fields in which grew rows of grey-green trees. Doves perched on the roof purring in the sunshine; dark cypresses nodded above the walls.

'See,' she said, 'in that villa garden they still grow plums and peaches. The man there claims to have no drop of any other blood but Roman since time began. His name is Aufidius and he will not even uncover his head when he speaks to Arthur himself.'

As Amleth stared towards the villa, he saw the gates open and men and women come out dressed in long white linen robes, leading children by the hand. As the Kymry clattered past, the men outside the villa held up their heads and raised their right arms in a stiff salute. Arthur saw this and called back to the trumpeters, 'Give them a blow, lads. Let them feel that Rome is still alive—dead old bitch that she is!'

Behind Amleth four silver trumpets screamed out, thin and snarling in the summer air. The family outside the gates stood as still as carved statues, then suddenly began to shout, 'Vivat! Vivat!'

Then the cavalcade was past them and the leaders were laughing to one another and saying, 'Vivat! Vivat!' in tones of mockery.

After a while, when the sun stood overhead, they came to a place where oakwoods reached away on either flank of the road. When Amleth first smelled them he remembered that he was the King of the Wood and felt a sort of royalness rising in him that set him above the men he rode with, though he made no show of this and enjoyed it only within his own body.

And here the Duke of Britain raised his hand and halted the squadrons. Then he twisted in his high saddle and called back to Elene, 'Is this the place you meant, daughter?'

She nodded. Then she turned to Amleth and said, 'Here I shall bathe and refresh myself before going in to the city. There is a clean stream that the Frisians dare not approach within the wood. Will you escort me there, guardian?'

Amleth did not answer but swung himself from the horse and then reached up and brought the girl down. Gautrek began to dismount also, but Kei and Bedwyr suddenly called to him, 'Stay, comrade, there is something we wish to talk of with you.'

Then the golden-haired boy Lacheu shouted out, 'I will come and splash in the water, Elene. There are frogs with gold in their eyes down there. I will take one back to Cornwall for my uncle, Duke Cador.'

But Arthur laid his hand upon the boy's shoulder and said, 'I intend to get such a frog for your uncle further south, perhaps in Leir's Caistor. There they have more gold in the eye, Lacheu.'

Lacheu said, 'Frogs or not, I want to go into the water with Elene.'

Arthur said, 'Princes do as they are bidden. You will bathe in Lindum, my son; the water there is Christian water. Here there is some doubt. Sit still.'

When the girl and Amleth were deep in the oakwood she said to him, 'How hot it is today. You must be smothered in all that wargear.'

Amleth said, 'It is hot. I will take off my helmet if you will permit it.'

She tried to twist one of his fingers and said, 'Silly goose! You can take all off as far as I am concerned. Indeed, if you are to bathe with me it would be better to take all off, or else you will ruin your fine armour.'

Amleth lifted off his boar's head helmet stiffly. He said, 'This gear takes an hour to get off and another hour to put on. I shall not go into the stream.'

After that Elene walked away from him pouting. But she smiled again when she saw the fresh clear water with the tiny minnows lying in shoals under the banks of high grass, and the leaning willows and elders and oaks and hollies, all green in the sunlight.

'Quick, quick!' she said, 'help unlace my bodice, guardian.'

Amleth's fingers were slow and thick and often she sighed and stamped her bare feet and even, once, pretended to slap him as though he were a woman's thrall in the bower.

But he paid little heed to this and at last he said, as he drew off her under-shift, 'You are dark-skinned for such a golden head, lady. Our women in the north are a pale white in the body.'

Elene dangled her long legs wide apart on a fallen oak-bole and nibbled at a grass-stalk. 'That is because I am a Roman and they are brutes,' she said. 'They are no better than the Frisians, you see. Do they eat their babies?'

Amleth rushed at her in mock-fury but she stayed there without moving and he halted before her half-ashamed. She stared up at him then, her blue eyes as clear as the brook water, never blinking, and said, 'Can you understand why Rome was the Mother of the world, Danishman?'

Amleth wiped the sweat from his eyes and nodded; 'Aye, lady,' he said, 'I see that we of the north may be a little backward in some things.'

Elene suddenly jumped off the oak-bole and touched him, then turned and plunged into the rippling water. For a breath, he almost followed her in to catch her and hold her under; but he drew back at the grassy bank and switched at the midges with a stick as he watched her in the stream.

She swam like a fish, like a water-nymph, laughing, spouting out the clear water, flicking her dark-gold hair back again and again over her dark shoulders.

And sometimes she lay flat on the waters, on her back with the sunlight through the oak-leaves dappling the dark ivory of her body, as beautiful as a water-lily, Amleth thought.

Then, 'Look,' she cried, 'I am a dolphin!' and she bellied her slim body up and down, sending foam flying, until at last even she was weary and half-crawled up the green bank, her hair now hanging before her face, to lie spread-eagled on the grass.

Amleth stood above her, his face clouded, his hauberk oppressive. She raised her head to him and said, 'Now dry me, slave.' Her eyes were bright, like a bird's, like a young hawk's. Amleth's hackles rose. He thought suddenly of Sibbi who should be Queen in Britain. He said harshly, 'That is for bower-women, not kings.' Then he turned away and stood for a while slashing at a thorn bush with the stick he had picked up again.

And at last Elene came to him quietly and clothed and touched him on the arm. 'I am sorry, guardian,' she said. 'I should not have spoken to you like that. I am not used to playing with princes from Jutland.'

Amleth gazed down at her like a sullen hound. In a low voice he said, 'I would hope for your own good that you do not play in this way with anyone very often. This is not a game which men are likely to find humorous, princes or not, Jutlanders or not.'

Then Elene began to cry and to cling to him like a child afraid. He ground his teeth and thought of flinging her into the reeds and treading her down with his heavy battle-shoes. Then this mood passed and he stroked her damp head as gently as he knew how; and at last she looked up at him, her full eyes no longer as sharp as a hawk's and said, 'Forgive me, lord. I will tell you now that there is a kingdom coming to me. It is in Powys, southward in Wales, and it will go to the man who weds me.' She halted a while then began to weep afresh and far louder than before. 'Oh, I would to Jesus Christ that the man should be you, my lord.'

Amleth thought again of Sibbi. But this time he let his great

142

mouth smile to show his stallion's teeth. He said thickly, 'Very well, Elene. You shall have your wish. If your father agrees I will name you my wife.'

She gazed up at him for a long space and then said, 'But it must be before a Churchman, my lord. We noble Romans believe . . .'

He put his hard hand over her mouth. 'What you noble Romans believe is your own noble affair,' he said. 'I have told you that I will have you and will name you my wife. Is that not good enough for you?'

When they got back to the military road the Kymry still sat their horses in form of squadron, the banners raised. Amleth was amazed that the men were not lying about on the grass, drinking from the ale-horn as Jutlanders would have done. It was as though these Romans had been waiting for him all the time.

Arthur saw the two coming up through the oak saplings at the edge of the wood. He turned to Medraut and said, 'Here they come, hurrying to tell us they will wed, I hope.'

Medraut glowered back leaning down hard on the saddle-horn. He said, 'If she has not persuaded the Dane by now she is lost. I cannot drag her behind me all over the land to make trouble for me. I shall cut her throat.'

The expression on the Bear's face did not change. Staring ahead he said, 'That would not please me, nephew. I do not wish to lose the support of the Lindissi-folk, or the Frisians will sweep across the land as far as Humber-mouth. One must be politic in these matters. I should be vexed.'

Medraut bounced up and down in the high saddle. 'Politic, by Mabon!' he said. 'Either we lose her, or you lose me.'

Arthur stared up into the blue sky as his charger pawed the dusty roadway. He said after a while, 'Then if it comes to it we will give her the poison-cup. That would be more seemly and it might be put out that she had died of a plague or of a snake-bite in the wood.'

Then he turned and bent from the saddle to greet Elene, who was holding on to his stirrup and smiling broadly, her blue eyes alight with joy. And when he gave the signal to move off again, he rode like a man ten years younger.

Archbishop Dubricius was close on ninety, could move only in a litter, was thick of sight and hearing and had knuckle-joints so crippled and twisted that he could not put a spoon to his mouth and had to be fed by a boy. Yet he was a merry Christian still who held that in dark times arrows must be made of any sort of wood if the Devil was to be put to flight.

So under a striped awning set in the ruined forum of Lindum, he baptized Amleth by asking the prince to step ankle-deep into a tub of holy water. While the old man instructed priests to touch the Dane on breast and forehead with the liquid, Dubricius went off into a devious form of ritual, spoken in a half-forgotten Latin down into his robe. Amleth accepted all this without qualm since all the while he held his right hand with his fist clenched after the manner of Thor-worshippers.

The marriage ceremony was just as informal. Amleth took off his helmet and gave Elene his sword to hold. She wore a chaplet of wild flowers in her hair and had a white stole across her shoulders. Dubricius pondered over them a while, leaning so far forward in his chair that he almost fell into the tub. He seemed to be trying to recall his lifetime in the service of Christendom, and often names like Ambrosius or Vortimer or Constans came into the sentences he mumbled. The Kymry stood about, waving flies away or smiling at the women who had come up from the market to see the Dane in his war-gear. Arthur and Medraut kept up a whispered conversation all the while, to do with troop-movements and supplies in the south-west. Kei and Bedwyr stood one on either side of Gautrek to keep him from shouting out abuse at the White Christ or from snatching his master away from the Archbishop's power.

Then all at once Dubricius seemed to lose interest. He suddenly said quite clearly in Celtic and then in Jutish, 'So under God and in the sight of the people I name you man and wife.' After which he nodded to his litter-bearers to take him away to his house and bed.

Then before all the company Elene fell to her knees in the dust before Amleth and kissed his battle-shoes. He raised her sheepishly and set the chaplet of flowers straight upon her head, then took back his sword from her and pushed it into the sheath.

'Well,' he said to Gautrek, 'what can't be cured must be endured.'

Gautrek came forward shrugging his great shoulders. 'They will want to hear me tell of this at Vendilsgarth,' he said. 'Torfi will enjoy it.'

Amleth said, 'Tell him I kept my fist clenched, do not forget that!'

Everyone was laughing and content save Lacheu, who was found in a corner by the city well weeping. When Kei asked him what was amiss, he said, 'Why must my friend the Dane-prince marry Elene? Why must I lose him so?'

Kei slapped the boy hard on the back and said, 'Elene is a lady of some importance now, Lacheu. She has been declared your sister and is the wife of a man who will one day be a king in Jutland. Is that not cause for rejoicing not tears?'

Lacheu wept more than ever. He said, 'She is still Elene of Lindissi from among the sheep-folk. She is not noble, she is a bitch. She is no true Roman, her folk were incomers in kitchen-tubs. Look at her hair and you will see.'

Bedwyr came over and ruffled the boy's golden hair with his one hand. 'There, there, prince,' he said. 'All the world cannot be Romans or there would be no value in the name. Let us Romans be generous and leave little Elene with her thimbleful of Roman blood. All will be well, I promise you. You will see, now you have both a Dane and a new sister to play with. Why, you are the most fortunate of fellows, isn't he, Kei?'

Kei nodded and then said gruffly, 'That is what I have been trying to tell him but these Cornishmen from Kelliwic are as thick as their own oak trees.'

Then at last even Lacheu was laughing with the others and trying on Elene's wedding-wreath and holding her by the hot hand.

Before sundown, most of the Lindum folk were drunk with the

celebration; had they known it, the Frisians from up the Ermine Street could have marched through the city gates unopposed.

Three mornings later Arthur, having gathered all outstanding taxes in coin and kind, bade a formal farewell to the Pilus Prior of the Lindum Militia, advising him to be of good heart and to keep his volunteers up to strength even if he had to conscript all able-bodied men of whatever status over the age of fifteen. To the farmers and their bailiffs he spoke sternly of the need to plough the last square yard up to the city wall, to bend their backs in the production of cereals, beans, onions, lettuce and beetroots. 'Waste none of your time and labour on celery,' he told them, 'for this food has little strength in it. Such leisure as you have, spend in gathering the natural foods which God has given you—I mean, the honey of wild bees, birds' eggs, blackberries and all the herbs. Do not neglect such humble creatures as the snail—yet do not push him into your mouth as the Frisians do and hope that he will be to your taste. Let me, in the moments before I must leave you, instruct your wives how our ancestors prepared their dish of snails: first remove this creature of God from his shell—that is important, my friends, since a shell has no nourishment in it—then place the snail in a dish of milk and salt for a day. After the second day, use milk alone for a week. So, on the seventh day, clean your snail every hour with salt to remove all excrescences and, by evening, fry him in the best oil you may lay hands on. Should you be able to provide a wine sauce, then he will be all the more grateful to you and you the more nourished by him.'

As Arthur said this a red-faced farmer whose family of eight lived on a quarter of an acre and the milk and flesh of one stark-ribbed cow and a sow worn out with farrowing, called, 'Aye, that is a good dish, Duke. Now give us the one about roast chicken stuffed with dates, nuts and honey.'

Arthur gazed across the crowd and fixed the man with his eye. Then he waved and smiled, 'Ah, my old friend,' he said, 'I see you have a good memory. Fabricius, isn't it? Did your daughter Claudia ever come to bed with the bastard that Angle put in her last Easter at Venonae?'

The folk in the crowd turned their heads to look at the man, but he had ducked away almost before the Bear had finished. Kei and Bedwyr winked at one another; Gautrek said to Amleth, 'This Duke is no easy man to make a fool of. He may look like a shrivelled stick, but he is a man and the master of men.'

Arthur then complimented the four chief civitates who had catered for the Kymry during their stay and told them that whenever they were in Caer Leon he would do as much for them.

Finally he looked round for Archbishop Dubricius, but saw only the sub-Deacon, a thin red-nosed man named Stuf who mumbled that his master was laid up with an ague from having been up all night praying for the heathen. Arthur told him: 'Pay my respects to him, Deacon Stuf, and bid him be of good cheer for I hear that half the heathen priests of East Anglia are abed with ague from having prayed too long for us Christians!'

The sub-Deacon did not take this well, but the crowd enjoyed it. The Kymry for the most part had heard its like up and down Britain from Eburacum to Winchester, and they could not be expected to laugh yet again.

Then moving out of Lindum along the Fosse Way, they came at last to Ratae where they picked up another squadron of errant Kymry stationed in wait for them under the command of Drystan, and so the whole cavalcade, now numbering upwards of one hundred and fifty lancers, followed the long road that would take them to Aquae Sulis where they would then turn westward so as to pick up the ferry over the Sabrina that would bring them into Caer Leon within a week, barring all unfortunate incidents.

There was only one such incident. Just outside the old fortress of Corinium a bone-faced rag of a man started up from the roadside and ran towards Arthur shaking a broken crook and shouting, 'Death to you Romans, all of you! Why do you keep this dead land tottering on its bony legs? Let it die, Arthur, let it die! For Christ's sake, let the Saxons have it and be done!'

Arthur had drawn in his horse and was quite willing to speak

147

kindly to the old man since he had suffered much and was hardly in his right mind. But just then the man fell in the dusty road and his long thin jaw creaked down onto his breast most sickeningly. One of the troopers rode up and rolled him aside so that the horses should not take fright from the corpse.

Gautrek whispered to Amleth, drawing close, 'Since Ratae this has been an empty deserted land, brother. I fear we are coming to the end of the world and that no good will result from all our journeying. Should we not break away and make our own road to some coast or another? I have it in my heart to smell the sea again. I have never been so far inland before.'

Amleth whispered back, 'Patience, patience, old brother. I have a desire to see this famous Caer Leon of his. And besides, have you forgotten, I am soon to be a king down here, somewhere.'

Gautrek snorted and said, 'Odin save you; it will be the king of dust and ravens I think, not of any place that living men would envy.'

Then they came to Corinium and saw the tottering, fire-blackened walls and the stripped and naked bodies strewn about the road. All the men had been mutilated and the women so ravaged that Amleth sent word back to Elene's litter that she was on no account to look out from the drawn curtains. It was impossible to clear the way; like it or not, the horses went over the bodies not only of men and women and children, but of dogs, swine and cattle also.

Yet, strangely enough, perched on their high parapets, guards still stood, the lances in their hands, looking out over the wasteland.

Arthur called a halt, then shouted up to them. It was Medraut who stopped him at last, saying, 'Look more keenly, my Bear. They will never hear you. They are the dead men whom Cerdic has propped against the wall again. He has a sense of humour, this West Saxon. It must be the Celtic blood that runs in his veins. No Saxon would have such wit.'

In her litter Elene, having broken her promise to her new husband, had looked out and now she was being sick.

The Kymry came at last into Caer Leon across the river by black painted horse-barges, since the bridge was now too ruined to bear much weight. The Danes looked everywhere with sharp eyes. They saw the graveyards, bath-houses, and the towering amphitheatre with its moss-grown circles of stone seats where once the Augustan Legion had howled for blood. Between this dark well of death and the curling river lay a huddle of low hovels over which smoke hovered in heavy whorls. But Arthur swung his horse away from these towards the huge square fortress with its battlemented walls and red-tiled roof-copings. Once inside the gates the Danes gazed, shocked into silence. Rising above the old legionary barrack-blocks stood temples and theatres with gilded roofs supported on fluted columns of cream-coloured stone. At the far end of the main thoroughfare reared a high white palace over whose portico fluttered an enormous samite banner embroidered with the figure of an enraged black bear, its red jaws open and screaming with fury.

As the squadrons clattered towards the palace two score of maidens ran out, chanting and scattering flower petals before the riders. Amleth had never seen such tender beauty before. It seemed to him that these women were of some sacred company; they seemed like sisters, their eyes being of the same blue and their long hair of the same golden shade. Each girl wore a silver fillet set with pearls, though their long robes were of different colours—such delicate colours as could only be seen among spring flowers: pale blues, gentle greens, sun-washed pinks, rain-faded yellows. Two of them ran towards the Danes then stopped and stared up at them with wide eyes as though they were gazing at monsters.

Kei twisted in the saddle and called to Amleth, 'Well, Jutlander, what do you think of these pretty Romans, hey? But they are not for you, lad! They are kept for the Kymry—why else would young noblemen cut each other's throats to ride with the Bear!'

Later, when the Danes were lodged in a chamber that lay alongside the cavalry dormitory, Elene, who had made the servants lay her a bed between the two men, said, 'I did not like the way you looked at the girl in the blue robe, husband. She smiled at you as a wicked woman smiles. I saw all this from the litter.'

She spoke seated in a tall chair, her lips drawn thin and forbidding, her long pale fingers clenched upon her thighs.

Amleth looked back at her calmly. 'Elene,' he said, 'am I to blame for being wet because it rains? Let it be understood that it was I who promised to protect you, not you who swore to guard me.'

She drew a deep breath through her flaring nostrils, her knuckles gleamed as white as bones. She said in a flat, harsh voice, 'You will learn that when a British princess commands it is better for her man to obey. Among us you will learn that women are not the fat cows of Jutland.'

Gautrek was picking his teeth as she spoke and when she had finished he strode towards her, bent suddenly and twitched her robe up about her waist. Then holding her hands so that she could not cover herself again he said, 'Fat cows, hey? The girls of Jutland would laugh to set eyes on such a thin-shanked heron as you, little one! They would say that your mother had reared you among the swine to eat husks.'

She stared up at him wide-eyed and spitting like a wild-cat, but could not break from his grasp. When she kicked out he turned so that her foot struck the hard side of his leg, causing her more pain than it did him. Amleth watched this with a smile on his face but when the tears began to run down Elene's cheeks, he went forward and said, 'Let her be now, brother. She has learned something.'

For a while after Gautrek stood back from the chair the girl sat with lowered eyelids, her shoulders shaking. Then suddenly she looked up as sharply as a bird and said evenly, 'Yes, I have learned something. Gautrek will be the next to learn something but what it is he will tell no one.'

Then she rose from the chair with a strangely graceful dignity and went out of the room. Amleth said, 'You held her uncovered too long, brother. It has shamed her. Now you would do well to keep a watch on her, I think.'

Gautrek shrugged his heavy shoulders and laughed. 'They are strange cattle, these Romans, Amleth. It is not easy to regard them as creatures like ourselves; they are more like some animal that lacks a name.'

Amleth was about to answer when Arthur himself stood in the doorway and motioned with his hand for Gautrek to leave him alone with the prince. And when Gautrek had gone, the Bear eased himself down onto the chair and said gravely, 'You are a stranger, a guest in this land. So, if by your lack of knowledge you break our customs, it is our place to pardon you. Yet there are certain customs which all men share and the breaking of such customs carries no pardon with it, Amleth.'

The prince wondered for a while what was meant. He said at length, 'Who has complained of me, Duke Arthur?'

The Bear looked him in the eye and said, 'Your wife, Elene. She complains that you have not lain with her since your marriage, nor have you shown her any tenderness of word or touch. Surely this is not the custom among the folk of Jutland, or how is it that so many of you get born to come plaguing us along our coasts?'

Amleth rose and walked about the room before he answered. Then he turned and said, 'My lord, I am, as you can see, a grown man and a very big man at that. The girl Elene is a child, scarcely more. Would it be the act of a man to spread his great weight upon such a child? Would it bring honour to him or pleasure to her, such a savage wrenching apart?'

Duke Arthur rubbed the side of his face wearily. He said, 'Perhaps you mistake the nature of women, Amleth. And certainly you mistake the nature of your wife Elene, who is hardier than you think. If my judgement were asked I would say that of the two of you the Prince of Jutland would be the first to cry for mercy.'

Amleth saw the smile in the Bear's eyes, but did not smile in return. Instead he said from a stiff face, 'At Vendilsgarth they made me the King of the Wood, if you know what that means. It seems to me that it would ill become the Green Man to plant his great oak root in such shallow soil.'

The Bear of Britain got up from the chair then leaned heavily on its arm for a while with the effort. He said thickly at last, 'I am not concerned with the dark gods of your forests. Here men hold to Christ and to the Virgin and expect even their guests to lay aside such pagan beliefs as they might have, for a while at least. If the purpose of your marriage with Elene was to get a child in the state of holiness then, by your delay, you are ignoring our Christian custom. I cannot command you in this, not being your sworn lord; but I ask you in all friendship to follow our precepts and to give your wife the rights she claims.'

That night Elene came to Amleth's bed in the darkness and lay close by him as though she had great faith in what the Duke might have said to her husband. Yet, though at last she was forced to use all her wit and skill upon him, it was as if a cold magic lay upon the prince, as if all the warmth in him was drawn away towards the north, towards Vendilsgarth. Then, struggle and sweat as she might, gnash her teeth and bite at him as she would, Elene could not move him. And at last when the agony of her threshing, driving body had brought her to weeping, the dead man whispered in the darkness, 'Leave it be, little one, or you will hurt yourself.' Then she struck at him and said bitterly, 'Are you a gelding, Jutlander? They promised me a man.' And Amleth said as gently as he was able, 'That you must judge for yourself.'

After a while she rolled from the bed and ran away into the darkness. Then Gautrek said from the other bed, 'Now she will hate the two of us, brother. Perhaps it would be wiser if we followed our noses to the nearest salt sea and took what ship there might be, back towards Jutland. I think that we shall do no good in this place.'

Amleth answered, 'I think you are right, Gautrek. There is a smell of death in the air of Britain. It is like those old stone pens where bullocks have been taken for slaughter since the world began. The scent still hangs about the stones though the ground is now dry. Foxgloves and willowherb grow there, showing the blood they have drunk in the colour of their flowers. Yet I cannot run away from the slaughter-pen because I smell a smell, or see a scarlet flower, brother. I have come far to gain a kingdom so that old Vendil in the Ale Hall shall know he sired a man. Now I am promised such a kingdom with such a wife—and I cannot walk with you to the nearest sea and leave it.'

And Gautrek in the darkness said, 'Then I shall stay with you, brother. But know that it is against my wisdom. Know that it is because of the love I bear you, only that.'

Then Amleth rolled closer across the marble floor to where Gautrek lay and putting out his hand touched the warrior on the arm tenderly and said, 'You are older than I am, brother. I listen to you though I may not obey you. Tell me, Gautrek, what will happen to us by staying here to gain my kingdom?'

Gautrek was long in answering. When he did he said starkly, 'It is in my dream that by staying here we shall bring our deaths upon us, Amleth. As we have seen, this girl they have given you is little more than a corn doll. Her breasts are no bigger than young apples. Her body and legs are as lithe as the willow. Yet this child might carry death where a company of warriors would fail to gain an entrance.'

Amleth lay on the chill marble tiles in the darkness thinking. At last he said, 'You may have guessed right, brother, and I feel it in my bones that you have. But if I left Britain now could I ever be the king in Jutland again? In the hall at Yuletide feasting, or about the fire with the sword-bearers in the night wind, could I ever hold up my head and be a man among them all in the North?'

Gautrek was as long in answering. He said, 'Thank you, my prince. A man must stay where he has things to do. Do not tell Torfi that I counselled you to smell out the sea and take the ship for Jutland, I beg you.'

Amleth said, 'Nor do you tell Sibbi that I must put a son into this hot child if I am to keep the kingdom I have got.'

Gautrek scratched his beard in the darkness. It made a sound like a host of rats running over a thatched roof. To himself he said, his face close against the cold stone wall, 'Sibbi! Sibbi! By the time we come into Vendilsgarth Haven with the pennants flying, she will have forgotten who fathered her last brat but one. Poor prince, poor thrall, poor man. If only the swords and the arrows could strike as nearly to the heart as these sharp women do!'

They were both sound asleep when Bedwyr blew on the war-horn to fetch the Kymry out to exercise in Mars Field, which, at Caer Leon in those days, the Celts called Prysg. It was the place where in past generations foot soldiers had slept in their narrow cubicles; but now the walls had tumbled down and farm-thralls had taken them to build byres. It was an open space, without the walls, and up to four squadrons of cavalry could move about in it as though they were lancing Saxon footmen and so keeping Rome still alive.

The days went slowly at Caer Leon. Duke Arthur locked himself away with Medraut or Kei and Bedwyr, listening to the tales that spies brought in of Jutes pushing up from Kent, or Angles crossing the Ermine Street into the midland zone, or wild and painted Picts rolling down in their wagons through Strathclyde. But the name that echoed most about the palace was that of Cerdic of Wessex. In the minds of the Kymry he was like an evil spirit that could move anywhere, silently, powerfully, maliciously, invisibly until the last screaming moment of attack. They thought of his hosts as of a my-riad bees swarming, black across the land. Few of them had ever seen him and they only in the heat of battle when a man's senses lie to him to turn a housecat into a leopard. Yet they told such tales of him that the women and children of the old fortress dreamed of Cerdic as a monstrous, black-faced hunchback who roared like the thunder and carried the hacked limbs of babies in his hand to munch, like the legs of chickens, when the battle gave him breathing-space.

Only Arthur and his captains had ever spoken with Cerdic and knew what manner of man he was. They had met him on the downs above Tribuit five years before, in a little hollow away from the wind in sight of the blue sea, to talk of the things they wanted in Britain. Cerdic had come with his only son Cynric, leaving his army squatting in the rough grass below the hill with their helmets off on that warm day. He was a small dark-bearded man with bright blue eyes and a stammer in his speech. He was at pains early on to point out that his father had been a Roman and he made a great thing of speaking always in the Celtic tongue, choosing his words so carefully and pronouncing them with such clarity that he seemed more like a scholar-monk from Winchester than a great and terrible warlord.

Cerdic and Arthur got on well together and laughed mightily at each other's jokes, sitting in the heather and sharing a skin of pale wine. Cynric stood away from them, tall, straw-haired and tongue-tied. He took after his Saxon mother and always felt like a thrall when he was in the company of Romans. Kei and Bedwyr tried to cheer him up but the young man backed away from them and made a great business of polishing his helmet on the sleeve of his hide jerkin. Medraut tried to tell the boy an indecent story that was then going the rounds of the Caer Leon taverns but Cynric blushed and lowered his eyes like a girl. After that the men left him alone.

It was during this meeting that Cerdic said to Duke Arthur: 'My friend, in a week's time I shall be fifty years old. At that age a man should be sitting by the fire with the ale cup at his hand, not sleeping on hillsides and galloping horses up and down the land. If you will give me your word, upon your shield that has the Virgin's image painted within it, that you will leave me unmolested in Wessex to sit by the fire with my ale cup, then for my part I will swear never to meddle in your Roman affairs again.'

Then Duke Arthur flung his great shield onto the ground and the men sat round it as though at the council table; and he said, 'In the presence of all here, Cerdic, I swear that in my time you shall hold Wessex undisturbed.'

They parted good friends that afternoon. Duke Arthur gave Cynric the title of Count of Wessex. Both armies were well pleased that it had not come to fighting on that sultry day up among the hills.

But Cerdic was the sort of man who forgets what he has promised after he has slept for a night and now each year he pushed a little farther northwards towards Caer Leon, occupying fortresses, blocking off the old military roads, laying waste to the standing corn to force refugees to take shelter at Caerwent or in the Bear's capital and so placing a great strain on the food supplies there.

Medraut once said: 'Young Cynric is visiting some woman or other at Aquae Sulis, Uncle. It would be no hard task for a brisk man to put a bag over his head while he was in bed with her and bring him back here as a hostage. Once we had him in Caer Leon, old Cerdic would see sense and would go back to his chimney corner.'

The Duke said: 'Well, why do you wait? See that you take a strong bag or he might bite his way out.'

Medraut was away for a week and came back alone. In the bag he brought two silver-gilt dishes and more than a helmetful of gold coins. He said that he had found them in an old well just outside Aquae Sulis. He said that Cynric must have got news that he was coming for him, because when Medraut arrived the West Saxon had left.

Kei watched Medraut as he told the tale, then said, 'He sets small value on his hide—two dishes and a few coins.'

Medraut rose and made as though to strike at Kei but the captain stood there smiling and the blow never fell.

At Easter tide Arthur held a feast such as the one his father Uther Pendragon had held in London half a century before when he had lusted after Ygerne, the wife of Duke Gorlois. The great hall rang with laughter. Bards plucked the strings and sang of Constantine. Amleth and Gautrek sat one on either side of the Duke, at the cross-table which was set above the long feast board. Gwenhwyvar was on Amleth's left hand, her eye-lids stained with blue, her lips reddened, her golden hair free upon her shoulders like a maiden's and covered with a fold of her white silk robe.

When the Bishop gave the first toast, to the White Christ and His spotless Mother, both Amleth and Gautrek made the hammer sign of Thor above their cups before drinking.

Arthur was too occupied with his old wounds to notice this but Gwenhwyvar glanced brightly at Amleth and touched him on the thigh, below the table level. 'Does that make the mead sweeter, Dane?' she asked. She left her hand a little too long upon him, he felt the warmth of it through his woollen feast-shirt. He put down his own hand and pushed hers away, then he said, 'It is something all my people do. An old dog cannot learn new tricks.'

Gwenhwyvar looked down at her dish with modesty. She said in a low voice, 'I think there are some new tricks I could teach a dog as young as you are.' Amleth looked away from her and called to the serving-thralls to bring him bread and pork sausages and more mead.

Gautrek was singing the old song of the Uppsala vingull, with Kei and Bedwyr urging him on to verse after verse. Even the Duke had forgotten his aches and pains and was laughing now. Wood smoke hung in the rafters. Men up and down the board began to remember old battles and comrades who had died beside them. They rolled back their sleeves and drew up their shirts to show the puckered relics of half-forgotten wounds, boasting whose sword had done this, whose spear that, and how long they had lain at death's doorstep recovering.

'On Carn Gwylathyr,' shouted Greidiawl Gallddofydd, 'I took three arrows in the left side when my shield was split. Each one went deeper than the last, and the third one came out at my back. The heather was red that year, but I was redder when I broke off those shafts and sought out the sender.'

Gwystol son of Nwython rose and yelled, 'Who saw me at Esgeir Cerfel in Ireland? Who stood by me when I faced Twrch Trwyth who had laid waste five provinces before I showed him my sword? And see the marks his tusks left on my belly. See the deep furrows that the great boar ploughed.'

Gwenhwyvar smiled at Amleth and whispered, 'He cannot wait to lift his shirt once the mead reaches his stomach. But that is the best he can do now, the boar eased him of other burdens, he is good for nothing save Easter-bragging.'

Amleth said, 'In Jutland the king does not allow edged weapons to be brought to a feasting. Here all men carry knives.'

The woman said, 'It is safe enough, they only spill blood in their dreams, the Kymry. It all ends when the mead-casks are emptied and never a head broken among ten squadrons of them.'

Amleth said, 'I have seen as many as five men propped stark against the wall after a Jutland-feasting. And all done with beef-bones.'

Suddenly he saw that Duke Arthur was leaning towards him, listening. Arthur said, smiling thinly, 'Aye, Dane, but there may be some things we can show you yet. Were you ever in a cavalry charge?'

Amleth curled his lip. 'In the north we fight on foot, Duke,' he said. 'A man who must sit on a horse to gain height should put dung in his shoes to gain an inch or two.'

The Duke's eyes were small and red, the spittle was running down his chin, he said thickly, 'When the horns blow and the lances come down in a line like the boughs of a pine forest, I have seen hard northerners spurt the piss of terror from under their shirts, Dane. When the hooves have drummed on the turf, I have watched Saxon kings slip in their own mess to escape the iron points.'

Gwenhwyvar snorted with disgust and looked away from her husband. Amleth smiled and said, 'I do not hear the captain Bedwyr boasting of how he lost his arm.'

He meant this as a pleasant jest but Kei jumped up and struck his fist hard upon the board. His face was so furious, it was another man's. He shouted out, 'It took three Danes to hack it from him, Jutlander. And then, even dead, its fingers would not unclench from the Danish king's throat it was gripped on. Is that your answer?'

Amleth felt the blood draining down into his belly and his heart go cold with anger. Gautrek was standing, ripping at his shirt to get it off and drumming on the floor with his feet. Suddenly all men along the board were silent, the bards let fall their harps, the serving-thralls set down their dishes. Medraut slid from his seat at the bench and came round by the shield-hung wall until he stood behind Amleth, his right hand within his feast-shirt where his dagger lay warm.

And then, as quickly as the moment had arisen, it went again. The harps struck up, the thralls hurried about the hall with their troughs of blood-sausages and cabbage.

Gwenhwyvar put her hand upon the prince again and said, 'It is a shame that your wife, the princess Elene, should not be here to enjoy the feasting. Yet it is the rule here, among Romans, that only the Duke's wife should sit among the men. One bitch among three hundred hounds is enough, they say.'

Amleth stared past the mist of mead that lay in his eyes and said, 'This Elene, this daughter of Arthur the Bear, is she from you?'

Gwenhwyvar threw back her head and laughed, she said, 'From me? Am I so old that I could have such a daughter? You see me, you see my breasts, am I so old and shrivelled, Dane?'

Amleth fought against the mead within him. He said, 'I cannot tell, my own mother, the Barley Queen in Jutland, seems no older. Who is Elene's mother then, and who are you?'

Gwenhwyvar leaned hard against him, taking his left hand in hers and placing it nearest to her. She said, 'Elene is from one of the northern kingdoms. Who knows her mother's name now? Not even the Bear himself will remember. But I have Duke Cador of Cornwall for my father, whose line was long, before the first Caesar trod on our soil. Does that answer you, my prince?'

Then a great madness swept over Amleth, for he remembered Sibbi and his own mother, and they were so high above these Roman liars that he could have retched with fury at being so far from home.

In a loud clear voice he said, 'This bread is flecked with blood. This meat stinks of the grave. And as for your mead, it is sour with rusty iron.'

In a voice as loud and clear Gwenhwyvar answered smiling, 'Should this surprise you, Dane? In a land that has been so much fought over, should this amaze you? Might not the corn grain spring best where old Romans had lain in their honourable graves? And are the rooting pigs respecters of noble warriors' remains? Do the bees, gathering honey for our mead, stop to consider if they suck their nectar from among old swords that lie rusting in the nettles?'

Now Gautrek was on his feet again, trying to drag Amleth away from the feasting, but the prince struck out at him and then called, 'You, the fair-haired harlot of the Duke, you who have an answer for everything ... Now I read you at last—you cover your head with a cloth like a bond-woman; you raise your skirts as you walk across the floor as though you had but one robe; you pick your teeth with a splinter after meat, and then eat again what you dislodge! By Odin, you are a thrall born of thralls! You are no noblewoman!'

As the strange dark eyes of the Kymry turned upon him lit with mockery, Amleth swung round towards the Duke and saw that he too was leaning back in his chair and smiling. Then Gautrek stood above him saying, 'Forgive me, prince, but there is only one way out of this.' His great fist came down like a hammer and Amleth fell senseless to the floor. The Celts sat as still as ghosts when the henchman bent and picked up his lord, then carried him from the feast chamber over his back.

Later that night Medraut came to the Duke's lodging wrapped about with his cloak of dark wool. Standing before Arthur he said in a low voice, 'So, at last you have met one of them, a true man of the north. I hope your whim has been satisfied now that you have seen the nature of the beast that snarls about our eastern shores. Say the word and I will see that he and his watch-dog do not wake from their drunken sleep.'

But the Duke looked up at him as though he was a stranger. He said, 'The Jutlander is serving his purpose, he has married this young fool of a girl off your hands, and by entertaining him here I have gained the promise of his uncle, King Feng of Jutland, that no Danish longship shall harry our shores for a lifetime. I see no good purpose in killing him.'

Medraut came a step nearer and said, 'It ill becomes me to tell my lord his business. I only wish your nose were longer so that you could see farther, for in truth you see no farther than your nose, Uncle.'

Arthur stared at him fixedly. He said, 'Medraut, there is a sort of darkness in you I cannot fathom. As a child you were always different from the others about the court.'

Medraut yawned and stretched his arms. 'Now you will go on to tell me that my brother Gavin was a born knight, who even sucked at his mother's teat with courtesy, while I spent my time tormenting the other palace brats and killing what creatures came into my grasp. I have heard it all before, many times. But I still think that the Jutlander should be put out of the way.'

The Duke said, 'He is a harmless enough brute. He broke a few dishes at the feasting and shouted a few words; that is no reason for killing him.'

Medraut drew his little dagger and tapped its point against his jutting teeth. He said, 'The dishes were poor enough ware, like most of the things we still have left in Caer Leon; but the words were different. What was said about your wife, Gwenhwyvar, merits no more and no less than death.'

The Duke tapped with his toe on the floor; he said, 'What the Jutlander said about Gwenhwyvar was true in all respects, though God alone knows how he should have come at that truth. She is a harlot, as you know better than most men, since you have used her as much as I have in your time. She is a thrall, born of thralls, as he said, although Cador brought her up like a daughter in his castle, to train his son in the use of a woman. No, Amleth must not be killed for speaking the things which you and I know to be true. Go you home to bed and let me go to mine, Medraut. We have said enough.'

Medraut put up his dagger and went to the door. There he turned back and whispered, 'Britain has come to the end of its journey when its ruling lies in the hands of five senile kings and a Duke who allows his woman to be dishonoured at the feast board by a sottish Dane.'

Arthur did not even turn. 'When Medraut speaks of honour,' he said, 'both Britain and the world must be drawing to their end. Go home, you bloody butcher.'

Medraut stood silent for a moment, then smiled and drew his right forefinger across his thick throat behind the Duke's back. He said, 'Sleep well, old man. No doubt the world will end when it will end, and nothing the Bear of Britain can do or say will change the date of that ending.'

Then he went through the door, hissing like a lynx into the dusk.

When Amleth woke the sun was shining. He had forgotten all that had been said the night before. He only recalled that men had mocked him across the feast board. So, leaving Gautrek still snoring, he burnished his gear and put on helmet and hauberk; then, with his sword Quern-biter in his right hand he walked out into Caer Leon to see if any man abroad would care to laugh at him in the daylight. And so that all should have a fair share, the prince strode down the middle of the road and not on the footpaths beside the high buildings.

Wagons and horsemen gave way to him. Men bearing swords turned up alleyways as though they had found urgent business they must attend to. Other men of the *bacaudae*-class stopped and waved to him, or even saluted him with the old Roman hand, bright-eyed with pride that there was a man to be seen at last in the city. Women of whatever class let fall their face-veils and smiled openly at him wishing to God that he would turn his stark face and smile back at them.

A boy pushing a barrow full of freshly baked loaves let fall the handles and shouted out, 'Sir, may I touch your sword blade? Is it true that you have come to save Britain, sir?'

But Amleth had the cheek-pieces of Battle Swine latched and could not hear him. The boy called after him along the street, 'Go to the old amphitheatre, my lord. There you will find the land's enemy. Kill him and the folk will put a crown upon your head.'

A stern-faced matron cuffed the lad and told him to be about his business delivering the bread or half Caer Leon would go without breakfast.

All Amleth saw was a sparrowhawk pecking in the road at a heap of horse-dung. He paused and spoke to the bird saying, 'Hail, warrior. It speaks ill of a land that has nothing to offer its blood-birds than that. Come with me and there may be better pickings.'

The bird gazed up at him with stark and golden eyes. It did not move even though he passed within a foot of it with mail rustling and sword clinking. It was as though the prey-bird sensed a brother although their weapons were of differing metals.

Medraut was walking in the pale sunlight across the sheep-cropped greensward of the old amphitheatre. He held the lady Elene by the hand. Her slim shadow lay small as a child's beside his on the grass. He said to her suddenly, 'Tell me, ward, is your Jutish husband good to you?'

He felt her hand go hot and damp in his. She said, 'Good? How do you mean, good, foster-father?'

He clucked and nodded his head like a wise old man and said, 'Is he pleasing to you in the night time, does he do the things that please you?'

Elene kicked at the turf and said, 'The Jute is a brute beast, foster-father. He lies and snores, with his henchman snoring beside him. I lie there on my straw-pallet and wait, but they only snore. I pray that one of them will get up in the night to make water, but these Danes have such strong stomachs, they sleep till dawn light and never wake. They are beasts.'

Medraut said softly, 'Tell me, lady, was I such a beast when you lived in my house at Lindissi? No, do not shake your head, tell me truthfully, I shall not be offended.'

Elene put her other arm about his waist and halted him, her face close to his breast. 'Oh, foster-father,' she said, 'Now I can understand that you were a god. You hurt me at first, but then all was well and I understood that this was as a young horse must be broken, for his own good in the end. How I wish that I were yours again, my lord. In the night, lying between the Danes, I think of what it was like with you. It is you I dream of, not my husband who does not want me.'

Medraut gently put her away from his body and walked on with her. He said, 'Hush, girl! A Roman must not utter such things. The holy Bishop in Lindum gave you to the Jute in marriage and it is of the Jute that you must think now. They are a cold folk, these Jutes, and you are a warm young animal. You must learn patience and so all will be well in the end.'

The lady Elene was weeping now. She said, 'Oh, foster-father, life is cruel. How long must I wait do you think?'

Medraut whistled a while like a blackbird, then said, 'Nay, lass, I am no magic-speller like old Merddin was. I am just a plain soldier. But they tell me these Jutes have a season, for three days, in the time we call Lent, once every seven years or so.'

Until they stood outside the old shrine of Vengeance that led down darkly into the ground, the lady Elene sobbed. 'Oh, oh!' she said, 'and I shall be old before then. I shall be shrivelled up. Why must I wait on this heathen's time, when you have shown me such magic, my lord? Why must the Duke punish me so? What have I done in my life to suffer, being married? And to a Jute!'

Medraut loosed her hand and said sternly, 'You are to be the queen in Powys one day. Then will be time enough for such frolics of the flesh, girl. Good God, to hear you talk so, anyone would think you wished me to take you down there into the dark shrine and do that thing to you again, and you married to this great prince.'

Elene smiled up at him through her tears and took his hand again. Now she began to drag him towards the place. 'Anyone would be right, foster-father,' she said. He glared at her from under his red brows fiercely, but she still laughed in the morning sunlight. 'Hurry, my lord, hurry,' she said out of breath, 'before the shepherd lads come down into the amphitheatre.'

Medraut took her by the shoulders and shook her, but not hard. He said, 'This is a wickedness and one day we must both confess to the good Bishop at Lindum. But this once I will act as you beg me in the hope that such will be thought a deed of mercy to one who might otherwise find less tolerable ways to quench the wicked thirst that parches too many young girls. But be it known that I act now at your will and I would even say under a certain Christian protest.'

'Come, come, you bad man. Hurry, hurry, or the lads will be here looking for their sheep.'

Medraut sighed deeply and let her drag at him with her right hand. He saw that with her left she was already ripping at the fastenings of her new blue robe.

So Amleth came down onto the cropped grass of the amphi-theatre and gazed about him like a leopard, sniffing the air and listening.

And at last from the shelving slope that led to the old shrine of Vengeance he heard a girl say, 'Oh, no! No! Not like that, my love!'

And then he heard a man's thick voice answer, 'Lie still, you fool. After all I have done for you, lie still.'

Inside the great bronze helmet he heard such things. In his right hand he grasped Quern-biter. Suddenly he called into the blue air of morning, 'Come out, man.'

The grazing sheep stopped in their grazing and gazed at him in surprise.

'Come out and face a man,' the Jutlander cried, for no reason but that at last he needed to test himself.

The sheep now unafraid went back to their cropping of the old turf. Inside the shrine Medraut felt the lady Elene shake under him with her spasm. He cursed her for knowing heaven before him: shook her to stillness, then whispered, 'For the love of Christ, do not move. There is a man outside who will kill us both if he knows we are here.'

Amleth stood on the grass, his sword-holding shadow long on the turf, listening and sniffing.

Medraut clapped his hard hand upon the girl's gaping mouth and whispered, 'If you love me, daughter, be still.'

She felt the fear in his shuddering wet hand. She lay in the ancient darkness and knew that great Medraut was a coward in face of the Jutlander.

Then in his own open green space among the grazing sheep the Green Man of Vendilsgarth started to roar in his bronze helmet like a black bull.

This sound echoed so terribly in the closed amphitheatre that the sheep left their grass and galloped away. Even the horned rams took terror and went.

In the close darkness of the shrine Medraut's great teeth clashed

165

like those of a man with the fever. He said in Elene's ear, 'Dog's blood! Dog's blood! For Jesus' sake, hold your breath. If you love me be still.'

And at last it was all over. Amleth had roared at the blue morning, had challenged the sky and the earth, and now he was satisfied. Gently he slid Quern-biter back into the sheath, waited a while, then turned and walked away.

In the broad streets of Caer Leon folk dropped to their knees as he passed and crossed themselves as though Lord Zeus walked the earth again. A black stallion waiting to serve a mare outside the livery stable in Prysg-field suddenly caught the smell of the questing man and gushed out his water with fright.

Amleth saw this and went to the horse and stroked his quivering soft muzzle. 'There, there, brother,' he said gently, 'be still. It is not you I am after.'

Down in the shrine of Vengeance, Medraut struck the lady Elene hard across her tender mouth. 'You bitch!' he said. 'For your worthless body I could have died under that savage's sword this morning. You are not worth it, you offal for dogs.'

The lady Elene fell back, tasting the salt of his blow. She said softly, 'You were a god once, Count Medraut. Now I see that you are only a man, and a most frightened man at that.'

He heard her and answered, 'I, afraid? Who can frighten Medraut?'

She began to laugh as she drew her skirts down again. 'Who?' she said. 'Why, a tall Jutlander in a bronze helmet and carrying a sword, my lord. I mean, my husband, the Green Man of Vendilsgarth. And I have such pride in him now that I think he would have frightened Caesar himself off his throne.'

Amleth was near the old barrack building when a horseman clattered up to him, bearing no shield or lance, but with the stern expression of *dignitas* on his face. He saluted briefly then said, 'My lord, the Duke wishes to see you now. Walk no further through the city, wearing helmet and sword, but go straightway to where he waits you. I speak his words.'

166

Then the man swung about and cantered off. Amleth spat in the dust and at last followed him, a string of children and young girls at his heels.

The Duke was pacing up and down his chamber, swinging his leg with the effort and glowering. He said, 'Sir, these things must come to an end. You will have the Kymry and the city folk against me if you keep on. I can forgive your mead-words in the hall, but to walk out in the morning sun bearing a sword is a thing which I would not allow even Kei and Bedwyr to do. Such behaviour can only excite my people, who are quiet enough now, getting on with their simple lives while I keep the Saxon from them. What have you to say, sir?'

Amleth clucked his tongue against the roof of his mouth and answered, 'I am the King of the Wood who does not account to anyone but tree-Odin for his comings and goings, Bear.'

The Duke frowned. He answered, 'While you are in Caer Leon, which is my city and mine alone, you will account to me, sir. I have learned to forgive much that my Kymry do but you are yet one of them. So you will answer me.'

Amleth came close to him and towered above him like a tree. He said, 'With this sword I could now put an end to all your troubles, Bear. That could be my answer and it would need no breath to make it.'

Then the Duke turned to him and almost put the point of his beard into the prince's face. 'Jutlander,' he said, 'if I clapped my hands now two men would run in and take the head from your shoulders.'

Amleth laughed. 'Clap them, Bear,' he said, 'but do not hope to see what your dogs might try to do to me. Your own head would be grinning on the floor.'

Duke Arthur turned away and sat down. He began to smile despite his hurt pride. 'Years ago,' he said gently, 'those would have been the last words you spoke, Jutlander. But now I am an old man full of a hero's dreams, but without the force left in me to bring them into life. My tongue and your strength would make a true king in Britain, Amleth. I can recognise a man when I meet one, my son.'

Amleth said, 'I am not given to weeping over old men's disasters,

167

Duke. You sent for me to thrash me like a dog. So, carry out your will, Bear.'

Arthur lowered his head and then shook it sadly. 'Let us not spin out the wool, my son,' he said. 'The moment has passed now and there can be no more thrashing done. You are too big for it and I am too old. I am too near to what you are to treat you like an enemy, Amleth. But let me advise you instead; leave Caer Leon for a while. Take your young wife and go to visit your kingdom of Powys. Let the fire you have started burn itself out a little and then come back and ride with me against Cerdic as one of my captains, sitting beside Kei and Bedwyr.'

Amleth nodded and smiled now. 'You do not mention your nephew, Medraut,' he said. 'Is he not a captain too?'

The Duke's face hardened. 'Medraut is a captain,' he answered. 'But such a captain as might put spurs to his horse and ride across the field to lead the other host if the mood took him, my son. He is a good sharp sword but at the moment of trial, he can twist in the hand and cut the holder. I shall say no more of him. One day and perhaps soon he will twist in my hand, and then he will either pierce me to the heart or I shall break him across my knee. There can be no other outcome.'

Amleth regarded him a while and saw that his eyes were moist with tears. He said to pass the moment by, 'I shall welcome a ride to my kingdom, and so will my henchman Gautrek who grows weary of living under a roof away from the sea.'

The Duke said gently, 'Gautrek will not ride with you, Amleth. Here we have customs which cannot be broken. He must stay in the palace until you return, as a hostage. Do not frown, this is an old habit of ours and casts no reflection on your honour. Consider this; you are going away from my eye with my daughter Elene. It is right then that you should leave behind someone you hold dear. Otherwise the thought might take you to travel on towards the coast and leave me, taking the lady with you.'

Amleth smiled. He said, 'That would be a poor bargain, to gain and throw away a kingdom in a day, Bear. Who then will act as my henchman on this journey into a strange land? It seems to me that the lady Elene will need more than one rider to care for her.'

The Duke said evenly, 'Medraut will ride with you. He knows the way and the customs in Powys. He knows how to deal with old Cuneglassus too, and that is a mystery which few have command of, since the old king is more often than not out of his wits, living among heather hills and sheep the whole time. Are you satisfied?'

Amleth placed his hand upon his sword. 'I am satisfied that if your kinsman Medraut offends me on the journey, I am able to rid both myself and you of a nuisance,' he said starkly.

The Duke nodded. 'There was some such thing in my own mind,' he said. 'But it is not a matter I wish to proceed with, my son.'

Amleth felt the warmth that came from this tired warrior across the room towards him. Taking the moment by the forelock he said, 'Yet there is a thing I still have to discuss with you, Arthur. On the Humber shore two men of my uncle's were killed at your command. Feng will wish to put their blood money into his coffers when I return to Vendilsgarth at last. You made me the promise that good coin should pay for them when you reached your treasury.'

The Duke looked away and smiled. 'I had hoped you might forget it,' he said, 'having been given a princess and a kingdom so freely. But you Jutlanders seem to have long memories. Very well, it has not yet been said that the Duke of Britain turns back on his promise. You shall have the money. How would you like it, in gold or silver or in cups and dishes?'

Amleth said, 'Small coin can fall through a hole in the saddle-bag, Bear. And cups and dishes are cumbersome to carry for a man like me who always travels light. Let it be gold, melted down and poured into two stout alder sticks with the pith removed. Then who will know that I carry two men inside two staffs? There will be less chance of being robbed if I take Godgest and Hake back to Jutland in that fashion.'

The Duke smiled again. 'It shall be done, Amleth,' he said. 'When you are finished at Powys, Kei and Bedwyr shall deliver the two sticks of gold to you.'

Amleth went to the door then stopped and said, 'So there is nothing more to keep us together, wasting the blue morning with empty words, Bear. I shall make ready for the journey.'

For long after he had gone, Duke Arthur sat on in his chair, rubbing his bearded chin and nodding. To himself at last he said, 'It is like cutting off your right hand. It is like losing an eye. God knows why I should be troubled with such things at my age, and after all I have given of myself to this decaying graveyard of a land. When will two men be allowed to come together and live simply as friends without all this scheming?'

His great hound Cabal pushed through the curtain and came to his hand to be stroked. The Duke took the dog's long ear and tugged at it in love. 'Can you answer me, old friend,' he said, 'when shall men live in peace together again, as they did in the old days of Rome?'

But the hound did not answer him. He beat his tail against the oaken chair and held up his grey muzzle for his old master to scratch it as he always did.

There was a place at the far lip of the amphitheatre where few folk ever went. There the paving and tiles had subsided to form a shallow pit overgrown with ferns. It lay in shadow most of the day even at the height of summer and there families of small brown vipers had an undisturbed home.

Medraut took Elene sharply by the arm when Amleth had gone away and led her to this spot. At first she thought that he meant to fling her into it and drew back in terror; but Medraut shook his head and smiled. 'You are a quick-minded child,' he said, 'but you cannot fathom my heart yet awhile.'

He drew off his Phrygian cap and turned it inside out, putting his right hand into it and holding its outer edge with his left. Then he bent to his knees over a viper that lay coiled in the warm sun. 'Look,' he whispered, 'this is how you take these little creatures.' He swooped his hands over the serpent, snatched it up, then shook it down into the cap. It lashed in fury for a while and then lay still. He

170

said, 'See, it was easily done. And now you have a little fork-tongued guardian of your own. What will you name him, my lady?'

Elene said, 'I have no need for a viper, sir. I hate these creatures. Throw it back into the pit and let us go.'

Medraut shook his head, but he said, 'Yes, we will go, for I have something to give you. As your foster-father it was my duty to see that you took a dowry of some sort to your new husband; yet I have been too occupied with other things to give thought to that duty. Now I know what you shall have. It is a little cedarwood box that belonged to my grandmother, carved on the outside with old Greek runes, and inlaid with ivory from the teeth of elephants. Inside that box I shall place for you a silver ring for every wicked finger of your hand, a necklace of gold that my own father brought from Rome when he made his pilgrimage there, and twenty coins minted in the days of the greatest Caesar the world has known. All this you shall call your treasure and I do not think that your Jutish husband will consider he has wed a pauper when he sees it.'

Elene went to him and took his face and drew it down to hers to kiss. 'Oh, my foster-father,' she said. 'And I thought you were angry with me! How can I thank you? Let us go back to the shrine now, where I can tell you in the darkness how grateful I am.'

But Medraut pushed her away, laughing. 'Nay, nay, girl,' he said. 'I have work to do and your gratitude would leave me ill-prepared for it. Come, you can tell me on the way to the palace with gentle words.'

When Gautrek the Mild learned that he was to stay in Caer Leon while his blood-brother made the journey to the kingdom of Powys with Medraut and Elene, he was angry. He struck at the wall with his sword-hilt and said, 'Am I to live among thralls? Is this the value you set upon me, Amleth? Have I journeyed from Jutland to be left behind like a dog?'

Amleth put his arm about him and said, 'Brother, we must bow to the Duke's command. Have no fear, once I have ridden the boundaries of this new kingdom of mine I shall gallop back to you. We cannot change things. And in any case you will find something to fill your days while I am away. You can have your pick of the maidens who came out to greet us when we first rode into Caer Leon. What with one thing and another you will not notice the time passing.'

The lady Elene came in to hear this, dressed in her travelling clothes. She took Gautrek by the hand for the first time and smiling said, 'My husband is right, Gautrek. You will not notice the time passing. I will leave orders that the prettiest of the Kymry women shall come to you in this chamber so that you may choose from them. And to show my trust in you, new friend, I shall leave with you the dowry-coffer that Medraut has given me so that you may keep it safely for me until I return. See, it will be a sort of hostage, a token of my feeling for you.'

Gautrek grumbled a while then smiled with her and nodded. When they left him standing on the tall steps of the palace his sadness had gone. Or, if it was still there, he made no show of it but only called out to the three riders to mind how they went and to avoid all sunken lanes especially after night-fall.

Medraut nodded to him and answered, 'We shall take good care of ourselves, Dane. See that you do the same.'

Then they clattered off towards the north, towards the grey mountains and the source of the Sabrina, whose curving banks marked the southernmost limit of Amleth's new kingdom. They started early to make what distance they could that day, for Powys lay three days' journeying away and was not the easiest of places to reach.

In that parched summer Powys lay like the carcass of a burned dog, its ribs of rock sticking up through the shallow grey soil, its heather as dry as tinder. There were no living trees to be seen but only the bare bones of ancient oaks and pines. Where in the winter streams had run down the hillsides were now dry gullies, with starved sheep nibbling at the brown mosses that sucked what little moisture still lay among the pebbles.

Amleth stared at this waste and said, 'In Jutland men would call this a poor country. They would scarcely think it worth while hoisting the sail to come for it.'

Medraut rode near to him and bending over whispered, 'Then they would be wrong, my friend. The harvest of Powys does not lie on top of the ground as in other kingdoms. It does not lie in the sheep that wander the hillsides either. It rests deeper than the eye can see—underground, my friend. Yes, underground.'

Amleth gazed back at him and said, 'You take me for a fool, Medraut.'

But the other shook his head. 'I take you for a most fortunate fellow, prince,' he answered. 'This Powys is full of gold. It lies under the mountains and men make shafts into the ground to bring it up in baskets. Old Cuneglassus is by far the richest of the Five Kings of Britain—though to see him you will not think so. He dresses and eats like a crofter-king so that no one shall realise he could buy Rome and Jerusalem and still not know he had spent a penny. You will see, aye, you will see. There are certain secrets that we have here which your rough sea-rovers would give their right hands for. Poor fools, they harry the eastern coasts in their tub boats—but if they knew what you will soon know they would forage in the west. Yet you will be the last to tell them, Amleth—for once you have got your own hands on the hoard you will not wish others to know of it, not even your own countrymen.'

Amleth was considering this and they were passing through a narrow valley with high black cliffs on either side of it. Inside, it was as dark as twilight although the sun shone at either end of the valley.

Suddenly Elene called out and pointed; 'Look,' she said, 'up there on the rock, carved out of the stone. Two horsemen bearing round shields with hawks on them. And what is that strange coiling thing they seem to be dragging behind them? It seems like the ripples in a lake when a stone is thrown into the water.'

Amleth looked where she pointed and a strange tingling came up from his feet to his heart. He said, 'That is a barley maze, lady. We

173

have one at Vendilsgarth, but I have never seen them cut into stone before. Ours is laid out on the turf where we dance at springtime each year.'

Elene said laughing, 'Not even a man as clever as Medraut here could dance in that maze unless he grew wings like a bird.'

Medraut shielded his eyes and stared up at the maze. He said, 'The birds on the shields are choughs, Elene. Our ancient legend says that when the Duke dies at last he must be buried here so that his spirit shall pass into those birds and live on for ever. Folk say that the Phoenicians came this way and amused themselves by cutting these shapes into the rock face. But the old country people in Powys swear that the maze was put here many generations before the first Phoenician saw day's light. I do not know. But I would not care to be here when the sun had gone down. It is not a pleasant place. The air is thick with the breathing of ghosts even now.'

He began to kick his horse forward to get out of the gully but Elene called him back. She said, 'Within the maze there is writing, foster-father. What does it say, I cannot read?'

Amleth waited as anxiously as she did for to him the great strokes of the runes were a mystery that baffled his head.

Medraut said, 'The letters are A–I–U–R–T. And you can puzzle your heads about them for a lifetime unless you know the answer to the riddle.'

Amleth said gravely, 'You who seem to know so much, what is the answer? Do not hold us waiting like a pedlar at a fair, keeping his best wares hidden until the crowd are ready to pay a higher price.'

Medraut clapped him on the thigh. 'I am no pedlar, prince,' he said with a smile. 'Like you, I am a lord in my own country. But unlike you, I was taught to read when I was a tiny boy. And that is a useful trick to learn even for a warrior.'

Amleth said again, 'What does the writing say? I am not used to being kept waiting, man.'

Medraut's thick lips curled with amusement. He said, 'When I have told you you will be little the wiser, Jutlander. But if you must know, then you must. These letters are to be read backwards and not as they are cut into the rock. So they make the word TRUIA. That is all.'

Then he swung his horse round and cantered off along the valley towards the sunlight. He was smiling all the while, waiting for Amleth to ask him the next question; but the prince would not humble himself further now and rode silent and sullen into the light. It was the lady Elene who could not stand any longer waiting and pleaded with Medraut to tell them what the word signified. Medraut shrugged his shoulders and said at last, 'It is the ancient word for Troy, daughter. Nothing more. There was a great battle there when the world was young, and many kings and captains died there. The greatest king of them all, the Lion of Mycenae, Resolute Agamemnon, came back to his palace in victory but was murdered by his wife and her lover as he lay in the bath, washing Troy's dust from his weary body. That is all.'

Amleth said, 'I have heard something of this before but I did not expect to meet signs of that old battle here at the world's edge, so far from Greece.'

Medraut was in a gay mood now and said, 'There are many things you do not know, Jutlander, wise as you may be in the small learning of your midden at Vendilsgarth. This land we ride over is as old as any land; it holds many secrets and many treasures. Who knows that kings coming back from this Troy did not sail here to find themselves new kingdoms? Who knows that they did not bring their treasures with them and hide them under the ground in Powys? I who ride beside you and this child who is your wife—may we not be of the blood of those ancient kings? When you take my hand, may you not be touching the hand of distant Agamemnon without knowing it?'

He was laughing up into the sunlight. Amleth was moody at this taunting. He said, 'When I take your hand again it will be the first time. And the last.' But Medraut went on laughing and did not answer him. Elene, her head now full of ancient kings, rode proudly, her back straight, her heavy blue cloak hanging down onto her horse's back, truly like a young queen.

175

Gautrek the Mild lay in the dusk at Caer Leon, a golden-haired Darling of the Kymry leaning above him on her elbows laughing. Her sky-blue robe lay upon the mosaic floor, tumbled in haste beside the bed.

She said, 'Is this how you treat the women of Jutland, warrior? Is this how you sleep when the game is at its best?'

Gautrek groaned. He would have tumbled her from him if he had had the force left to do it. 'Our women are not like this,' he said. 'They bed to get bairns, without all this mischief and trickery.'

She bit at his thick red ear and with her teeth clenched on it said, 'They should be shipped to Caer Leon, those brood-mares of Jutland, where the Temple Master could instruct them in the many ways of Rome.'

But Gautrek had fallen asleep, as sudden and as deep as death for an instant. The girl left his ear and spat with disgust. Leaning over him she put her hand down towards the ivory-inlaid dower chest that lay under the bed in his protection.

Gautrek woke as she began to grope open the lid and said, 'Leave well alone, woman. I shall pay you, never fear.'

She kissed him for the hundredth time and said laughing, 'Men say that but do not always do it, Dane. What is in the coffer? Is it your war-gains?'

Gautrek said starkly, 'My war-gains would need a longship to carry them, not a small box, woman. Stop meddling and take your hand away or I will trap your fingers under the lid.'

She pouted her lips at him and whispered, 'You are cruel folk, you Incomers. You would cripple my most precious instruments. What is in the box, Dane? Is it jewels? Is it coin?'

Gautrek said, 'I have not looked, woman. I have only obeyed the orders my lady Elene gave me when she went with my prince, I have guarded the box. Nothing more.'

She said, 'You northern simpleton! Let us look what is in this pretty box. I have let you know my secrets, now do me the courtesy of showing me yours, Dane.'

Gautrek's teeth showed out of his beard in a snarl. 'You are

176

meddling with things that do not concern you, woman,' he said. 'Get from this bed.'

She laughed again and pulled in mockery at him, then she suddenly reached across and thrust down her narrow hand towards the coffer. Gautrek growled like an angry bear, flung her hand aside roughly and glaring up at her made to close the ivory lid.

Her face altered with the shock of pain. Viciously she said, 'God, if you were as hard in other ways there would be payment enough in lying with you, without any talk of money. I think I have a broken wrist now, you barbarian.'

Gautrek laughed without pleasure and groped for the lid. His great hand went inside the dowry coffer and the little brown snake, alarmed from his sleep among the jewels, lashed round and struck.

The girl, nursing her own hurt, stared down at the Jutlander at last and said, 'Very well, Dane. There is no need to froth at the lips and thresh about so. I will not touch your precious box. It is full of sea-gull's droppings, no doubt. I have no wish for them. Pay me and I will be gone back to the barracks where men value me.'

It was long enough before she understood why he did not answer her. And then she began to scream and could not stop.

Cuneglassus had once been known as the tallest man to be seen in the five kingdoms of Britain but eighty years of lust and warmaking had left him as stooped and bent as a windswept hawthorn tree.

He came forward to greet his guests, his chin hanging down, his head thrust out upon its vulture's neck, his filmed old eyes glaring up from beneath his brows. He was dressed in a patchwork of sheep-skins and old hide. A heavy stench came from him and a swarm of black flies buzzed behind him wherever he went. He was not the most handsome king to be found in the west: but he was the richest, and the wickedest, and there were many wicked men in the world in those days.

Gazing past Amleth, he returned Medraut's formal salute briefly then made straight for Elene who sat apart from the others smiling at this strange king more from fear than from friendship. Then, without courtesy of any sort, Cuneglassus steadied her pony with one hand and put the other where she was least protected, pinching and kneading as though he was in the cattle-market.

Amleth began to urge his horse forward but Medraut placed his hand upon the Dane's bridle. 'Be still,' he whispered, 'let the old fool please himself, then it will be over the sooner. Do not frown, he is capable of nothing worse after a life of raging.'

Cuneglassus now lifted the woman's robe as she sat shaking with insult. 'What god do you pray to, girl?' he asked, his old sheep-head nodding without control. 'Not the Virgin it is plain by what I find here! Who put that into you, this big-shouldered Jutlander?'

Then without listening to her answer he called back at Medraut, 'You have brought me a poor bargain this time, you lying hound. I have paid for fresh fruit but you bring me a half-gone apple. Hey, well, all's one at my time of life, and no doubt this will be no worse than others I have bought from you.'

He spoke without anger or feeling of any sort. All his mind lay in his searching hand until at last the lady Elene could tolerate no more and pulled her pony back so hard that it almost knocked the old king to the ground. Even this did not upset him. He nodded and clucked and said, 'Aye, there's something left in her yet. We'll make do, the pair of us, we'll make do.'

Medraut leaned over to Amleth and said, 'He is mad, my friend. He has lived so much among the sheep that his mind has left him. He still dreams that he is a man full of fire, and believes that any woman who crosses over into Powys has been brought as a gift to him.'

Amleth said starkly, 'In Jutland they would have hung one part of him on a thorn bush years ago, the fathers and brothers.'

Medraut smiled and said, 'Nay, nay, Dane. Here we are not so vengeful. Here we still hold to the ways of our Roman fathers, who could think of another use for that part than hanging it on a thorn.'

A brown-haired thrall came over the hill with two shaggy grey dogs. He beat hard on the ground with his stick and shouted out, 'The supper's ready, old man. If you like to stay out here until it gets

178

cold, that's your affair.' Then he turned and went back, the two dogs barking their own defiance at the King of Powys.

Cuneglassus came out of his senile dream and laughed. 'We are all men of spirit here, you see,' he said. 'Let us do as my seneschal advises and go to the table before the flies fall into our mutton-broth.'

In Caer Leon Kei and Bedwyr saw to it that Gautrek's body was decently burned, down by the river beyond the old amphitheatre. What was left after the fire had cooled they threw into the water and crossed themselves as the stream carried it away.

His weapons and other gear they put into a cowhide bag and dropped down a well behind the palace for whoever should be lucky enough to find this hoard in future years.

When this was done it was as though Gautrek had never lived. In that city only the woman in the blue robe still remembered him, and once she had been to the bath-house and had put on fresh garments she forgot him too.

With the Kymry to serve there was small space for anything else, of past or future. It was enough to live through the present, which was more like a raging and engulfing sea than anything else, until they rode out again on their patrols and let the ancient city sink back into its dream of decay.

In the grey slate longhouse of the Powys king thick blue wood-smoke swirled at shoulder height from the round hearth-stone in the middle of the chamber. Four shaggy white horses snorted and stamped their hooves in the straw at the further end, swishing their tails to drive away the flies. A sheepdog bitch suckled her litter behind the king's granite chair. Amleth coughed in the smoke and drank deeply yet again from the horn beaker at his elbow. The heavy thatch of the roof hung down only a foot from his head and sent off a thick scent of mouldering age that seemed to mingle with the amber-coloured fluid that old Cuneglassus poured out from the red clay amphora on the oaken board. The lady Elene was already swaying and giggling with tipsiness, but drinking turn for turn with the men as though she wished to prove her nobility. Medraut leaned back against the slate wall, his eyes reddening but his hands under control. He spilled no drop in raising the horn beaker to his lips. Amleth whose senses were starting to swim with drink and wood-smoke said, 'This liquor, my lord, what do you call it in Powys? I have not tasted its like before.'

The old king replied, 'This is metheglin, Jutlander. Men say that it is as sweet as the lips of a princess and as strong as the axe-blow of a warrior. It is made from the honey of wild bees who have sucked the essence from the herbs which grow only upon one mountain in Powys. The single family who know the magic of making it must wear stone anklets about their legs from the time they leave the cradle so that they shall not leave Powys with their secret. In the cruel ancient days their tongues used to be taken from them as soon as they reached the age of speaking in words; but we are no longer savages in this kingdom, as you will have seen.'

Medraut said, 'It is a pleasing enough drink, for those who have never tasted the liquor that the Picts distil. It does well enough for women who like sweetness in their drinking.'

The old king's head was beginning to loll but at the mention of women he twisted round with an effort and gazed towards Elene. She smiled back at him now, seeing that his shaking hand could not reach to where she sat. Medraut watched this then said, 'Down in the south in Caer Leon, men do not praise your metheglin, my lord. Down there the talk is always of your great treasure. Some say that there is a whole burial-mound of it; others laugh and say that it could be placed in a fish basket. What is the truth of it all, my lord?'

Cuneglassus looked up at him directly and said, 'You have the reputation of being a very clever fellow, Count Medraut. Now tell me what you think my treasure may be like. You have come far to visit me and you must have thought about it much along the way.'

Medraut glanced at Elene before he spoke. Her eyes were bright and her mouth was partly open as though she waited anxiously to hear every word that might be said. He answered the king, 'You are an old man and so in the years you must have put by more than most. Yet you have had many women in your time and it is known through the world that wives have cleverer fingers than night-thieves in picking the locks of a weary husband's coffers. So I would argue that though you may have gained much in your life there is but a moderate amount left by now.'

He spoke gently and smiling as though he bore great love for the old man. Cuneglassus thought a while then smiled. He said, 'There are few men alive in the five kingdoms now who would speak to me as you do, Count Medraut. There are those in Britain who talk of you as being black hearted and a forked tongue in speech. Yet I always answer them by saying that Duke Arthur loves you and keeps you beside him, and that if you were not an honest man he would have been rid of you long ago.'

Medraut helped the old man to pour out more metheglin. He said, 'They speak of your wisdom down in Caer Leon, my lord. Now that I have heard a little of it I know that they do not praise you without good cause.'

The old man reached out his foot until his toes touched the hem of Elene's robe. He seemed to gain some comfort from this for he said, 'You are said to be a hard bargainer, Count Medraut, yet I have not found it so. This girl is as pretty as a lark. That you should have journeyed so far into the north to bring her to me shows you to be a good Christian man.'

Amleth's senses came back to him a small way. He said, 'When we came to this place, my lord, it was for another reason, as I was told it.' But Medraut cut his words off short before the king could understand what they were and said, 'This is the Green Man of Vendils-garth, my lord. He tells us that he can talk to the oak trees and the hunting birds in the place where he comes from.'

Cuneglassus stared hard at Amleth. 'I am the Green Man of Powys,' he said stiffly. 'It is an ancient title and one which I have not thought to use for many years. But if you doubt me see what I have to show you. It speaks more truth than anything a scholar might set down on a sheepskin.'

With a great effort he tore at the waist thongs of his breeches and dragged them down to show his legs. They were brown and scaly and the hide of them had all the look of roughly furrowed bark. His knee-joints were like the gnarled and knotted places in old trees where the wind has broken away a bough. On the under side of each leg there was a faint scum of green, like the lichen that grows upon damp boles towards the seaward side. The lady Elene turned back to her drinking cup and blew through her nostrils as though to clear them. Medraut nodded gravely and said, 'Such noble growth can only come with age among storms, my lord. This young Dane will have nothing like this to show us. For all his great bulk he is but a sapling.'

The old king chuckled and drew his breeches on again with much struggling and grunting. He said, 'Aye, aye, I do not judge a man lightly, and I spoke truth when I said that you were a wise and honest man, Count.'

Amleth was trying to find the words that would say what he felt but before he could do this, Medraut had risen and had taken the old king by the arm. 'Come, my lord,' he was saying, 'settle this argument about your treasure and show us what little your many wives have left you.'

Amleth and the lady Elene followed the two towards the end of the long house. There beside the slate wall lay a great fire-blackened log, as long as a sea-going dug-out boat. It was bound round with rough bronze strapping and covered with chiselled runes. Cuneglassus slapped the wood with his hand and said proudly, 'This is my hoard, Count Medraut. Within this coffer lie such golden chalices, such silver dishes, such amber and jet and garnets, as would buy back the freedom of Britain and still leave a king enough to live on richly for a thousand years.'

Medraut was feeling about the bronze strapping, searching for the locks. But the old king touched him on the shoulder and said smiling, 'Nay, nay, lad, when old Merddin the druid made this chest he called on all his skill. Only one man alive knows how the latching works and that man stands beside you now but will not speak of it.'

The lady Elene put her hand upon the old man and whispered to him, 'Would you show me how the box is opened, my lord?'

He turned to her slowly and said, 'Aye, that I shall do in time, my pretty blackbird. But first you shall show me how your box is opened, hey?'

The lady Elene laughed at his jest and bent and bit his ear. She said, 'That could be shown without delay, my lord, if these others would walk outside on the hill a little while to leave us some privacy.'

But Cuneglassus shook his head. 'Nay, blackbird,' he said. 'Not so fast, not so fast. There is still something left in the mead-jar. The other will come in good time but now is not the time. Nay, for an old man now is not the time, so let us go back to the board.'

He sat there for a space, looking at his three guests and rolling the metheglin about in his mouth as though to draw the last ounce of savour from its harsh-sweet herbs, then he flung his arms wide and said, 'To be so smiled upon by God! To drink with one's dear friends about the board! If I were taken now, my dear ones, I should have lived a happy life.'

Amleth looked up at him stupidly and wondered why the old king's cheeks were wet with tears.

Later two dark-cloaked riders on great horses pushed into the fire-glow under the hill where the brown-haired thrall and his woman sat among the king's henchmen. The taller of the two called, 'How does the feasting go, up at the king's long house?'

The henchmen did not answer because this man spoke like a lord from somewhere too far to the south. But the brown-haired thrall cried out, 'So far, so good; but once the metheglin jar is emptied it will be as always. We are well used to cleaning the floor by now.'

The tall rider swung his leg from the horse and said, 'Very well, we will wait here by your fire. It is cold up here on the hills of Powys.'

The thrall woman shrugged her brown shoulders. 'There will be colder places before morning comes,' she said. 'If I had my way I would journey up to Pictland and live in the forests there among the free folk.'

The tall rider held his hand out towards the blaze. He laughed and said, 'Men eat each other up there, woman. They talk in grunts like swine and lie with their own daughters.'

The woman spat into the darkness. 'That is where I would go,' she said. 'I do not care how men talk.'

Amleth felt the sense coming back to him, but slowly and being stopped before it took shape. His eyes were open but there was a dark cloud before them that only lifted at the edges now and then. His body was deathly chill and when he moved his left hand onto his belly he found that his gear had gone. His right hand would not obey him and when he forced it a sharp agony came into him. He tried to cry out but almost choked with the salt in his throat.

He lay so for a long while. Somewhere beyond the black curtain that hid all, he could hear the distant buzzing and the restive stamping of horses' hooves. He would have died then but a fly lighted on his open cheekbone and bit greedily at him. Amleth roared in fury. The sound came from him like the last whisper of a drowning man among great tides. He roared again and almost stifled. Now the fly was joined by its fellows who fluttered here and there to find their feasting. The last spark in him flickered and caught flame: I am the King of the Wood; I am the Green Man of Vendilsgarth.

Then what was left living of him knew who he was, recalled his strength, his pride again. Groaning he rolled onto his face, then as a man might strain to heave up a rock, he raised himself on hands and knees and began to move. It was a long journey across the dark place. At last he fell against a great log carved with runes, its coffer-lid split and splintered now. Amleth's toppled mind thought that it was the black ship come to carry him away, but his groping hands told him differently. Though now it was empty of all the old king's boasted treasure. His hand rested upon a stiff and hairy mask with teeth as broken and sharp as ancient flints. He drew away from this with pain

184

and turned slowly towards the draught that seemed to come from an open door.

It was a lifetime before he felt the cool hillside wind upon his bare body. He fell many times and lay moaning, but always he rose again and journeyed on, knowing that he was a king and must end like one and not like a pole-axed bullock patient in the straw.

And in the end with the first sunlight of day upon him he crawled past the byre and touched the torn edge of the lady Elene's blue robe. For long he did not know what it was he had come upon that lay in his way so spattered and crying out and ruinous. But her agony spoke to his in its own language and made itself understood and then he fell beside her in the dust and wept. 'See,' she moaned, 'see what the red beast did.' But he could see nothing save the earth below him now. 'See,' she moaned, 'how he has left me, with the child gone from me all bloody.' But Amleth did not know what she was saying.

Now he was praying wordlessly to Odin and to old Vendil to put the strength back into his arms and legs and to let him stand upright like a man again. And when they would not listen to him, he prayed to his mother the Barley Queen to let the force sprout in him like the little green shoots of spring. And she seemed to be listening to him across the long and bitter grey seas so that he was able to kneel once more and take his weight upon his hands.

The lady Elene saw him rise and start to leave her. She clutched at him and cried out, 'Take me with you, my lord. I cannot rise, the red beast has crippled me. Take me with you.'

For a while she clung to him and was dragged along the ground, then the power of the terror in her gave her the moment's strength to lie across his back. He went on down the rough slope like a mindless animal, not knowing why his movements were now so much slower or what the weight upon his back was.

And just before the sun had climbed to its highest in the blue sky of Powys he came to the foot of the hill, away from that house of death, to a place where gorse and bracken and hawthorn struggled with each other to gain a living from the parched dust. And there in the dim shade covered by the tangled branches Amleth fell at last.

185

There was a little trickle that came from beneath a flat rock. Elene rolled from him with her face into the water which she sucked thirstily like an animal for a while. Then she remembered him and cupped her hand in the water and put it to his white lips. At first it ran onto his caked breast, but in the end he learned again how to drink and even said, 'Sibbi . . . Mother . . .', before his wits left him.

It was almost nightfall before Elene heard the men's footsteps treading warily among the gorse. She whispered in fear to Amleth to hold his breath and when he did not hear her clapped her hand over his mouth and nose. This caused him to choke and gasp so she drew her hand away and did her best to roll further from him into a deeper part of the thicket. Once she saw their legs as they stood at the far end of a brushwood tunnel as though waiting for the creatures they hunted to come out. Then she heard them beating with spearshafts onto the gorse as though to start up a sitting hare. She almost screamed with fright at this but when she saw the bright iron point dart down here and there among the undergrowth she learned how to be silent though her heart almost burst with the effort and her teeth almost broke themselves striking so hard upon one another.

And at last the waiting was over for they pushed through the bracken and stood over where Amleth lay, looking down at him but not seeing her in her dark hiding-place.

Kei spoke first and said, 'The Dane has carried little away from the feasting, brother.'

Bedwyr laughed sadly and replied, 'What little he has will not be with him long it seems. This is a lesson all men might profit from, never to drink with our noble friend Medraut.'

Kei stirred Amleth with his foot then said, 'It would be a mercy to put the javelin into him but as he lies now I cannot bring myself to do it. I should carry the memory of such a killing with me to the grave. What are we to do, brother?'

Bedwyr thought a while then said, 'The Duke's orders were plain enough; we were to see that old Cuneglassus came to no harm and we were to give the Dane his two alder sticks and send him on his way from Britain. The old king is beyond protection now—and the Dane will soon be beside him wherever dead men go. All we can do is to give him the alder sticks. Perhaps he will need them to lean on, hobbling to Heaven.'

They laughed without merriment then laid the sticks beside Amleth, pulled the branches over him again and made their way through the brushwood up the hill.

Elene dragged herself back towards Amleth and reached out for one of the sticks. In her weak hand it seemed very heavy, as heavy as doom.

A day later the brown-haired thrall and his wife passed along the rocky road that led away from Powys. In the general looting of what was left in the longhouse on the hill these two had gained a strong horse and a grey sheepdog. There had been a long-shafted iron spear lodged across the rafters which the thrall had always coveted; but one of the henchmen had got to that first. The thrall regretted this for such a weapon would have been useful in the long journey they meant to make into the Coit Celidon of Pictland, the forest where at last they would be free.

The woman was saying: 'If we had had the courage earlier we could have put the axe to Cuneglassus as Medraut did and have had our share of the hoard. Then we should have left Powys as rich as kings ourselves.'

Her husband was saying: 'The Great Mother did not put that in our heads and so she could not have wished it. If we had done as you say either Duke Arthur would have hunted us down or someone else would have heard the gold and silver clinking in our bags and would have left us dead under a bush for it. All is for the best, wife, as the Mother ordains it. She takes when she chooses and gives when she chooses. There is nothing more than that in a man's life.'

It was then that they saw Elene sitting beside Amleth, bathing his wounds with a strip torn from her woollen robe. The thrall-woman laughed in mockery and said, 'The Great Mother does not choose to give generously today, man. An old ewe with foot-rot would fetch a better price in the market than these two.'

The thrall slid down from the horse and went towards Elene. She cowered from him in fear as far as the gorse-spikes would let her go; but he put out a hand and drew her back and felt her as he would have done an animal he was bartering for. She began to howl but he paid no heed to that and went on searching for broken bones. Then he turned to his woman and said, 'She will mend. What has happened to her has happened to many and they have lived.' His woman said, 'You took long enough in finding out.' The thrall replied, 'Take care or it may be you I sell in the north and not this one.'

His woman said, 'It matters little enough to me as long as I have the warrior to keep me company.' The thrall turned Amleth over then wiped his hands on his leather breeches and blew down his nose. 'This one has the smell of death upon him,' he said. 'On the battle-field he would fetch no ransom. They would leave him for the crows.'

The woman said, 'A man who could crawl so far from the house on the hill must be a hero. Such a man must lie in the lap of the Mother herself. If she has decided that he will live a hundred years, shall we prosper in leaving him stark on the roadside for the wolves?'

The thrall did not argue with her any longer but took out his knife and cut down willow-withies to make a hurdle. These he lashed to two small saplings with a length of hide and fastened them to the horse's neck so that they dragged behind like a sledge. The woman ripped off a length of Elene's robe to wrap about Amleth. Her husband jested about this but she made no reply.

It took both of them all their strength to get the prince onto the willow sledge and they let him fall many times into the dust. Always his hands clenched on the two alder sticks. With Elene it was different, she was so light; though when the thrall slung her over his shoulder she screamed out so shrilly that the stony valley echoed as though all the pigs in Powys were being put to the knife.

The thrall-woman said bitterly, 'Be silent, you little whore, and bear your pain like a woman.'

The thrall said, 'Now, wife, now! She is only a child yet. She will know better when she is as shrivelled and as long in the tooth as you are.'

The woman answered, 'We have a score of rivers and a hundred hills to cross before we come to Pictland. They will both be stark when we reach Deva and perhaps it will be just as well.'

Yet the woman was wrong. It seemed almost as though the Great Mother mocked her in giving back life to the wounded ones. By the time they reached Deva Elene's hair and eyes were bright again and she had begun to fret that she had no blue for her lids and no red for her lips. And though she would now walk always with a limp, a soldier beside the northern gate of Deva whistled after her and called, 'Come, dance, pretty one! You are a dancer, are you not?'

The thrall said to her sternly, 'Do not answer him, girl. Now that you are mine you will do my bidding.' So she let the new smile fade from her face and hobbled on beside the horse, her head bowed, the ragged hem of her robe trailing about her thin legs in the dust.

Amleth sat on the hurdle staring behind him like a blind god and holding the two alder sticks stiffly crossed before his matted breast. The merry soldier who had called after Elene caught Amleth's eye, so turned away and discovered something to occupy him under the city wall.

The thrall-woman went beside her husband as he sat on the horse and said, 'Did you see how he put fear into that javelin man though he only carries two sticks? When the full strength comes back to him Christ knows what we shall do with him. It is like dragging a crippled god about the land.'

The thrall said, 'It is more like dragging a crippled bear behind one. When his claws grow again he might take it into his head to tear off the hand that fed him. If I had my way I would sell him over in Eburacum and keep the girl. She is growing to be a pretty, docile thing.'

The woman said savagely, 'Pretty, docile! You are already lusting to have her. I have known you many years and I know all the signs.

If you sell him you must sell her too. I will not have that little bitch taking my place.'

He leaned down and struck out at her. 'You have no place, old woman. Or if you have it is not a place I wish to visit.'

After that the thrall-woman treated Elene more harshly than before and always saw that the girl was safely tied up outside any lodging they found on the way to Eburacum.

Then one evening just at sunset when they had pulled up beside a wayside shelter, Amleth drew in a deep rattling breath and rose from the willow sledge like a great corpse striding from the grave. His teeth were broken and his beard all shaggy but he moved once again like a man, although a thin-legged, thin-armed man.

And he walked to where the thrall-woman was putting the hide thongs about Elene's wrists and growled like a man from some distant place where words were not used. Then he took the hide thongs from the woman's hands and snapped them in his own. And when he had flung them onto the midden he turned and took Elene by the neck, but as gently as a father, and drew her towards a sheltered place beside the hearthstone. She went with him willingly and then sat by him, silent and smiling, while he out-gazed all men in the room like a lion, or an eagle staring down from a ledge.

That night the thrall-woman said to her man, 'The time has come. These kings and queens are not ordinary folk. They rise from the dead and put on their crowns again. If we do not get rid of them we shall be slaves again, husband.'

He nodded in the darkness and said, 'That was in my mind also, wife. As soon as I can, I will find out where we may get the best price for them.'

To himself he mourned that he had not found the chance to use the girl before she had grown too proud. It had always been his dream to learn how queens differed from other women. Now he feared that he would go into the grave without knowing and this thought made him weep in the darkness as though he had become a slave again.

III

Pictland Dream

AMLETH came out of his long time of suffering to see a beautiful creature walking by the shore. When he clenched his eyes hard he could see that it was a woman and not a fairy from under the hill or the mere.

First he saw a long white cloud like the wall of a castle and under this the dark blue sea sending in its white-crested rollers to the golden shore. He saw a hundred mussel pools along that gold, and then nearer still walking on that sun-bleached sand that no tide had darkened, that was as white as flax, this woman.

It was as though he had not seen a woman ever before and he looked carefully at her lest his life should end now. She wore long robes of silk so thin that the shape of her body came through shadowy from the sun that stood behind her, above the sea. The colours that floated about her were faint blue and pale red. Now the sea breeze lifted the silks and he saw the long brown legs striding; now the breeze dropped and the robes fell gravely to the sand and dragged like those of a great queen. Yet whether the robes rose or fell the long stride was the same, the arrogant swaying of hip and shoulder the same, the free majesty of the walking. This woman's skin was a light brown as though she had been long in the sun, or as though her folk had come from another place in the world. Her hair was deep black and hung in one long plait below her waist, as Sibbi's had hung long ago when they went into the green wood together.

Amleth shook the tears from his eyes and looked at this woman's long thin hands as she moved them talking to an older woman in brown robes who struggled to keep up with her along the shore. He looked at the high carriage of this woman's chin, at her bare feet, at the small round wicker buckler she bore between her shoulder bones and the jet bracelets that reached almost as high as her elbows. He

N   193

could hear them clacking as she moved whenever the breeze blew his way.

She strode so heroically that for a while he could not tell how she was different from a man until the breeze held the thin silk against her upper body. Then he turned and said to the brown-haired thrall, 'They are a noble folk, these Picts.' The thrall shrugged his shoulders. 'Not all men say so,' he answered. 'You must wait until you know them better.'

The woman on the shore began to laugh at something her companion had said. Amleth shook his head. 'Nay, men have reported them wrongly,' he grinned. 'They are a merry folk.'

The thrall-woman said darkly, 'Tell yourself that when they put the pointed stake up you, slave.'

Amleth gazed down at her until she looked away. Then he said to Elene who was holding his hand like a child, 'Shall we go down and speak with this Pict woman, little one?'

Elene looked back at the thrall, afraid, but he was staring at his feet, so she nodded to Amleth and they began to walk over the spiky dunes and down towards the shore.

They had gone no more than twenty paces when Elene said in fear, 'Look, there are men watching us, below the cliffs, with bows drawn at us. They are her guard. If we go on we shall be hit.' She began to drag away but Amleth took her hard by the wrist and went on. She had to go with him, fearing with every step that the arrows would thump into her back and breasts.

But this did not happen. The woman in the red and blue saw them and stopped still, the wind whipping her robes behind her like a goddess, and held up her hand in a signal. When Elene turned again the men with bows had withdrawn into their hiding-places of sea-grass along the shore.

Then the woman called out in a deep-throated Celtic, different from the thin tongue men spoke down in Caer Leon, 'Come forward wanderers, and let me see what you are.'

Amleth's heels dug deep into the sand, sending it scattering as a stallion does the earth. Elene hung behind him in case there might be blows to receive. And when they got closer to the woman she saw how broad her face was and her hips were, yet how narrow her nose and her hands. But three things Elene saw which were wondrous to her: this Pict woman's eyes which were as wide as brooches and thick-lashed with black hairs; her breasts which were as great as helmets but yet as well-formed; her waist which was so thin that she thought Amleth could have spanned it with his two hands joined.

Then the sea-breeze blew the woman's black hair from her forehead, and they both saw something they had never seen before—a great blue-tattooed eye in the middle of her forehead, directly above her nose, its outer edges ridged and raised, its pupil picked out in red. When Elene saw this she drew back on Amleth's hand but he pulled her on and bowing slightly said, 'Greetings, lady, I am from Jutland; this girl is a Roman from Lindissi and is daughter to the Duke Arthur who has given her to me in marriage.'

The Pict woman's lips seemed about to smile then they stiffened again and she said, 'All this I know. Why do you tell me again?'

Amleth said, 'It is well for travellers to greet one another, lady. That is the old custom.'

The Pict smiled now and turned her dark eyes up towards the blue sky. 'Mother, Mother,' she said. Then she looked down sternly and went on in a thick whisper, 'It is hardly the custom for slaves to ask for news of their mistress, is it, strangers?'

Amleth said stubbornly, 'We are not slaves, lady. As I have told you, I am from Jutland and this girl . . .'

The Pict woman suddenly held up her hand with a jingle of bracelets and said, 'Let us have no more of this, man. I am Elekt, sister of Orest, and I have paid good Roman coin for you both from the man who brought you here. If you do not walk to heel like the good dogs he said you were, I must whistle the warriors to come out and teach you your manners. Now behave.'

She turned then and walked on, talking in a strange tongue to the old woman who went beside her. Amleth and Elene followed, hand in hand, wondering at this greeting but glad at last to be going freely as they wished with the warm wind upon their bodies and the open sky over their heads.

They passed through a tall stockade beyond the dunes with a hundred warriors treading behind them, dressed in hide clouts and holding their long lances and wicker shields in the left hand. They were all small dark men who walked like leopards without sound.

Elene shuddered to see the line of wizened bodies high on the impaling stakes, their arms and legs dangling in the wind, their heads lolling forward onto the breast like rotting fruit about to fall. Amleth looked at them and said to her quietly, 'You Romans are no gentler. At least these folk do it in the open and not in secret at the friendly mead-board.'

She began to whimper then but Amleth shook her and said, 'Behave, they will be watching us. We must go in like lions or we shall live like dogs for ever.'

In the compound, surrounded by a score of low stone huts, a crowd of folk awaited their queen's coming and raised their right arms. 'Cruithin! Cruithin!' they shouted in greeting.

Black dogs herded flocks of brown-fleeced sheep through the narrow streets. Cattle lowed from open-sided byres. Fires of sea-weed sent up a thick brown smoke that swept just above the roof-thatch of the houses, warding off the sunlight and turning mid-day to twilight until sudden gusts of sea breeze swept it away for a while.

Elene whispered, 'This is a dark town, lord. One can hope for small mercy here.'

Amleth walked on. 'Where can one hope for mercy,' he said, 'in dark towns or light towns?'

They came to the queen's house. It was of grey stone blocks which stood to the height of a man with a boy upon his shoulders. Its roof of stitched cow-hide towered above this like a great tent. Yet the door of this place was so small that, even on his knees and twisting sideways, Amleth found it hard to enter. The Pictish soldiers who stood behind him made great fun of this and even threatened to help

196

him through with the point of their lances; but though they made the gestures, no one touched him.

There were no window-holes in this place; the only light came from shallow stone lamps whose wicks floated in oil, and from the smoke vent that opened to the sky in the tent-roof.

All about the square hearth, set with four long stones, the floor was covered with heather and dried bracken. A throne-chair of slate slabs stood against the wall opposite the tunnel-door, and set over it two crossed stone axes, bigger than anything the prince had seen before, their blades in the form of the emergent moon.

And when his eyes had grown used to the dimness of that house he saw, all about the central room, low doors that led into passages and other rooms. From one of those rooms came the smell of meat roasting. His mouth began to water. The Pict-queen, sitting on her stone chair, said, 'You are hungry, Jutlander. From the look of your body your last master did not feed you well. A man is worthless unless he has a full belly. Send your slave-girl to help in the kitchen and your dinner will come to you all the sooner.'

Amleth answered, 'She is no slave, Lady Elekt. She is a daughter of the Duke Arthur who married her to me before the Archbishop Dubricius in Lindum. Nor am I a slave, lady, but the Green Man of Vendilsgarth who one day will be a king in Jutland. Whatever you paid the thrall for us I shall return to you when I lay hands on my own things again.'

Elekt lowered her head until all Amleth could see was the great staring eye pricked in the middle of her broad forehead. This silenced him. And then the queen said, 'Along this shore there is no one who would dare to tell me that the sky was blue if I had said it was red, Jutlander.'

Amleth sank down upon the heather. 'I am too weary,' he said, 'but perhaps when I am a man again I may dare to tell you what colour the sky is.'

Elene did not wait when the queen signalled to her to go to the kitchen, nor did the other dark-robed women who waited about the walls. And when Elekt and Amleth were alone the Pict-queen said to him as to an equal, 'The pleasantries of princes are not for thralls' ears, Green Man. Tomorrow I will have another chair set up for you, so that you may talk with me at the same level and not crouching on the floor like a beaten dog.'

Amleth laughed in self-mockery. 'What am I but a beaten dog, my gear gone, my body gashed and weakened, with only two alder sticks to call my own?'

Queen Elekt gazed openly at him with her great dark eyes and said, 'I will tell you what you are. You are two things that you did not know before. News travels fast among my folk for they learn many secrets and their ears are everywhere. And when they learn a secret they pass it to their fellows, by smoke fires on hilltops, or by signs tied to the legs of tame pigeons, or by other means which I shall not tell you of yet awhile. And one thing I know is that you have no cause to love Duke Arthur or his bastard nephew Medraut.'

Amleth turned from these words with pain at the memory of such a man. He said, 'Then what am I, Lady Elekt?'

She smiled and said, 'You are the sword that the Mother has put into my hands to destroy these Romans and to take Britain for my ancient people. Now it is a hacked and bent weapon but it can be reforged in time and in my hand it will cut deeper than it ever plunged before.'

Amleth waited a while then asked, 'You said that I was two things, lady, yet you have only told me one of them. What is the other?'

She made him wait long before she answered, then she said, 'You have named yourself, my lord. You are the Green Man, but now of Pictland as well as Jutland. For too long while I have been waiting for a sign my brother Orest has been King of the Year, now you shall sit beside me and lie beside me and take his place as Lord of the Cruithin.'

Amleth stood, hearing this honour, and said, 'In Jutland I am given to the Maze Queen, Sibbi. That is one reason why I never lay with the child, Elene, daughter of Duke Arthur.'

Elekt smiled. 'We Cruithin have always found it hard to understand the customs of outlanders,' she said, 'though we have lived and fought beside Saxons and the Attacotti of Hibernia for as long as our grandmothers can recall, working to drag down these Romans.'

Amleth said stiffly, 'Among us it is the law.'

The Pict-queen drew her narrow hand across her painted forehead and laughed. 'Then it is an unnatural law, Green Man,' she said. 'Does the stallion stay with one mare until he falls with his grey muzzle in the dust; and does the mare not draw back her legs for more than one lord in her life? It is good that you came to us when you did or Jutland would have had a Green Man that the rest of the world would have called a fool.'

As the summer waned and his strength returned, Amleth learned much from the lady Elekt; more than he had ever known of life before. She told him of many different things, just as a child will thread beads of various shapes and colours onto a string to make a necklace—amber against jet, red clay against Egyptian blue. He did not wonder that she went from one story to the next, for all was new to him who had passed his life in a stark stone castle imprisoned by the grey seas of Jutland.

She said, 'The Romans called us Picti because they thought we put paint on our foreheads and bodies. They laughed when they named us so. But they did not laugh when their Caesar, Constantine the Great, died by the dirk of my great-grandfather. This Constantine, son of a peasant woman, thought after seven short months in Britain that he ruled the world. He took my great-grandfather's only daughter into an apple orchard and was upon her when my kinsman found them. That is how the Caesar ended, on the knife of the Cruithin. Much did they laugh then! Their next Caesar, who called himself Constans, was so afraid of us he gave us land, here on the north shore, and in many places south of that wall of theirs. He gave it to us out of fear; he took many of our young men to be Romans and wear their helmets. But they never stayed with him.

They took what he had to give and then went home to their own people as the Cruithin always do. So in the end this Constans fell to the knife, as all Romans must do when their dice is thrown.'

Amleth said, 'In Jutland the men speak of Romans as though they were gods, each one of them. And the young girls dream in their beds that they have a Roman on them to love them, as though this would be better than gold coin or Valhalla.'

The lady Elekt laughed and said, 'They were worn-out old dogs, gone in the teeth, before ever they came to this land which we named Priten when they were still grovelling in their reed huts by the Tiber, waiting for their Trojan lords to whip their backs. No, Amleth, it is the Cruithin who are the gods. At the world's dawn-time we sprang up and slew the shag-haired monsters who were spawned from darkness and lived in trees and caverns. We, the Cruithin, gave the world to men as a generous gift of our hands. So since that time we have walked the earth as its rightful lords. Would you expect otherwise? We do not deign to weave cloth, to sing songs, or to grovel in the earth for iron. There are folk on this earth who are so fearful of being forgotten that they make runes upon clay and stone and even the skins of sheep. We despise such remem-brances. Those who meet us as we swarm like hornets up and down the world remember the proud sign of Mother Dia we wear on our foreheads. And some of them recall with fear the old dirks we have carried since the time of our oldest grandfather Indra, who drank strong liquor sitting in his wagon among the steppe-reeds, his beard upon his breast, from Mickney Brae to India.'

Amleth said, 'This Mickney Brae, men do not speak of it at Vendilsgarth. Where is it to be found? Could a brisk warman find work there?'

The Pict-queen would not talk more then but sent him from the wheel-house and said she was weary.

But another time she called him to her and said, 'You asked of Mickney Brae and I dismissed you. My dreams have troubled me a great deal since then. The Mother has whispered in my ears that I should hide nothing. So I will tell you.'

Amleth said, 'This is for you to decide. I would as soon hear of anything else you have in mind, lady.'

The queen put out her hand and drew him towards her. She smiled and told him: 'You will hear what I have to say now, or you will go into the kitchen and pick mussels from their shells. No, do not draw away, it must be told. You must know that at one time in the past years we were great in the middle sea. This was in the time of the Pharoah Menos of Crete, I think, or perhaps at a time later or earlier. My fathers lived in Mickney Brae then and put gold on the face of their dead. It was always summer there and they were rich in corn and cattle. But then droughts came and all the gold had gone onto the dead men's faces. So my kinsman Agam the Bull must seek gold and cattle in another place. He took his men in their tall ships beyond the blue islands to Horse Truia where they had gold still and there they fought for ten months until the Horse-tamers gave up their gold.'

Amleth said, 'When my own folk have done that they have been called barbarians by the Romans. Yet your people do it and you call them heroes and gods. How is it that two folk may do the same thing and be judged differently, lady?'

She saw the smile at the corners of his mouth and so put off her own stern face and said, 'My people were not savage ship-foragers, Jutlander. They had a purpose in all they did which was beyond a mere harrying of coast-peasants. First they let one of their great queens be stolen and taken in a ship to Truia. She bore the same name as that pale-faced cripple girl you brought here, the little Roman who carries our sea-shells and sheep-bones to the midden heap and cleans out the pot you use. But the woman I speak of was not a midden-carrier; she was made in the Great Mother's image. Her breasts were as fine as mine, her waist as slender, the wicker-tattoos upon her legs were as delicate. She was in all ways worth sailing for, past the blue islands, and worth standing under the arrows for.'

Amleth nodded and said, 'So she was the excuse of your folk for laying waste to this city you talk of. Was she worth it in the end, lady?'

Elekt the queen pinched her nostrils in tightly. 'When there are such women you do not ask yourself if they are worth anything as though you were haggling in the market-place among traders. These women are beyond all judgement, Jutlander. They are here on the earth for men to guide their lives and deaths by. They are as gold and jewels, as fierce stallions in battle, as the keen old swords from out of the grave-barrows, all without price.'

Amleth nodded, thinking of his mother and of Sibbi, but he did not ask anything more. Then the queen Elekt said, 'This you must learn, that of all things created the beautiful queens are the greatest. Without them the men would lose their direction, like a horse without reins, or a ship without a steering-oar. The world is only for women, only what the women make it to be. There is no more to be understood in life.'

Another time, beside the hearth stone of Hestia, Elekt told him, 'Even the cruel queens are great ones, Jutlander.'

He said, 'Come, come, lady, it is the men who are the bulls, the stags, the lions, who tear and put in the horn and the sword—not the women. Do not tell me that you women, with all your soft parts, can be so terrible.'

The lady Elekt lowered her head at him so that he should see the mark on her and then she said, 'You are learning many things but in some you are as slow as a Jutlander can be. Because we are soft in our parts and less strong than the warriors, we are not less fierce. The great cliff will topple down and crumble into sand when the high seas come at it; but the small and pretty pebble on the shore remains unmarked. Then, long after men have forgotten that the cliff was ever there, a warrior fits that pebble into a sling and with it destroys his greatest foeman.'

Amleth laughed and shook his head. 'You go beyond me,' he said. 'Tell me about women not pebbles, lady.'

The queen placed her hand upon him and said, 'Here, where I touch. This is a man's strength, is it not?'

Amleth nodded smiling. Then she said, 'It is the custom of our people to bear their swords unsheathed always. This shows their courage. This astounds the world. When that unsheathed sword is seen, men say, He is of the Cruithin. He is brave, for look! Now I will tell you it is the will of the women that their sons should bear this token of courage. It is they who decide when and say, "Now is the time for my son to show his bravery and go forth without a coward's scabbard to hide his dirk." And so they lead the boy forward and sit him on their knee while the priestess teaches him the lesson of manhood and the chief warriors bow their heads that another one has come amongst them.'

Amleth yawned and said, 'This mead makes me sleepy, lady. I will go back to my bed.'

The queen smiled and said, 'It is not mead you drink tonight, Jutlander. What it is I will tell you another time but not now. For now I shall tell you how my kinsman Agam Bull came back from Truia and found that my grandmother Celest was lying with her chosen lover. Mother, but he was angry with the sweat and dust on him from the tumbled walls he had burned down. And so being a man and simple he dragged her from the bed in Mickney Brae and struck her before all the men with him. Here in Britain they speak of the three fateful blows of Arthur the Roman. Dia, but they have yet to learn what a blow can do! This Agam Bull went off to the bathhouse and never walked out again. He who had tumbled Truia never walked again, my Jutlander!'

Amleth lolled back against her chair and smiled stupidly. 'He took a cramp in the legs then, lady,' he said thickly. 'After those months in Truia, to get a cramp in the legs!'

The Pict-queen said starkly, 'He took a cramp in the neck, my friend. One that never let him speak again or strike another blow against Celest or against anyone.'

She gazed down at him a while then said, 'As he stepped from the bath, so standing between earth and water, poised in the air, the great queen my first grandmother paid him for his bull-like lack of understanding. She took him on the neck with the moon-axe that has always been in our house. It was after this that the cramp in his neck and tongue and legs began. But know you, my grandmother Celest put him away in the beehive with a mask of the finest gold to be his memorial. I have seen it, in the grave-cellar at Mickney Brae, and I can tell you that he was a handsome man. As handsome as you are yourself, Jutlander—though with an older face.'

Amleth tried to rise from the floor and had to grasp hard at the lady Elekt's legs to help himself. She bent and helped him and then said, 'Nay, Jutlander, you are the more handsome man. I made a mistake there—but it is long since I was down there in Greekland at Mickney Brae, looking over their treasure house.'

And when she helped him to her bed, staggering, she said, 'You have become the most proper man in Britain, Amleth. One day they will recall you here as a great one. They will remember you when this little Arthur is worm's meat and gone.'

Amleth said heavily, 'The Duke is great though he is small, lady.'

Elekt said back, 'He will fall, my love, and you shall help him to tumble into the dust.'

For a little while Amleth's senses stayed and he said, 'He is too great to put his mouth to the dust, lady.'

Then she said quietly, 'The axes on my wall, Jutlander. One of them took the great Bull's head down. The one on the right lowered his horns as he stood in the bath-house. But the one on the left is a virgin axe, Jutlander, and has not yet bitten a king's neck. It is too heavy for me to shake, but you could use it and be the King of Britain.'

And after this there was no more talking, but such other things that Amleth wept at dawn-time that he had betrayed his mother and Sibbi. Yet his weeping was short since by now he was understanding life differently.

Only the lady Elene went on weeping for she had looked through the hide curtain in the night and had seen a true queen in the hive at last; and she had cursed the foot of Medraut with all the curses she had learned from the sheepmen of Lindissi. And the smallest curse was that he should take the rot from damp grass and at last walk upon his hip-joints.

When he had healed again and could laugh about life and its ways, Amleth the prince said, fingering the Pict-queen's forehead, 'This sign—how can it be an eye when its centre is red?'

The lady Elekt put her arms about him and answered, 'It might be Dia's mouth, caressing you as I do now.'

Amleth thought and said, 'How did they make it? Did they use fishbone needles as northern folk do in decorating deer-hides?'

The lady Elekt held to him silently a while then said, 'When they outlined what it is they used needles. That was painful for most of us in my year-group. But when they made the eye they used the small flint knife and one of the queens, my youngest cousin, died of it.'

Amleth waited a while then said, 'To die of a little prick in the forehead? She must have been a sickly child.'

The lady Elekt drew him closer and said with pride, 'None of the Cruithin is sickly, my lord. The sickly ones go out onto the hill before their eyes are opened. So, only the strong ones stay. But what you ask about is not on the forehead, prince; it is not for the sheep-herders to look upon and jest about. It lies deeper.'

He rolled her about a while then said, 'This strong mead you give me, from what bees does this come?'

The queen answered, 'From no bees, my lord. In my brother's kingdom of the north beyond the wall we build our round houses, the glass castles where no men live; only the liquor lives and ferments itself and then refines itself. So from the heather honey we create the water of life. And that is what you drink. Is it good?'

Amleth said, 'If we had this water in Jutland we would rise from our benches and march down to take Micklegarth, my love.'

Queen Elekt said, 'Then I shall give you no more of it for I would rather lose my eyes than lose you, my lord. Come, let us run down to the shore and go with the fishermen in their boats.'

But run as he might the prince could not overtake her. In her coloured robes with her black hair flying behind her she seemed like the west wind. The golden sand of autumn spurted from her bright heels. Her long legs cast back a rainbowed spray into his face.

Later as they lay in the bottom of the leading dugout boat they laughed together and their people laughed down on them as they hauled in their lines.

'If this Jutlander stays, we shall gain Britain,' said the captain of the first outrigger.

But already Amleth was whispering to the queen, 'If only I had word that my brother Gautrek was well, I would think of learning to sail one of these craft towards Jutland.'

She answered, 'Be still, be still; one thing at a time, my lord.' And later she said, 'When the spring comes maybe we shall hear of Gautrek and then we can decide what is best.'

But the spring was long in coming. Word came that Duke Arthur was gathering new cavalrymen from among the Armoricans, and even that he had sent squadrons to Ravenna to aid Count Belisar, so that the two of them should sit as Caesars in Rome at last.

The lady Elekt told Amleth one evening, 'My brother Orest has massed his folk about Mount Agned. Arthur's spies will tell him of this and so we may look for a visit from the Kymry before too long. If the Duke is abroad then Medraut will lead them. Would that please you?'

Amleth said starkly, 'I would put my foot down his throat, heel first.'

She smiled and answered, 'I expected that you would. But I hope that you would give me time to visit him as my grandmother Astarte did, with her sickle, and as my cousins in Libya still do.'

Amleth said, 'When I had finished, lady, there would be small point in that.'

But she pinched him sharply and said, 'Nay, nay, my lord, it is a ritual that must be observed among the Cruithin. You would not have his spirit rise and beget other Medrauts to eternity, would you?'

Amleth answered, 'Once I have my foot on his neck I will take my chance on that, lady.'

Then the queen said, 'If that is how you think now, my lord, it is time that I gave you your sword.'

206

She rose from him and opened the stone coffer beside the limpet-boxes. She drew out a bronze dirk so long that it reached Amleth's chin when he turned it back with curved wrist. He had never held such a weapon, no, not even Quern-biter. It was so light, so keen, so agile. It flashed like the morning sun all golden when he flicked it out and back again.

He said, 'Lady, I have held two swords in my life before this. The first my mother gave me. The second was old Vendil's blade.'

The Pict-queen laughed into the dying sunlight and said, 'And now you have the greatest of them all, the one that Agam Bull took in his hand to Truia.'

Then Amleth almost let fall the light bronze blade in his fear. He had held swords before but never one on which the story of the world turned as on a pivot or an axle.

But Elekt the queen came up behind him and clasped him round the waist warmly. 'Courage, my man, courage,' she said. 'Before the tale is told, you shall be the Caesar in Rome holding such a blade before you and leading such a wife beside you.'

The lady Elene heard all this as she cleaned out a broth-pot in the kitchen. She bit her lip until the blood ran down her chin. Then she hobbled outside and shouted into the wind, 'I am the Queen of Powys! Hear me, Christ, and tell me if I must bear their taunts any longer.'

But there was no answer. Only the wind blowing a little harder, flinging the sand grains into her sore eyes.

Through the cold winter he came to depend on the queen's wisdom as she came to rely on his growing strength. Once after she had told how her kinswomen had danced their way back from India in the ancient days, sometimes before the Ark of the Covenant, sometimes before the image of Dagon-Poseidon, and often over the long horns before Menos in Knossos, Amleth asked, 'This maze, this labyrinth we always come back to, what is its meaning, lady?'

Then the lady Elekt let fall her heavy blue-painted eyelids so that their thick black lashes seemed to lie upon her russet cheeks. 'You have been into the maze, Green Man, with the woman, Sibbi. Do you need ask me?'

Amleth said, 'I know well enough what is done there. I ask what the maze itself is.'

She opened her eyes for him and let him gaze into them, their lids flickering like the wings of a moth. She let him run his great fore-finger round her smiling lips and once she came forward suddenly and bit it quite sharply. But he did not draw away for in the time he had been with her she had taught him the kingly lion's strength and pride.

She said, 'The labyrinth-maze and the sword, such a dirk as you now call your own, are the first things in life. All else grows from them. Without them there would be no kings, no men, and none of the things men do. There would be no palaces, no fields, no harvest-ing of corn or of fish from the sea. They are the beginning and the end of all things.'

Then Amleth said, 'I can understand that with a sword in his hand a man may become a king and cause other men to build him palaces, or plough his fields, or bring fish in from the sea. The sword is like the thunder-stone, it can destroy those who do not obey the man who holds it. But the labyrinth, the curling maze, surely this is but a floor for dancing?'

She said lying before him, her wide eyes upon him, 'In that old Knossos where my ancient cousins danced and bemused the bull, cheating his horn when they chose, bringing him to his knees in the sand after their skill had weakened him—there lies the start of the story. There was a queen of our folk there, at time's beginning, whose womanly pride was so fierce that she swore to topple the Bull-king himself and, in view of all the people, left him gasping on the ground. And when the artful Duke, Daedalus himself, saw this, he vowed that this moment should be remembered through the world until the last night fell upon men. So he had made in every place that men visited memorials to that great queen in her secret image. This was his praise of queens and the tokens of their power over men.'

Amleth said, 'A dancing floor?'

She answered, 'There is a dance, to be sure; but without help it is not easy for a man to enter the maze. And when he reaches the centre at last, he may fall as though a thunderclap had sounded in his head, and lie gasping like the Bull-king of Knossos.'

Amleth shook his tangled head. 'I do not understand all you say, lady.'

She said, 'I have made it plain for you to see if you will only look. The beginning of all truth is open to you.'

Before winter was over, the artificers among the Cruithin made for Amleth new war gear. This was not of metal like that he had sailed from Jutland wearing. Among the Cruithin there was little metal but stolen gold and heirlooms of old bronze. With them, all was speed and light movement. Their round bucklers and their breastplates were of tight-woven wicker covered with bull's hide. Their lances were of straight ash tipped with hard flint. Their small bows were of slim yew branches, strung with finely cut deer-sinew. Yet with such weapons the Cruithin could bring down a heavy Roman charger or could pierce that spot in a man which his metal chain did not cover.

Once Amleth had become used to his gear and weapons, he laughed at what he and all the warriors he had known set such store by.

Then the Cruithin taught him to wrestle, taking his adversary by the chain-mesh, drawing him off-balance, and kicking his legs from under him. The captain who taught Amleth this said, 'Have no doubts, my lord, such a little trick would have brought down the Emperor Alexander—if there had been a Pict to set against him at that time.'

They taught him to steer their great dugouts, sliding them with the paddle along the side of the mountainous waves and not trying to plunge through the rollers.

And when at last he stood before all the people to dedicate his forelock to Apollo Apple-king, Elekt who held the shears herself said, 'They are proud of you, my lord. Now they would follow you anywhere—even to Jutland across the grey sea-waste, if you asked them.'

Then in sight of all she kissed his forehead from which the lock had been cut and the Cruithin sent up such a cheering that it could almost have been heard down in Lindissi.

Elene watched from her place on the midden and when all had gone away to the new king's feasting, she limped out and took up the forelock. While she had this part of the Jutlander, she thought, she would have power over him. Queen Cedda in Caistor had taught her this. The old woman had kept Duke Arthur's nail-clippings in a small bone box, from one occasion when he had come collecting taxes in Lindissi; and these, she always maintained, could set her beside him on the throne at Caer Leon as the fourth Gwenhwyvar whenever she chose to say the right spells over them.

When the year had fully turned and the last of the aconites under the beech woods had faded back into the ground, a tall runner of the Cruithin came gasping into the encampment by the shore with the message that Orest was on the move southward with his swarm and wished to talk with his sister the queen by that part of the Roman wall that lay above the crag lake. Elekt turned in her stone chair in this man's presence and asked Amleth, 'Are we to go, my husband?' Amleth nodded and when the runner had been fed and sent off again with this answer he said to Elekt, 'Why did you ask my opinion? This is a matter for the Cruithin and not for an outlander.' Elekt said, 'We must have gone in any case but it is as well for the messenger to take back word to my brother that I depend on you in all things. So he may respect you and treat you well. But if I had sent back my own word without consulting you my brother Orest would have had you murdered. He would have considered that you must be too small a man to decide such a thing; and among the Cruithin a man must always be strong.'

She smiled a little when she said this and Amleth, taking her other meaning, nodded and smiled too. He said, 'I hope that your brother will not be a hard man to handle, lady.' She answered, 'He will be as hard as you let him be and no harder. He is hammered of the same metal as I am. When you come face to face with him you must treat him as you see best. But, I warn you, if you do not master him before a day is out you will lie stark before the next one ends.'

Amleth sat staring ruefully at his finger tips. He said, 'In Jutland it takes longer than that to find ways and means, lady. We are slow to action though once we are roused I must say that things are never quite the same again.'

Lady Elekt smiled and stroked his staring mass of hair. She said, 'You are a man, my brother is a man. Surely one man knows how to deal with another? It is no mystery, such as that of a man dealing with a woman, say?'

Amleth drew her to him and said, 'I think that I would rather deal with this man's sister than the man himself.'

And afterwards she said, 'That is enough dealing for this time, Jutlander. We shall go north in separate wagons so that when you face my brother you shall not say with your last breath that I stole the force from any blow you tried to strike at him.'

Amleth took her in his arms again and rubbed his stubbled beard so hard against her that she cried out. 'If your little brother has the better of me, lady,' he said, 'I will abide by that and make no excuses.'

She clung to him then and wept against his matted breast. 'Mother, mother,' she whispered, 'to have found a man at last and then to put him in danger. Amleth, let us leave this place together and go towards the south. Let us forget the Cruithin and my brother Orest.'

Amleth said gently, 'Nay, nay, my lady. If I did not go north to see your brother and this Roman wall by the crag lake, I should never forgive myself. I tell you, I should be no use to you for the rest of my days.'

The evening before the Cruithin of the Shore went northwards, Amleth sat under a windbreak with three of the captains drinking the water of life after a long day's running in the heather behind a fallow deer. He was in the middle of telling these men what the ale was like in Jutland when one of them, a hooknosed warrior named Breachan, pointed behind him and said, 'There is someone to see you, lord. She has been peeping round the shelter for long enough, waiting to catch your eye.'

Amleth said, 'The lady Elekt would walk among us, not hide like a slave.'

Breachan answered, 'It is the slave, the Roman midden-girl, lord.'

Then the three captains rose so that Amleth should speak with the slave alone. They went away high-nosed and looking straight ahead as though he had gone out of their lives all at once. He began to call them back, but sensing that they would affect not to hear, silenced the words before they were spoken. Then without turning he called softly, 'Come here, Elene.'

She limped to him and fell at his feet, weeping and holding his ankles. 'Oh, husband,' she said, 'the women in the kitchen say that you are going away and that I must stay here on the midden for the rest of my days. Take me with you, I beg. I am your wife, do you not remember? We are the kings of Powys, you and I.'

Amleth put his hand out of pity on her tangled yellow hair. Once she had seemed so proud and even queenly and now she was like a girl that blind beggars take through the streets to collect offerings after the flute has been played. Her ragged clothes were stiff with kitchen grease. Her hands were callused and deeply engrimed with dirt. She who had loved to wash her lithe body now sent up a sour smell of sweat and sheepskins.

He said, 'Elene, little one, you must not weep so. Nothing is got by weeping in this world. You would not have the Cruithin see a Roman crying, would you?'

She glowered up at him from the turf. 'You, you say this to me, and you are the king of these Cruithin! You tell me not to weep but you lie warm at night in a bed while I grovel among stinking shells on the midden to find my rest. Take me with you, I command you, or I swear that I will get word to my father the Duke and beg him to take revenge for me.'

Amleth drew his hand away from her. He said, 'Duke Arthur is far off, Elene. You might die a hundred times before your message reached him.'

Then she rose, so painfully and crookedly that his heart was touched; and she flung herself across him as though he were her father or a trusted brother. 'Oh, my lord,' she cried, 'if you do not take me with you I shall find a sharp cockle-shell and cut my throat with it before your door tonight while you are lying with the black queen. I swear it. I have that little much of a Roman in me to do that, Amleth.'

He set her gently onto her feet again and tried to smile into her face. Then he placed his hands upon her thin shoulders and said honestly, 'You shall come north with the Cruithin, Elene. I do not know whether I do right for you in promising this but it is my word and it shall not be broken. Are you content?'

She tried to kneel at his feet again, but he caught her and straightened her. 'There,' he said, wiping her eyes and streaming face with his neck-cloth, 'it ill becomes a daughter of Arthur's to make such a fuss about a little journey to the north. Why, Elene, when you and I rode from Lindissi all the way to Caer Leon there was not this great weeping and clawing of the heather. Have courage, Roman. Your life will live itself again if you are brave.'

When Amleth returned to the wheel-house at dusk the lady Elekt sat upright in her stone chair looking ahead. She had put on a black robe and had her face painted white with ochre. Her dark eyes, rimmed round with scarlet plant juice now, looked like those of the Furies. She gave him no time to greet her but said outright, 'Stand, Jute. If I blow upon this bone whistle five of the captains will run in and hold you.'

Amleth leaned upon his ash shaft and smiled. 'Hold me, lady?' he asked. 'Why should they wish to hold me?'

The queen stared beyond him as though he were of glass and said stiffly, 'So that I should geld you, Jute.'

He put his hand up to his forehead in weariness. 'My lady,' he said, 'this is hardly the welcome I expected at this time.'

She answered as through a clay mask, 'And this is hardly the husband I had expected—to go with a midden-thrall into the windbreak on the high hill. Do not lie to me, my captains have told me of the meeting.'

Amleth flung down his ash spear and sat beside the hearth fire, his back towards the queen. He said into the ashes, 'So among the Cruithin a crippled shell-wench is envied by a queen whose kinswomen danced before the Ark of the Covenant and the image of Dagon-Poseidon! Odin, but it is a strange world when a man who is to sit on the throne of Britain must be called to account and lose his very manhood because he wiped a little girl's tears away from the face that Romans kept clean but Picts wish to see fouled.'

He stopped then and waited for the sound of Elekt coming at him with the flint knife. He thought that he might let her strike once to satisfy her pride and then take her over his right shoulder and put her head into the ashes. He was so savage then that he even tried to picture what she would look like with her great black mane of hair burned away and only the white of her head showing. The old Jutish fury came into him so strongly then that he even hoped she would run across the floor at him and strike. He bunched his right shoulder up so that her knife would hit bone not muscle.

But she did not come.

At last after a long silence she said quietly, 'I am not the bird to be caught by such lime, Amleth. I shall not strike you and you shall not singe off my hair either. Now turn about and face me as a man should.'

He sat staring at the glowing fire. He said, his great horse teeth thrust out, 'Do as you please, woman. If you want to know what manner of man you have bought then get off your backside and come to face me. You may be a queen of the painted sheepherders, but by Thor and his great vingull I am the only King of the Wood in the north.'

It was long before she came but come she did. And then with the same look in her eyes that Amleth had seen in Elene's. He stared her down until she lay before him and held at his ankles. Then he said quietly, 'Now let me see you weep, my lady!' And she wept, every bit as sadly as Elene. And when he had dried her eyes and face on his neck-cloth Amleth said, 'Now let there be no more talk of gelding, my lady. It is not the sort of talk that should pass between high ones. It is a matter for farmers and butchers. The sooner you learn that the better for us both, Elekt. I think that you Cruithin have been too long in your ancient dream. Perhaps it is I who have been chosen by the gods, whoever they are, to raise you from the slavery that you have always suffered and never admitted. Very well, I will do that if my father Vendil will let me have my way. But no more talk of gelding, little black one, hey? It is not good for a man's pride.'

She came to him then and put the knife in his hands. 'Destroy it, my husband,' she said. 'It was given to me by my mother, who had had it from hers. It goes back to the dawning of man. I beg you, Amleth, take this sickle-curse from women. Let us be lovers again.'

Amleth looked down at the little knife, turning it over in his great hand. He said, smiling, 'What a small thing to cause so much distress. Tell me, lady, how many have you used this on?'

She hid her face under his arm and said, 'Only on three, my lord. All of them were Cruithin. Not one was a Roman or an Outlander.'

He said, but sternly this time, 'And did they merit it, woman?'

She kneeled before him, her face in the ashes, and said, 'My brother Orest commanded it. They were good enough men but he did not like the way they sat their horses.'

Amleth kicked cold ashes over her as though he was thinking deeply. He said at last, 'This brother of yours seems to be a very great man. Is that not so?'

She nodded, rubbing her ochred face against his foot.

Amleth said with his hand in the small of her back, 'He loves you deeply, lady?' And she nodded again.

Then he said, 'Tell me, when I love you, is it deeply too?'

She drew her face from the ashes and said, 'My lord, it is as though

I am a small tree in a great storm. It is as though you have reached up and have taken me by the very throat.'

Then Amleth rose from the heather and said, 'And this great brother of yours, this Orest, does he take you by the throat, lady?'

She rose and followed him about the chamber like a dog. 'Oh no, oh no,' she cried. 'There is no one in my heart but the prince of Jutland, my lord.'

He turned to her and handed back the small flint knife. 'Destroy this yourself, my lady,' he said. 'I think that you have the power to do it now. And as you go to the shore to cast it into the sea, tell the little Roman girl that she will go north with us tomorrow. And when you tell her this, smile and place your right hand upon her shoulder gently as though you were her elder sister. Will you do this?'

For a while she rocked and flared at him, but at last she nodded, splashing him with her tears of fury. 'I will do it, lord,' she said.

And when she was by the tunnel-door Amleth called her back, 'Beloved,' he said smiling, 'would you have me different from what I am?'

Then she ran to him and took him about the hand. 'Dia, no!' she cried. 'By all the gods, but you are what our queens have waited for since life began.'

Amleth put his lips against hers then said, 'So, you have me, lady. There is no cause for tears. Now go and tell Elene that she will travel north with us. And on your way back tell your spying captains that there is a greater captain walking among them now.'

The Picts went north beside the Ermine Street through Deira and into the southern tip of Bernicia. Then they struck west towards the wall. They saw few folk in that empty land, only old people and cripples who could not move out of their path. The great roads were now overgrown with weeds, the villas were in ruins, and most villages they saw were black with burning. Above them and behind them flew hordes of carrion birds, wheeling and crying out for feeding. Amleth rode sometimes in his great wagon and walked sometimes among the captains at the forefront. He stood over a head taller than the tallest man among them. Now Elekt was like a sister to Elene and had washed her and given her fresh garments. The two women sat in a wagon together among the thick of the warriors. The queen had hoisted her great standard of the bleached stag's head with its antlers, so that all folk should know where she was to be found if they had grievances to bring to her.

It was a long journey; some of the old ones and the very young ones did not come to the end of it. But at last as the spring sun grew stronger, the host came in sight of the rolling moorlands that separated Britain from Caledonia.

Amleth stared in amusement at the wall that ran along the hill top. He said, 'Such a little thing for so many tales to be told about! Is this what the great Romans boasted so much of? Is this the memorial to the great Hadrian? Why, a young horse could leap it!'

Elekt said shrewdly, 'Then the young horse would leap to his death. On the further side he would fall down the cliff and drown in the great lake that waits below.'

For a while it seemed that they had reached the meeting place before Orest and his horde but, suddenly as they came round a headland, they saw the army on the great hillside waiting. Even Amleth drew in his breath then for he had never set eyes on so many men. It seemed as though half the world had turned out to meet him. The moorland for as far as he could see was covered with folk, all sitting silently upon their haunches, their hands dangling as they waited, their lance-points bristling into the blue air like the spines of a great hedgehog. Most of the folk were naked. The sun shone on their dark skins and their glistening black hair. Only the clan leaders wore coloured cloaks.

Beyond them on the hill crest were lined their wagons, and near these the women sat and the children played.

Elekt said smiling, 'These are the Lords of Britain, not Arthur and his few hundred Kymry cantering up and down in the south, playing like children at being the guardians of Rome.'

Amleth nodded gravely and said, 'Such a sight would have terrified even the Great Caesar, lady. Why is it that you have not taken all the land long since?'

Elekt answered, 'It is not for want of courage, my lord. It is for lack of bread and meat. Even the bravest cannot fight without food and when we move we eat up all that lies in our way. So there is nothing left for our return. We lose more folk by starvation than by battle wounds. Have you not wondered why our enemies give us the name of eaters of human flesh? But this time all will be different; we shall draw Duke Arthur and his Kymry up towards us at Agned and he shall be the one to eat his fallen comrades.'

Amleth thought of Gautrek who still lay in Arthur's hands. He turned this thought aside and said, 'Where is your brother the king among so many folk, lady?'

She said, 'You will see him soon enough, husband. Our kings do not declare themselves until the moment has come. But once they have made the declaration those who see it do not forget it while they live.'

They had gone fifty paces further up the slope when suddenly it seemed that the whole hillside shifted and shuddered. As though at one instant every man rose and held his lance high. 'Celest, Elekt! Celest, Elekt! Celest, Elekt! Hail! Hail! Hail!' they roared, until birds flew high from them in black swarms like thunder clouds, adding their screeching to the great earth bellowing below.

Then, as the men sat again as still as images, a black cross of fir wood was hoisted and burst into red and yellow flames. Elekt beside Amleth whispered, 'There is your sign. The king Orest stands beneath his burning cross. Now is the time of your trial; you are a dead man if he can dominate you, my lord. May the Mother put her skirts about you.'

Amleth slid his dirk behind him so that he could not draw it from his belt easily and then walked forward holding the two alder sticks full of gold that were the blood payment for Feng's henchmen.

The man who rose and came to meet him was dressed in a floating robe of blue like that worn by Elekt. In his right hand he carried such a bronze dirk as Amleth himself had pushed out of sight. Orest was so like his sister in looks that at first glance Amleth thought they must be twins. But as he came closer, moving stiff-legged like a hound, Amleth saw how the battle-scars had coarsened his face and how broad in the shoulder he was beneath the pretty blue robe. Then Orest spoke so that all the folk could hear and said to Amleth, 'Are you blind that you walk leaning on two sticks? I see that you have given your forelock to the apple-god, yet you are not of our folk. Whose dog are you then?'

Amleth moved on towards him smiling. Then in a gentle voice he answered, 'I am such a dog that no wolf has yet stood in my path, carrion-eater.'

Orest laughed lightly then flung his bronze dirk up into the air and caught it again, hardly looking at its fall. A great sigh went across the hill at this. He said loudly, 'This wolf's fang lies in his right hand. Where is your fang, Jutland dog?'

They were now less than two paces from one another. Amleth said gently, 'Where is the rotten meat you munch upon, black-face?'

Orest held up the dirk until it pointed at Amleth's eyes, his arm out stiff, his tattooed face a mask. He said, 'It is here and now I shall carve it.' Then as he spoke his blade went out like an adder's tongue. Amleth saw its coming but did not shrink. He felt the sharp pain in his cheek and the keen point grate upon one of his upper teeth inside. Orest stood before him still smiling. 'That is how the fang bites, Jutlander,' he said. 'Now let us make all equal and nip at your other cheek.'

Amleth shook the blood away from his mouth and said, 'If this wolf bites twice he will remember it all the days of his life and will weep in the night at its remembrance. That is the warning.'

Orest laughed now, his dark eyes bright with savage merriment. The massed folk upon the hill laughed with him, proud of their black king and his ancient sword. Then they were still again for they saw his hand come out once more in the sunlight towards the Out-lander's other cheek.

But this time Amleth was not there to take the blade's bite. He bent sideways so that it passed over his right shoulder and, as he did, swept one of the heavy metal-loaded sticks across Orest's face. The men squatting nearby heard the nose bone break and saw the laughing face become crimson all at once. Orest roared like a black-maned lion and plunged forward, but as his foot left the ground the other stick took him across the eyes. He staggered back, but could not escape the whistling staves that smashed against his mouth, then across his throat and, as he fell in the heather, again and again over his arms and legs and at last, when he rolled face downwards to hide, his back.

And with each stroke Amleth yelled out, 'Godgest! Hake! Godgest! Hake! Godgest! Hake!' in a ghastly rhythm of baresark destruction. Now horror swept the hillside below the Roman wall as the folk heard their leader scream with each blow. But no man stepped forward to end this meeting of kings.

And at last Elekt herself went to Amleth and drew his arms to his sides. Her face was white with pity and her legs trembled so hard that she could scarcely stand upright. She said hoarsely, 'Enough, my lord, enough. You have humbled him. Do not kill him, I beg you.'

But leaning from the wagon, her lips apart and wet, Elene cried, 'Finish him, husband! End him! Make him yell louder, then finish him!'

All at once Amleth shook the Pict-queen away, then putting the two sticks under his left arm, bent and took Orest by his long hair plait and dragged him up, shuddering and bleeding. 'Stand, king,' he shouted. 'Let your folk see how merry you look after the little jest I have told you.'

Orest stood with a great effort and turned his face towards the men on the hill. It was another face from the one they had been so proud of a moment ago. Many groaned, some wept; then all were silent to hear the bubbling sounds that came from their leader's torn throat.

As well as he was able, Orest called, 'You have a new king among you now, Cruithin. You have a wolf of the north. You have a man at last, one who will face the best sword of our people with only two sticks in his hand. Give him his due.'

Then the hillside stirred again, and the roar went out, 'Celest, Amleth! Celest, Amleth! Hail! Hail! Hail!'

Orest heard this, tottered towards the Dane, placed his bruised hands upon his shoulders, and then fell senseless at Amleth's feet in the red heather.

The queen Elekt said proudly, 'We have two men among the Cruithin at last. Let the greater one raise the smaller and carry him to his booth.'

It was night time before Orest, lying upon his bed with his face and body bandaged, spoke again. Beside the smoking fire in the turf-roofed booth sat his sister and Amleth. Orest said, 'My heart is glad, brother.'

Amleth spoke with pain too and said, 'You of the Cruithin choose strange pleasures. I could think of entertainments which have made me laugh more.'

Orest shook his head and said, 'All this was for the people on the hill. I knew well enough the sort of beast I was tormenting and what might come out of it, but our people had to see it for themselves.'

Amleth said quietly, 'You are a brave man, brother. I have met few who would have stood as you did.'

Orest looked away. 'It is a king's duty to the people,' he said. 'And I have not come badly out of it, all told. If you had fallen into the heather I should have taken your head for my standard pole.' He smiled as well as he was able and Amleth smiled back at him, yet with some pity that he had been forced to ruin such a handsome man.

Elekt said, 'We are well content, husband, for this battle of sticks is our first step towards the crown of Britain and the tumbling of Arthur. We have made a good bargain in losing a few teeth and in gaining a war-lord.'

Amleth gazed at her. He said, 'What is to be done now, lady?'

She answered, 'We shall wait here until our messengers have spread the word in Caer Leon that our host is gathering, then when Arthur and his cavalry move north we shall return across the wall and into our own country to lengthen their lines. And when we have them lost in the woods of Coit Celidon, we shall take them from all sides by night and destroy the Kymry. Word has already gone down to Cerdic in Wessex that soon we shall give him permission to sack Caer Leon. So Rome will have withered at last.'

Orest lay back on his bed, coughing and spitting, but Amleth paid little heed to him now. He said, 'This plan is well enough for you, my lady, but I have a dear friend in Caer Leon. My blood-brother Gautrek the Mild waits for me to come back and fetch him away, and I cannot do anything that would cause Duke Arthur to take vengeance on such a hostage. I cannot lead you in battles until Gautrek is safe and away from that city.'

Orest struggled up onto his elbow and smiled sadly; 'Then,' he said, 'you will have no hindrance. Word came north to us many months ago that this Gautrek died guarding a little jewel box that the girl Elene left in his keeping.'

At first Amleth could not understand what the Pict said, and when he did understand he said, 'Gautrek died fighting robbers, then? While we drank the metheglin of Powys? My brother died fighting and I did not know?'

Orest said with pain, 'He died from the bite of a little brown snake that your lame Roman put into the box to kill him.'

When Amleth heard this he stood up and began to yell hoarsely and without words. The Pict-queen and her brother shrank from him, seeing the froth on his lips and his eyes rolled back in his head.

Then he turned and staggered from the booth, hitting the doorpost with his great shoulders and causing the place to rock. Beside the women's wagon Elene was sitting, playing with a child. Amleth swept the girl up in his hands and flung her against the solid wagon wheel. Then as she lay howling he went at her again and tried to stamp her to pieces like a furious warhorse. Men ran shouting at him with poles and beat him away from her. It took eight of them to hold him down and put thongs about his arms and legs. In the fighting three of these men were so mauled that they would never stand straight again.

By the morning his rage had gone and he lay under the wagon as white-faced as a dead man. When Elekt came to sit beside him he said in his old voice, 'How is the Roman? Did I kill her last night?'

Elekt shook her head. She said, 'She will not die so easily, husband. She is more terrified than hurt. Her broken arm will mend but she will fear you for the rest of her time.'

Amleth said, 'Get the men to untie me, lady. I have had the night to think about Gautrek and now I mourn him no longer. It has all gone out of me now, the anger and revenge.'

And when they had set him free he went to Elene who shuffled back from him screaming, and said, his hand upon her face, 'You are a poor thing, child. You are that weak creature they have told me of who can bring death to the greatest. Well, that is your fate and you are not to be blamed. I am not sorry for what I did to you, for something had to be done. But you may be sure that I will never again raise a hand against you, or may Odin strike the light from my eyes. You have been hurt enough in this world. What other hurt you may suffer belongs to the next, if there is such a world.'

Then he went to where Orest lay with his wounds and said, 'Brother, our plans must be changed now. Have no fear, we will drag Arthur down and take Britain from him but we must do it differently. There is revenge to be got for Gautrek now and I wish his brother Torfi to share it. I must go back to Jutland and fetch Torfi and all the warmen we can find longships for. Besides, I have a vengeance of my own to take in Vendilsgarth soon and I have sworn to my mother that this will be taken at the proper time.'

Orest said, 'Will you swear to come back, brother?'

Amleth answered, 'Ask that again and I will crack your neckbone.' Then he quietened and said, 'Yes, I swear, Orest. I will make landfall in the Humber with a score of longships, and we will go direct to Caer Leon. I know the way now, never fear. So while you are destroying the Kymry at Agned, I will tear down Caer Leon, stone from stone, and put every Roman to the sword, men, women and children. This I swear, and I pray to Odin that Arthur may leave Medraut behind to guard the place for I want his heart on the end of my dirk.

And I vow to you, brother, that I will eat the heart as you Cruithin do in view of all our people. Does that satisfy you?'

Orest bowed his head. The queen Elekt said, 'What of our ally, Cerdic the West Saxon?'

Amleth shook his head. 'Cerdic is such another snake as Arthur or Medraut. From now on he is no ally of ours. When you have picked the bones of all the Kymry clean and I have laid waste to Caer Leon, then we will join and push this Cerdic southwards into the sea. So all Britain will be ours. We can decide then who will rule which parts. But one thing I shall do—or may I die as old Vendil did—I shall wipe out all traces of Rome as though it had never been. Not a house, not a palace, not a fortress, not a wall, not a road shall remain. No, not a garden or orchard. So Rome shall know what it is to betray a Dane with a little brown snake.'

Then Elekt said gently, 'I have consulted the Maze disk which is our calendar of all the barley dancings in the world, husband. If it was your promise to your mother the queen that you would return to Jutland for the feasting, then we must go now. The tides will be right to sweep our outriggers across to Jutland. We must waste no time or tide or wind.'

Amleth said, 'This is my affair, wife. I shall go alone.'

The lady Elekt shook her head and said, 'No, this you cannot command me in, however powerful you have become. My place is by your side now until one of us lies stark. We shall take thirty outriggers filled with warriors, and with such a host you will regain your throne in Jutland and at the same time show your own folk that you are a king to be followed back across the sea. I do not think that you will feel ashamed of the men I shall choose to sail with us.'

Amleth bowed his head before her. He said, 'I am proud to have such woman beside me. But tell me before we set our plough to a furrow from which there is no turning back, will you promise to accept my Maze-wife Sibbi as your sister, and to live with her in all friendship?'

The queen nodded her head and smiled. 'There is enough man of you for two of us to share, husband,' she said. 'I will kiss her on both cheeks when we meet and she and I will be your women.'

Amleth said then, 'And the child, Elene, you will agree to her sailing with us too? I owe her my protection after what she has suffered from me.'

Once again the queen nodded and said, 'She is a poor harmless thing now, husband. Why should we not take her? She can carry your two alder sticks for you, until we can find some husband for her who will not mind having a lame woman in his bed.'

IV
Vendilsgarth

IN the high-gabled hall decked with harts' horns and many-coloured bucklers, at the tip of Crabland beside the roaring Gut, King Beowulf turned with the ale cup in his hand and said to the man at his side, 'So you think we should do well to take the longships down to Vendilsgarth, while they are in the midst of their Maze-feasting, and sack the castle?'

This man was a small fellow, who spoke with a foreign clip to his words. His hair was long and brightly combed, his sparse beard spread out in thin forks upon his narrow chest, each of his fingers bore a gold ring. He wore a long tunic of red wool, a cloak of blue worsted fastened with a jet brooch, and breeches of fine white linen cross-banded with plaited black braid. In his right hand he held a silver-lipped ale-horn; in his left a small halberd no taller than a boy of twelve, with a narrow blade so pretty that a hedge-cutter would have laughed at it for lopping hawthorn.

And this man told Beowulf the king, 'When I suggested that you built a hall here on Crabland to station your longships against all who passed north or south, was I wrong? See, my friend, you have milked Jutland dry by my advice. Where else, until you get to Kiev, is there a pirate-king to equal you?'

Beowulf glanced round quickly to see that none of his men was laughing at him under the little fellow's onslaughts, then said, 'Yes, yes, Gilliberht, but I would not wish to run into Vendilsgarth Haven and have these Jutlanders skin my arse with their swords. A king has to be wary, he has to keep a balance in all things.'

Gilliberht surveyed the nails of his right hand, found them sufficiently polished, then answered, 'If you will not take my advice then I must seek elsewhere. No doubt the Emperor in Micklagard would find a place for me.'

Beowulf frowned and said, 'You are too hasty, little friend. I did not spurn your counsel. When have I done that since they flung you at my door? Never forget, Feng sent you as a slave, but I with my knowledge of good men saw that you were more and made you my chief bailiff. Did that not show judgement?'

Gilliberht answered, 'You are still a savage, Beowulf. Yet with God's aid I shall make you a king fit to travel into Frankland or even Greekland one of these days. But if you employ a teacher you must do as he commands; this is known by the smallest schoolboy in Rome. Why does not the King of the Geats know it also?'

Beowulf said, 'Look, master, you are always too hard on me and especially in front of the warmen. After all I am a king.'

Gilliberht raised his red eyebrows and said, 'Yes, my boy, you are a king—and what a king, until I came north to show you what kings were meant by God to be.'

Beowulf said, 'I have taught you to swing that little halberd of yours. I had it made specially for your strength. Is that nothing?'

Gilliberht answered, 'Sheep's dropping, king!'

Then Beowulf said, 'If it had not been for me you would have gone north and still north until you fell off the edge of the earth into boiling pitch.'

Gilliberht answered, 'And if it had not been for me you could have sent no letters from Scania to Novgorod, Kiev, Byzantium, Sicily, Rome, Colonia, Caer Leon or Alexandria in the last year. What sort of king is it who has no counsellor-scribe to make out his letters for him? God, I would as soon go to Carthage and dig beans among the cannibals as stay in this north where my king can neither read nor write and thinks that by giving me a little halberd he has become the match of the world's emperors.'

He stood up then and flung the halberd down into the straw. The drunken Scanians about him blinked up from lashless eyes, then went at their ale again. He said quite softly, 'Farewell, my king. I shall now take my finest black horse and ride southwards into a land where scholars are respected.'

Beowulf had grown heavier in the year and took longer to get out of his drinking-chair. But he caught Gilliberht before the scribe reached the door and almost fell at the little man's knees. 'I beg you, friend,' he said, 'do not leave me now, when you are on the edge of making me into a great one who could walk among the Caesars without being ashamed.'

Gilliberht looked down on him severely, his tight little nostrils pinched white with authority. He said, 'Beowulf, you have killed many in your time and you have frightened still more. But when you meet a true Roman you sense the quality that has gone into that man. Oh yes, with your thick northern arm you could break my delicate back easily; of that I am well aware. But, my hairy friend, where does that leave you? It leaves you exactly as I found you, a dim king in the cold north, unloved by most, unknown by any who matter, and immediately forgotten when he is dead.'

King Beowulf beat his great shaggy head on the cobbled floor. 'For Thor's sake, do not say that,' he cried. 'To live a hero's life and then be forgotten! No! No! Oh, God, no!'

Gilliberht led him gently back to his ale-chair and even put the cup into his trembling hand. Then like a father he said to the king, 'In this brief life, Beowulf, a man gets his just deserts; no more and no less. Treat me properly as I deserve and you shall be remembered for all time. Treat me badly, and you will most certainly fall into an endless stinking darkness when the axe takes you at last, as take you it must, unless I find you a way out.'

Beowulf drank three horns of strong ale before answering. When he did his voice was as smooth as silk. He said, 'My dear little friend, there has never been such a one as you in the north before. All credit to me that I found you.'

Gilliberht did not reply but drew his nose in thin again and stared over the king's head at a spider that was weaving a web from a rusty spear point to the boss of a shield. Beowulf could not stand the delay any longer and said, 'Very well, master scribe, for Thor's sake, tell me what I must do. If you want me to be great in the world, tell me and gain eternal credit for yourself at the same time.'

Gilliberht spilled some of his thick ale onto the oak board and then drew in it with his pointed fingernail. He said to the table, 'So I

231

would set down the saga of Beowulf. I would tell how he sailed into Heorot, slew the marsh-monster and her son, swam in the cruel sea among the drowned ships, then grew to be a Caesar and slew the dragon of fiery breath. Yes, I would even claim for him a great funeral pyre with all the folk bewailing him. And so I would set him down for all time, to stand beside the Caesar and the Pharoahs.'

He glanced sideways at the Geat-king to see whether he was listening; then he added, louder than before, 'God knows what Agamemnon would seem now if the scribe Homer had not sat in his hall with him to write down his life.'

Suddenly Beowulf rose and kicked one of the Scanians off his stool. 'You sorry swine,' he called, 'run to my coffer and fetch out the biggest gold cup that you find.'

Then he bowed to Gilliberht and said, 'Master, it comes to few kings to find such as you are. Set down the tale of how I slew the monsters, I beg you. In return I have sent for a new cup for you. What further am I to do?'

Gilliberht felt the strong ale reaching up into his skull-bone and drawing the brains out of his nose. He belched and then said, 'Sack Vendilsgarth and, if they are there, put to death that fool Feng, his two henchmen, Godgest and Hake, and then give me the first two prisoners you take as my slaves.'

Beowulf stared at him solemnly, finding it hard now to see where he sat, then said very carefully, 'You are a most reasonable man, on my heart, Gilliberht. If all men were as reasonable who would wish to go north to Valhalla for a perfect life? Of course, my dear little friend, of course you shall have your wish. Thor, to think that I have such a scribe for my own, to write my letters to Count Belisar and King Theodoric, and all he asks is three dead men and two slaves for his labours! Frig, Frig, Frig—but when was a king so lucky!'

He slid under the table into the straw. Gilliberht waited a while then edged his way along the board, past the snoring Scanians, to his own chamber where he had a little Frankish girl waiting for him, lying wide-eyed in the darkness, terrified of his coming.

Gilliberht stumbled about a while finding the bed and how she lay.

232

Then, after he had assured himself, he said sternly, 'No, that would not please me. Recall, child, you are dealing with a Roman of Marseilles now, not with any chance-met tow-haired cow-herd. Be good enough to save your tears and to turn the other way.'

After a while he said crossly, 'And for the love of God stop calling for your mother. She is in Colonia, she cannot hear you.'

Then he began to think how he would start the poem about Beowulf and the monster.

He strained hard to get started. This rude northern style was almost too much for him. It was so jerky, so violent, such hard-going for an ageing man who liked smooth sleek things.

'Sigon pā to slǣpe . . .' he hacked out.

Then he drew back and struck the girl on the back of the neck in the darkness. 'For god's love,' he groaned, 'be still, be still. I have my work to do.'

'Sigon pā to slǣpe. Sum sāre angeald
æfenrǣste . . .'

He cursed the uncouth words, the rough metre. He cursed the shuddering Frank again and again. Then all at once she was quiet and breathing regularly in sleep like a child; but his old mind went on jerking, his old heart went on palpitating, his old tongue went on mouthing the northern crudities: 'Grẹndel warode . . . wunian scolde. . . . Heorote fand . . . sōna wearđ.'

Then at length even he fell off the edge of the swimming world into a darkness as black as pitch. The young girl wakened, still sobbing, and for a while thought of cutting his knotted throat with her scissors. But in the end she remembered that she was a Christian, so she rolled onto the floor and let him live.

The sea-going to Jutland was hard and five of the outriggers were lost, turning turtle in high seas, or breaking their backs on skerries, before landfall was made. Few of the Cruithin loved water enough to swim in it so that those who went into the sea perished helplessly, swept away on heavy tides, while the others in their dugouts watched them go, sprawling on the black seas until they fell from sight.

Yet at last the rest came into Vendilsgarth Haven and saw lights burning in the great hall there, half-hidden by trees.

Amleth drew his queen to shore and said, 'We are only just in time, Elekt. Already the feasting has started. My mother will be wondering if I am indeed dead since I come so late.'

The Pict-queen said faintly, 'The journey has been hard, my lord. None of us is rested enough to fight such a battle as might be thrust upon us if we go before your uncle now. Can the warriors not lie outside the walls until the time is ripe to call them in?'

Amleth put his arm about her. 'Yes, my queen,' he said. 'They may do that and if Odin wills it we may have no need to call them in at all for this matter may settle itself.'

Yet the queen would not leave him to go alone into the dark castle so, as they made their way heavily up from the shore across the dunes, Amleth said, 'Behind this clump of alders there is a cottage where old Ragna, who was my mother's first nurse, lives. She will give you mulled Jutland ale to warm you before we go into the hall.'

But Elekt said, 'I smell blood about this cottage. Let us go past it without entering. I had rather stay cold than drink from what cup awaits me there.'

Then Amleth laughed and dragged her along. 'What!' he said. 'A queen and talks of fear! Come, seed of all great ones, if you can walk from India you can walk inside this cottage with me at your side.'

He bent under the hawthorn and pushed the hurdle door open. Beside a small charcoal fire two women sat, both of them very old and withered, their white hair hanging uncombed about their bent shoulders. Old Ragna looked up in fear as the prince strode in, but the other woman stared into the heart of the fire and munched at the ends of her hair without looking up.

Amleth went to Ragna and took her in his arms. 'Old one,' he said, 'see, I have come home again. See, it is Amleth the prince.'

Ragna let fall her arms and leaned against him weeping, so that he had to hold her lest she should fall into the charcoal fire. 'There,

there, old love,' he said gently, wiping her eyes with his sleeve, 'I am not such a troll as would frighten an old friend, am I?'

Elekt the queen went to her then and helped her to her stool. The other woman turned and gazed at them, her tongue lolling about her lips as she tried to speak. Amleth looked away from her wide mad eyes and whispered to Ragna, 'There, old one, you know me, don't you? You remember how you used to bake new loaves for me and I would catch fishes for you? Do you not remember that, Ragna?'

The woman nodded then put her hands over her face and rocked back and forth in misery. Amleth stood over her, knowing now that there would be no mulled ale in this house; but he said to her kindly, 'My mother, is she well?' Ragna turned her white face up at him and whispered, 'Odin, my son, who knows, who knows? I have not set eyes on her for a month. I have been here alone, tending the poor lass. Your mother has not been to see us, Amleth.'

He bent to warm his hands by the small fire and in bending caught sight of the gown that the other old crone was wearing. It was of russet cloth, trimmed with white fur at neck and wrists, embroidered in fine silver thread to show the shapes of dragons and serpents winding about the bodice. But now it was so torn and bespattered that he hardly knew it again. He said, though in some doubt, 'Sibbi had a dress like that. Aye, it is Sibbi's dress, the one she wore when we went into the green wood together. Why are you wearing it, old woman? She would never have discarded that gown, that of all gowns.'

The old crone looked away, her long chin upon her breast. Amleth took her hands and shook her with impatience but he could get nothing from her. Then old Ragna stared over her own cupped hands and said in desolation, 'Do not torment her, Amleth. Have men not done enough to her already, without you who swore to love her adding to the pain?'

Now Amleth gazed at the old crone then back at Ragna. 'Is this Sibbi?' he asked. 'Nay, you are jesting, old one. But such jesting is cruel, to a man who has come across the grey seas from Britain.

235

Come, come, Ragna, who is this ancient one who wears my love's bridal gown? Who is she?'

Then Ragna went to the old crone and put her arm about her to hold her upright and looking over the snow white head at Amleth said starkly, 'After you went Feng swore that women should rule no longer in Vendilsgarth. He vowed to make an example of them before the world and the first he took was Sibbi. For three days she lay across the log on the shore for all to take as they chose, midden-thralls, strangers in the Haven, wandering baresarks. Then at the close of the third day Feng's judgement was carried out; his hench-men poured the scalding brine into her through a horn funnel so that she should be cleansed of her sins. The sins you brought on her, Amleth, in the Maze dance. This that you see is Sibbi. This is what she has come to from that cleansing, my lord.'

The Pict-queen glared in the firelight. 'We are called savages,' she said with bitterness. 'We paint our foreheads and keep life within ourselves by eating the forbidden flesh when we are starving but, by Dia, we do not deal in logs and scalding brine. If this is Jutland, then I had rather be in Celidon, rooting for acorns among the swine.'

But Amleth could not bring his mouth to utter the words that wished to come forth. His face was drained of blood and the sweat stood in beads on his brow. He beat at his head for a while and at last cried out, 'Torfi! Torfi, the treacherous dwarf! He swore to guard her! Torfi!'

Old Ragna left the crone Sibbi and went to him. She took his great hand as though he were a little boy again and said gently, 'Speak no ill of the black dwarf, Amleth. Torfi struck such blows as left four of Feng's henchmen useless at board or in bed, until they dragged him down and did to him what they did to the little bear that came into the kitchen long ago. Then they hung him on the tree as they hung the bear, in memory of Odin, they said. So speak no ill of Torfi who served you as well as any man could.'

Suddenly Amleth began to stamp and to snort like a stallion when he scents cold iron coming. The froth came from his mouth. His eyes went wide and fixed in their sockets. His great teeth jutted forth and his limbs began to twitch.

The lady Elekt put her hand out to him and said, 'Husband, my husband!' But he flung her aside as though she were a fold of cloth from his robe sleeve. Then like a blind man he went out of the door. Now he did not bend to make his way under the thorn bush but walked through it and it faded before him like wood smoke.

Old Ragna said, 'He is the King of the Wood again, now God alone knows what will happen in the hall.'

And though the lady Elekt ran fast hoping to turn him away he had vanished. So she did the only thing that came to her heart and followed towards the rush-lit hall of feasting.

In the great hall, where doves perched in the rafters and the horses kicked at their stalls beyond the long board, Feng stood above all the henchmen and noble-folk to give the horn-hail. He was saying, 'We have shaken it off at last, my people, this old savagery, this King of the Wood, this Barley Queen. We have put them away, the wizards and witches, at last. The young whelp, Amleth, was put away by our good friend, Arthur of Britain, and we have dug up the Maze. That dance has finished now, my lords. But we shall begin another soon. This is the Feast of Easter that comes after the long fasting. What better than that we start a new life in Jutland and take a vow to serve the Kristni who gave the Romans so much glory in their day? I have had brought a Bishop to Vendilsgarth. He waits outside this door for my call to come inside and baptize us all. Are you with me, my people? Shall I call in the good Bishop so that we may become glorious among men? Shall I?'

About the board the henchmen beat on the wood with their ale-horns and called out with laughter, 'Aye, Feng! Call in the Bishop! Call the old fool in!'

Feng, slopping the ale down his chest, swung about and yelled, 'My lord Bishop, come in, we are ready, come in!'

Then amidst all the shouting and flinging of beef bones the door of the hall was flung open and Amleth stood there, his face as white as chalk, the eye of Dia staring blue and blood-red from the middle of his head, his clothes stripped off in baresark-wise, a bundle of stakes under his left arm and the bronze dirk in his right hand.

For a while there was silence, then one of the kitchen-maids pointed at something that was different now and began to laugh. So all began to laugh and Feng said, 'God's miracles are great. I called for the Bishop and instead got my dear son Amleth. But what a change is here, my dear son. Come, put down those stakes and let us look at you. Come onto the table so that we shall see the better.'

Amleth flung down the stakes and then leaped onto the long board. Then throwing back his head he began to crow like a cock. One of the henchmen shouted out, 'So he should, by God, so he should!' Then they began to throw pieces of barley bread at him and say, 'Cock, cock, peck, peck!'

Even the women joined in, crowding close to the board so that they should miss nothing. And for a while Amleth danced for them, up and down the board, until they grew tired of this entertainment and turned back to their ale. Then all at once the queen Elekt stood in the doorway, her black hair like a troll's, the eye in her forehead fixing them all with its stare.

Feng turned and said, 'Great Odin, but who is this?'

Amleth leaped from the board and ran to stand beside her, his hand in hers. He said aloud, 'It is the new Sibbi, come to lead the Maze dance, Uncle Feng.'

The King of Jutland swayed until he almost fell, then suddenly he kicked back his stool and ran along the hall. Amleth let him go then called out to the feasters, 'Is this not a pretty queen? Who has seen a prettier queen?'

The feasters at the table sat silent, wishing they had their daggers with them in the hall.

One of the horse-Jarls' women cried out, 'See, Amleth, we have hung the new tapestries about the room for this feasting. Your mother stitched at them until she almost went blind. But are they not worth blindness?'

238

Amleth began to crow again like a cock, shaking his sword about. One of the lords stood up and said, 'My lord, let me lend you a scabbard for your sword. If you shake it about so you will cut yourself.'

Amleth let him take the ancient sword and put it into a sheath. He saw the man wrap the peace-string round it quickly, so that it could not be drawn without great effort. Then he took back the sword and bowed to the man who had muzzled it. 'You are kind, sir,' he said.

The lady Elekt came to him and took his arm. 'Husband,' she whispered, 'they are laughing at you. They are mocking now that your sword is muzzled.'

He said to her starkly, 'Soon the laughter will cease, lady. Soon there will be no more mockery. Have you still the little flint knife you once threatened me with?'

She nodded and passed it into his great hand.

He smiled. 'You are the best wife I could have found, beloved,' he said. 'Now go outside into the stack-yard for what is to happen here must not touch you, whom I love now beyond life itself.'

She waited a moment, then his glaring became so fierce that she obeyed him and went outside into the night. Among the straw-stacks she whistled like a blackbird three times. From outside the stockade her captains whistled back. Then she knew that whenever Amleth needed them the Cruithin would be at hand to run in with their lances. So she sat down on a moss-grown stone and waited.

The queen Gerutha hung high above the moat, over the battle-mented wall, in an osier cage. They had not cleaned it out for a month. They had not fed her for days. The clay water-pot that stood among the straw and filth had been bone-dry for two days and nights. Even the raven that had perched beside her for a week had gone away for better pickings on the shore among the limpets.

She heard Elekt whistling down below in the stack-yard, but could not answer for her own throat was as dry as the clay pot.

Dimly she thought: He has come back. He has come to take the vengeance. Now it will not be long. Soon he will come to cut me down.

The tapestry was of the thickest wool and hung from a side-beam to the floor, the length of the hall, by a thong which curled about that beam and was threaded at every foot through the great wall-hanging.

At its end, near where Amleth stood now, the Queen of Jutland had stitched a tall oak tree in brown and green and yellow. Its boughs seemed to hang over all the feasters as they sat at the board.

One of them, a red-nosed youth with a cast in his eye, famous for mockery, called out, 'Now, King of the Wood, you have met your match there. That is one oak you could not climb.'

Amleth went to the tapestry and touched it. He said, 'If I cannot climb it, I can spread my wings and fly up to its top. Cock-a-doodle-do!'

As he jested his fingers weighed the cloth. It was of the heaviest and he felt a great love come into his heart for his mother. He wished that she could be here now to see how her tapestry would be used.

Then a merry-eyed girl shouted out, 'Go on, then, fly if you're going to—or are all your feathers clipped, cock?'

Amleth turned and bowed to her quickly, then taking great handfuls of the rough cloth, hauled himself towards the beam. Quickly he drew the little flint knife and, poised over the feasters, he cut the first thong that held the curtain secure. No one saw what he did, they were too full of ale and laughter. So he slid down again and stood before them, a fold of the tapestry in his right hand. He said, 'I found no eagles nesting there, no doves either. This cannot be a real tree.'

The red-nosed youth cried, 'No, have no fear, Green Man, it cannot fall on you and pin you to the ground as old Vendil's oak did!'

Amleth smiled back pleasantly at him then gazed at the far end of the hall where the horses were, as though he saw something. The feasters followed his stare, looking away from him. And when all eyes were turned, he shouted out, 'Nay, but it can fall on you, to pin you where you'll never rise again.'

He gave a great drag at the curtain and watched the thong uncurl, whipping loose from the beam the length of the hall. As the heavy cloth bellied down some of the feasters looked round in bewilderment, a few turned and saw what was coming onto them and tried to rise, but most had their heads upon their hands, stupid with ale. Those who rose did not stay long on their feet when the curtain reached them. It would have held down four cart-horses.

Now Amleth's smile left him. He ran to where the sharpened stakes lay and snatched them up. Then wrenching off the trestle-end of a bench he went round the humped and writhing cloth-covered heap, driving the pegs into the trodden earth of the floor. The drunken men had not tried to save themselves and the less drunk, finding themselves below the curtain beside women no less tipsy, began to make the best of their good fortune in the dark.

Amleth yelled out, 'Is it warm under there? Can you hear me? Is it warm?' But no answer came back to him, so he shouted again, 'Ah, I see that you Jutlanders are too polite to tell me you are chilly in my hall. Well, well, courtesy is its own reward. Here, have more warmth, my dear friends.'

Then he ran from one wall-sconce to the next, tearing away the resin torches and flinging them onto the staked tapestry. The dry wool took flame straightway. Now the heap began to move with a vengeance. Now the silent ones below there in the darkness found their tongues and shrieked out.

Amleth stayed a while shouting, 'Torfi and Gautrek; Torfi and Gautrek; Vendil and Sibbi; Vendil and Sibbi! Is the list long enough, feasters? I can add Hake and Godgest to it!'

Then the fierce flames drove him back. He snatched up the two alder sticks and ran along the far side of the hall to Feng's underground chamber.

Vendilsgarth was like a stone chimney. Each draught of air sucked up fire. Thatch crackled, beams roared and thudded down. Stone

Ω   241

went white with heat, then cracked like great whips and flew out into the darkness. The queen in her osier cage roused herself with the strange glow in her eyes. She did not know what all the roaring and crackling was, but she felt the floor of the hanging prison growing hotter and hotter and tried to pull herself up the bars away from it. Always she fell back and at last the hem of her robe, hanging over the edge of the floor, grew hot, then singed, then took flame. Little fires ran along it and onto her legs. She looked at them a while then tried to beat them out, but more came when the first were dead. The straw began to change colour, then smouldered and sent off thick smoke that made her cough.

'Where are you, Amleth?' she cried. 'Will you leave me here, my son?'

The floor turned black beneath her, fire climbed up every bar of the osier cage. Gerutha began to sing like a bird. Below in the stack-yard the lady Elekt heard this strange singing but could not see where it came from. At last she put her hands over her ears for it was not the sort of singing that a woman likes to remember.

Then Gerutha smelled a new smell as the fire took away her white hair. 'Oh, oh,' she sang, 'they are shoeing the horses at the forge. That is the scent of horn, the scent of horn!'

The osier cage began to rock as the flames climbed onto the rope that swung it from the battlements. It swayed hard sideways then fell, the rope eaten through. It struck the white wall of the castle and broke into charred pieces and the queen went on down alone into the dry moat.

She heard the thudding of the swine as they rushed at her, and the wet chumbling of their jaws, but when the first sow laid her tusks at this fodder Queen Gerutha had slipped away from more suffering.

King Feng tossed in his bed, feeling too warm. Sweat ran down his face. He drew the hide curtain from the window-hole and saw a red glow outside in the night. The thought came to him that the feasters had lit a bonfire and he called them drunken fools.

Then he saw Amleth standing in the doorway with a sheathed

242

sword in his hand. 'So you have left the feasting, my son,' he said. 'I do not blame you, the folk here at Vendilsgarth are not as they used to be. They are no fit companions for a prince now.'

Amleth shook his head and smiled. 'They are no fit companions,' he said. 'They lie about the floor with black faces, saying nothing.'

Feng nodded and drew up his legs in the bed. 'It is our curse, Amleth,' he said. 'We in Jutland spoil ourselves with too much drinking. Then we lie about, black in the face and silent, looking like fools to sober men from other lands.'

Amleth said, 'Our courtiers will never learn any better now. They are beyond all teaching. Now tell me, where is my mother?'

Feng looked across the chamber to where a great iron sword hung on two nails against the wall. He could not get to it before Amleth got to him, so he said, 'My wife Gerutha has not felt well while you were away in Britain, Amleth. Women are strange cattle, my son, and have fancies that men do not know. Sometimes they must be treated with a seeming harshness to bring them back to their senses, you understand? Yet it is for their good, whatever others think.'

Amleth came close, swinging the Pictish dirk. He said, 'But where is she, Feng?'

King Feng drew himself back against the wall and felt that it was very hot. He wondered if he had a fever from too much pork at the feasting. He wiped his hand over his streaming face and said, 'We made her a bower outside, where she could be private, where she could meditate on all things without the interruption of those chattering bower-women. You shall see her tomorrow, my son. I will bring her to you, never fear. Do you find it warm in this room, prince?'

Amleth said, 'I wear fewer clothes than you, Feng. And perhaps my blood is colder since I have just come up out of the sea. But if you feel too warm, let me help you.'

He stood over Feng and taking the neck of his linen night-shift ripped it down, leaving the king naked on the bed.

'Now,' said Amleth, 'tell me about my wife Sibbi. How does she do these days?'

Feng felt his jaws beginning to chatter. He said, 'Ah, poor Sibbi, poor lass! Who can account for the ways of womankind? Who can guess what they will do, my son? To tell you the truth, I think she went mad at the loss of you. You should not have stayed away from her so long, my son. We gave her all attention, I can assure you. But she missed you, Amleth, here on her own. It wrung my heart to hear her pitiful cries. I have dreamt of them often, I can tell you. Nay, you should not have been away when she needed you, my son.'

Amleth walked towards the old sword on the wall and ran his thumb down part of the edge. It was as sharp as when it first left the smith's anvil. He turned and said, 'And Torfi, the little black dwarf, is he well, Feng?'

The king began to ease himself from the bed, almost sure now that if he took his chance he could get to the sword and drag it down before Amleth might draw his own blade from the scabbard. He smiled and said, 'Ah, Torfi the dwarf. You left behind a poor fellow there, Amleth. It was not long after you had sailed that he went into the woods and none of us has set eyes on him for many months. Such fellows are not to be trusted, prince. They are like animals, not men.'

Amleth said, 'In some ways he reminded me of that little bear who came into our kitchen, Feng. Does he remind you of the same?'

Feng now put his feet upon the floor gently, feeling the stones beneath him and getting poised to leap forward. He said, 'Torfi was bigger than the bear. Though I grant you he was no prettier! Now you must tell me your news. What of my dear friends, Godgest and Hake? Are they drinking down in the ale cellar here? They should have come to see me without delay. They should know their duty.'

Amleth flung the two alder sticks onto the bed beside the king. He said, 'Here they are, uncle. As you will see they have not been drinking. They are as dry as a bone.'

Feng put out his hand and felt one of the sticks. He said, 'This is very heavy for alder, my son. What does it mean?'

Amleth leaned by the wall and said, 'The sticks are full of Roman gold, uncle. It is the blood money for your two henchmen who got themselves butchered as soon as we landed on Humberside. I insisted on this payment and Duke Arthur sent it as a gift to you. Did I do right?'

Now Feng's mouth began to twitch and his eyes to grow wider. The breath down his nose came in fierce spasms. It was too late to get to the great sword now for Amleth was standing before it.

Then Amleth said, 'I too shall give you something.'

For a moment Feng thought there was hope, he even tried to smile. He said, the spittle running into his beard, 'You have brought something for me, my son?'

Amleth said starkly, 'No, I shall take something from you. The same thing that you took from the little bear and from Torfi.'

Then Feng began to roar like a trapped lion. 'I have no sword,' he cried. 'If I had a sword, you would not torment me so.'

Amleth laughed by the wall and said, 'That is soon arranged, take mine, my lord.' He flung the dirk across to the man and even waited a while to watch him dragging at it blindly, unable to untie the thong that kept it in the sheath.

'Oh, God! Oh, God!' Feng was gasping on the bed, the sweat springing from him like dew.

Then Amleth swung round and snatched the great iron blade down and leapt across at the struggling king. 'Come, come, no fuss, Feng!' he shouted, grasping and then dragging at what must be shorn. The old blade hissed like a snake and Feng screeched and flung himself onto the stone floor, rolling everywhere and dirtying the place. Now he had forgotten the sword that had caused him so much care before.

Amleth stood back to give him more space to roll in and said, 'Did the little bear take on so? Did my brother Torfi roll about and squeal?'

Now Feng had got to his knees, glaring with bloodshot eyes and biting through his lips. He spoke no more words all the while that Amleth was with him, though he knew well enough everything that happened.

245

The first blow of the old sword was a poor one. Feng saw it coming and slid his shaggy head aside. His left ear lay down upon his shoulder like a red jewel. This caused him more distress even than the other thing. He jumped up and started to run at the prince just as Amleth struck again. This was a better blow than the last but still Feng saw it coming and held up his arm to ward it away until he could grasp his nephew by the throat.

But the cold shock halted him and then he gazed down at his right hand on the floor like a man seeing part of himself for the first time. Amleth said quietly, 'That was for my father, Vendil.'

Then he shortened the sword and drove it in at waist height. 'And this is for myself,' he said, putting his foot against the king and kicking him off the blade back onto the bed.

And that was how it was done, blow for blow and word for word. Whoever sets it down differently has no respect for the truth.

And so it was that Amleth left the two sticks, and came away with two swords. This he considered was a fair bargain.

The burning of Vendilsgarth was the greatest thing that had been done in Jutland for many years. The flames could be seen from as far away as Crabland. Certainly Amleth wished to make no secret of them.

Now he was in old Ragna's cottage by the shore, sitting in a chair and feeling that only the exact payment of all debts can bring peace to a man. He wished that his mother had been there to see Feng and his henchmen paying the price for Vendil and Sibbi and Torfi. But if his luck held and the Jutlanders sailed with him now she should see Arthur and Medraut paying for Gautrek.

He said to the lady Elekt very quietly, so as not to wake Sibbi where she lay rocked in old Ragna's arms, 'I feel now that I am the man in Jutland, my love. It is a good feeling to be the man. Soon I feel I shall be the man in Britain too. I shall be a proud king with you beside me.'

She stood close to him so that he felt all her body against his though her face was sad.

He put his arm about her and held her strongly. 'If my mother could see us now,' he said, 'it would wipe away many of her sorrows.'

Elekt whispered in the firelight, 'It is as well that she is not here, my king. To have three queens at one time about a king brings on his end. Arthur will learn that soon enough with our help.'

Then the girl Elene, who had been lying in the corner nursing her arm in its withy-splints, said hoarsely, 'There are three queens here. I am the Queen of Powys and the woman Sibbi is the Queen of the Wood.'

They glanced at her as though she was a dog whimpering for scraps from under the table, but did not answer her. They went back to their love-play until in the fireglow Elene saw the king in his proud rising and beat her head against the wooden wall in misery.

And then there came the scratching at the door. For a while Amleth did not hear it because of other things. But when it came again he rose with the old sword under his arm and said, 'It will be one of the captains come to know where the Cruithin shall sleep tonight. I will go. It is my duty.'

When he flung open the low door he could see no one because of the hawthorn bush, so he bent and pushed his way through the thorns. In the dying glow of the burnt castle he saw three men waiting but could not tell who they were. He said, 'This is a fine time to come scratching at the door.'

The tallest of them with a black bearskin about his shoulders and a helmet that glinted in the glow said evenly, 'It is the proper time, Amleth.' He sounded like a king and looked like one as far as Amleth could judge from the sword he carried over his right shoulder. But the other two were not kings, he thought. One was a short squat fellow in a horsehide, carrying a stone hammer; the second was a little bent man in a fur gown, whose thin beard blew in the night wind. He held a halberd so small that a hedge-cutter's son would have mocked it as a toy for lopping hawthorn.

Amleth saw that they were placed in a half-moon round him so did

247

not go any closer but began to edge the old blade round from under his left arm as quietly as he could. And while he was doing this he said, 'I think I have met two of you somewhere before.'

The tall king laughed with white teeth in the glow and answered, 'That is more than likely, we move about here and there in our long-ships as northmen should.'

Then Amleth felt a sort of chill coming up into his legs and said, 'Well, that's as may be. I am a northman myself and stand on no ceremony. You are welcome after your voyaging. There is no castle for you to sleep in now but I am the king here and I give you leave to go among the hutments and find yourself a roof to shelter you and your folk. Take what you need but treat my people well.'

The little man with the thin beard said in a high voice like a goat's bleating, 'Aye, Amleth, we shall take what we need.'

Amleth looked down on him and then said to the tall king, 'I see you have brought your monkey with you.'

The tall king said, 'Aye, and I have brought something else.'

The fireglow shone on the sword as he began to shift it from his shoulder. Amleth stepped back and had got his own blade halfway free when the girl Elene ran behind him and wrapped her arms about his, hampering his sword-hand.

'You have betrayed me, husband,' she was saying. 'You have deserted me for the Pict. You have set a barbarian above a true Roman.'

Amleth knew who it was, though he kept his eyes on the tall king. He said gently, 'Get away from me, Elene. You will be hurt. Go now or I may hurt your arm with my struggling.'

But she hung on so tight with her hair flying and her crippled legs flailing that the three men did not move for a while. They seemed to be more interested in what they were watching.

Then all at once Elene in her frenzy swung Amleth round so that his back was towards them for a moment. And the tall king nodded to the little man in the fur gown who stepped forward and most delicately swung his shining halberd. It was not well done, but it was done well enough. Amleth arched back so hard that Elene flew from

248

him among the thorns crying out. Then ham-strung the prince fell backwards, the great sword clattering away from under his arm to where he could not reach it.

The man with the stone axe came forward swinging his blunt weapon but the tall king swept him away with his foot like a dog and stood over the Jutlander. He said, 'Do you recall how you scorned me once on Crabland? I wished to be your friend then but you had other friends in mind. Now where are they all?'

Then as Amleth opened his mouth to answer the tall king put in his sword-point and drove it through to the turf behind. And when all the writhing and twitching had stopped he said to the others, 'It never fails to amaze me how easily this may be done.'

But the little man in the fur gown was not listening. He was bent in the grass heaving with the memory of what he had seen. Beside him lay Elene crying out that she wanted to die. Only the one with the blunt stone axe showed interest. He was feeling about the still body for rings or bracelets and cursing that there was not more fire-glow to see by.

This much must be said of Beowulf that he denied no king the right to a proper funeral. On the dunes in sight of Gannet's Ness he had men from his longships gather all driftwood to build a high pyre. They worked unstintingly all the day at this, then Beowulf told the lady Elekt, 'Since I am now the king in Vendilsgarth, I give you leave with all my heart to carry out such ceremony as your folk are accustomed to. You are visitors here and should be shown all court-esies, my lady.'

Elekt stared past him, stark-faced, but did not answer. When she gathered her folk together Beowulf withdrew his men towards their ships so as not to hinder them in what they wished to do.

After they had washed the prince and combed his hair, and put a green laurel crown on his head, they dressed him in fine red wool but with his shirt drawn back so that the most important of his wounds should be shown. Then they tied a thong under his jaw so that his mouth should not gape as though he was crying for mercy. His dangling legs they bound with calf-skin to keep them firm and stiff. They clenched his hands about his old iron sword so that no one should ever take it from him again.

As for the Mycenaean dirk, the lady Elekt took it when she was alone with him and hung it from a thong about her hips under her robe since this was an heirloom which belonged to the Cruithin. Her skirt was so wide that no eye however sharp would see the blade hanging as she moved.

They carried him on a hurdle down to the shore and laid him on top of oak, ash, alder, willow, hazel, yew and hawthorn, which were the trees over which he had the greatest power. As the Pictish captains put fire to the pile the lady Elekt came forward in her black cloak and flung cups of wine and milk onto the pyre. Then turning so that all the folk should see what she did, she drew the keen flint knife across her two breasts and squeezed them sharply till blood flowed from them into a cow's horn that one of the chieftains held for her.

So, climbing up among the flames, she bent and kissed Amleth on the white lips and then poured her offering over his face and breast. When she came down her robe was already burning but she walked seven paces with it flaring about her legs before she would allow one of the captains to beat out the fire.

King Beowulf saw this and came to her, his helmet held under his right arm. Bowing before her he said humbly, 'My lady, I honour you. If you will have me my crown is yours and you shall be the queen in Scania.'

She clenched her white teeth and looked into his face. 'My lord,' she said gravely, 'I have become so accustomed to a man that nothing less will do now.'

She said no more. So King Beowulf stood aside to let her lead the Cruithin down to their boats.

And towards sunset when they were riding the outgoing tide well away from shore one of the captains in the leading dugouts called across to his queen, 'Look, lady, his fire is still burning, sending up its black smoke.'

She did not look back but said with scorn, 'Only fools would think that they could ever destroy the Green Man.'

That evening Beowulf set course with his longships back towards Crabland. He did not sack Vendilsgarth as he had planned. For once in his life he took nothing away from a foraging, though a few of those who were with him took something.

AFTERWORD

From Gilliberht Voyager, Lawspeaker and Captain of Halberds to Beowulf by the Grace of Odin King of Scania, Overseer of Jutland, Guardian of Crabland Gut. To Manuel Chrysostom at Puteoli.

With this under the protection of the Geat, Wiglek, who is a free man and must not be kept beyond his will, I send three women; to wit the Briton Elene and two Jutlanders called Ragna and Sibbi. They are either crippled or old beyond usage. But if they reach their journey's end they will have achieved more than the two sorry mules your munificence once allowed me.

Furthermore, I send by Wiglek a hide bag containing twenty pieces of Baltic amber and ten of jet from Whitby. These will compensate you for the cloth and coin you saw fit to set me off with. I hear that amber and jet are much sought after in Italy in recent times. Knowing you, I have no doubt that you will dispose of them in the most profitable market. So I am out of your debt.

You will see from this letter that I am now well situated in the northlands. I commend to you this precept: that a man must make his way by his bravery and wit, and not sit a sluggard in the south depending on inheritance. Bear this in mind. Moreover, have a care about religion. There are such as you who claim that the truth may be discovered only in the Christian book. When you have travelled more and suffered more you will come to a fuller understanding. I will say no more but will leave you humble, I hope, before my revelation.

Ere the grave takes you Odin, Thor, Freyja and Frigg look with pity upon you. Take warning, the Summer of the North is now at hand.

Gilliberht Viking.